THE
TROUBLE
WITH
McCAULEY

THE TROUBLE WITH McCAULEY

GUILDHALL PRESS

Published in July 2012

GUILDHALL PRESS
Unit 15, Ráth Mór Business Park
Bligh's Lane
Derry
Ireland
BT48 0LZ

0044 28 7136 4413
info@ghpress.com
www.ghpress.com

The author asserts his moral rights in this work in accordance with the Copyright, Designs and Patents Act 1998.

ISBN: 978 1 906271 49 7

This publication is available in various e-book formats from www.ghpress.com.

A CIP record for this book is available from the British Library.

Guildhall Press gratefully acknowledges the financial support of the Arts Council of Northern Ireland as a principal funder under its Annual Support for Organisations Programme.

To Margaret and all my family,
with thanks and love.

ABOUT THE AUTHOR

Born in Derry in 1935, with strong Donegal connections, Charlie Herron grew up in the Marlborough area of the city. Charlie was a keen footballer in his youth and his claim to fame remains his time with Derry City FC reserves in the mid-1950s. For many years principal of Foyle View School, in his retirement Charlie's love of spinning tall tales has stood him in good stead as a stalwart of the Colmcille Debating Society and as a four-time winner of the 'prestigious' Baron Von Munchausen competition. More recently known for his story-telling on local radio, Charlie continues to write with storylines never far removed from his native Derry and Donegal. *The Trouble With McCauley* is his second novel.

ACKNOWLEDGEMENTS

When I began, at the request of Guildhall Press, to write this sequel to *McCauley's War*, I was immediately conscious that I was once again at the beginning of another journey. And a very enjoyable journey as it turned out.

Like most novels, *The Trouble With McCauley* is a series of interlocking tales which, when joined, become whole, complete, and meaningful. At least for my sake, and for the reader's sake, I trust that is so.

As I put pen to paper just over eighteen months ago, I was soon reminded of the words of the poet Eduardo Galeano from Montevideo in Uruguay whose thoughts on writing seem similar to my own. The city of Montevideo continues to inspire Galeano. Derry, in Ireland, along with its people, does more than inspire me.

Every day I walk the city that walks me.
I walk through her and she walks through me.
At the edge of the river-sea, river as broad as the sea, the clear air clears my mind and my legs stride on while stories walk inside me.
Walking, I write. At a stroll, words seek each other and find each other and weave stories that later on I write by hand on paper. Those pages are never the final ones. I cross out and crumple up, crumple and cross in search of the words that deserve to exist: fleeting words that yearn to outdo silence.

This novel was first written by hand, a lot of it on crumpled paper. It was then painstakingly edited and transferred by the skilled hands of my daughter Mary to a word-processing screen for which I am very grateful. Thanks to Declan, Peter, Joe, Kevin, Paul and all at Guildhall Press for their unfailing guidance and tireless professionalism in the eventual production process.

A most grateful tribute also to Marilyn McLaughlin for reading and correcting the many flaws in the first draft and guiding it most successfully on its way to its real sense of purpose. Thank you, Marilyn.

To my grandchildren Aideen Herron, Niall Herron, Adam Coyle and Clare Coyle whose brilliant artwork contributions enhance the pages of the novel. Well done, kids!

Profound gratitude to my daughter Ciara and to the rest of my family for their constant advice and encouragement of my writing efforts. Bless you and thank you.

Finally, to my wife Margaret who continues to inspire and support me when the need arises and who never complains of my frequent self-imposed but necessary seclusions – thanks for everything.

These pages are never the final ones. I will continue to write by hand, and cross out and crumple up. And I will always search for the words that deserve to exist.

PROLOGUE

Constable Johnny Johnston was gazing out of the Rosemount Barracks window at the two young boys who'd brazenly climbed into the station yard from Rosemount Terrace. Within seconds, they'd lifted the best three marrows from Sergeant McBride's special plot and hurled them unceremoniously over the perimeter wall and into the waiting arms of two young ruffian types. McBride wouldn't be too pleased about this, thought Johnston with a smile, if he could see what was happening to his precious marrows. But Johnston wasn't too pleased himself when he saw his own seven-year-old son, John, watching the whole carry-on from his very doorway. The child's mother shouldn't have allowed it. Indeed, it made him very angry that the boy should even be a witness in any way to this riffraff behaviour.

But all that worry could end soon: hopefully, within a few days, his sister would be on her way from Dublin to take his daughter, Eva, and the boy across the border to safety until the war was over. Although there hadn't been any German bombings in Derry since the attack on Messines Park last year, when about twelve people were killed, that didn't mean that it couldn't happen again. And with their house being practically next door to the police barracks, Constable Johnston was taking no chances. If his wife didn't like the arrangements he was making for his two children, she could take a running jump to herself. This time, he was putting his foot down.

The two mischief-makers down there in the Terrace looked familiar. Yes, he knew them all right. Sure didn't they live in the same street as himself, just a few doors away? Part of that Mc-Cauley gang they were. And as bold as brass, the whole lot of them.

With regard to the two even bolder boys in the barracks yard below, when he peered more closely, he couldn't help but notice that their faces were identical. And they were dressed exactly the same. Definitely twins, he mused whimsically. He didn't know these two but he'd make it his business to find out shortly who they were.

What Constable Johnston didn't see was the grinning face watching *him* from a bedroom window across the Terrace. If he had, he might have wondered, and worried, if something bigger was afoot, because the face belonged to Dickie McCauley from that Republican family down the street. The same young boy who spent his days hanging about the area and up to no good with his rowdy gang of delinquents. And, unfortunately, the same boy that his young daughter, the headstrong Eva, had now taken up with, even playing football in the street with him. But not for much longer, he hoped.

Maybe it was just as well for the constable's present peace of mind that he hadn't spotted young McCauley.

CHAPTER 1

He's Back, Dickie, Back Up In Our Attic

I knew from the policeman's reaction that he hadn't seen me, even though he was only thirty feet away. I'd made sure of that. My ma's net curtains are useful at times like this. You could see out through them but you can't really see in.

The cop was only interested in what Joey and Hughie Deeney were up to, progging marrows for a dare. It was me that organised it, as a trial for them to get into the gang. If the boys got away with it, they were in. And identical twins could be very handy in the future. They could cause confusion in the ranks of the enemy. And even though the Marlborough gang had broken up, the word was that a crowd called the North Street Bunch were out to take over the whole area. If you could believe the rumour.

'Dickie, you're going to be late!' It was my ma shouting to me from downstairs. 'The meetin' starts at eleven o'clock, and it's well after ten. Mr Kelly's waiting for ye in the van.'

I took one last look through the net curtains. Joey and Hughie were back over the wall. They began to play football with the marrows, up and down the street. Danny Doherty and Kevin Doherty, two of my other gang members, who'd caught the flying marrows, stood there watching. They weren't related. I'd sent them there to check up on how the twin Deeneys did on the test. They'd report back to me later, but I already knew that the twins had passed. I'd even seen the cop nodding his head up and down with the hint of a sneer on his face. Maybe he didn't like marrows. Or maybe he just didn't like Sergeant McBride.

It's a pity Eva Johnston hadn't appeared out of her house in the Terrace, what with all the noise. She'd surely have joined in the marrow-kicking immediately. That's mainly why I liked her, because she was game for anything, and she wouldn't have cared if her da had seen her, even though he would've been raging. It was great, too, that Eva was now an official member of the Dickie McCauley gang. I'd allowed her to join us last year, on the day after she arrived in the Terrace. The others didn't like the idea of having a girl in the gang, but I did. Well, just this girl anyhow. So I changed the rule – because I'd made the rule in the first place – and if they didn't like it, I told them, they could lump it and leave. Nobody left. Now they all like her. But I like her the best and they know it. A lot of adults in Rosemount who know Eva say she's a real tomboy. I looked that word up in the dictionary. And they're right.

I'd heard my ma roaring up to me again. 'Dickie, will ye for God's sake hurry up? Mr Kelly can't wait any longer.'

'Right, Ma,' I shouted, 'I'm comin'.' I thundered down the stairs, jumping the last three onto the hall lino.

'Where's Da?' I called to her as I reached for the door handle. 'Isn't he comin' with me to the College?'

'Naw, son. You'll have to go by yourself. He's not feelin' well the day. He must be comin' down with something.'

I knew by the look in my ma's eyes that she was lying. Covering up for him like she normally did. He was still drunk, that's what he was, drunk since last night. Still too drunk even this morning to go with me to the meeting at the College. An important meeting the letter had said, to inform us about the rules and regulations, and about the subjects we would be studying, and the classes we would be in, and about the school uniform and everything. And we would be seeing round the school and told about its history. Now everything was mucked up. I'd been looking forward to this day for weeks, ever since I'd got word

18

that I'd passed the entrance exam. You'd have thought that my da would have made a special effort, especially after the way he was talking yesterday, telling everybody about how proud he was that his Dickie had got the College exam. Aye, even shouting about it again all over the street when he was coming home last night from the pub. Waking the whole neighbourhood, that's what he was doing. Roaring his head off and singing rebel songs when he was staggering down the Terrace. It was a wonder the police didn't come out of the barracks and arrest him. Me and my wee brother Liam had heard him from our beds. Liam said nothing. He just put his head under the blankets to shut out the noise. He was embarrassed. I was embarrassed, too, but I didn't show it.

My ma interrupted what I was thinking.

'There's something I have to tell ye, Dickie, before ye go,' she said suddenly. 'It's about—'

But then it was me that interrupted *her*.

'Would *you* not come with me, Ma?'

But I knew by the way she was shaking her head and looking at me that she was going nowhere.

'Please, Ma?' I repeated. 'Sure I need some big person to come with me.'

'I can't, Dickie. You'll manage okay, son. I have to stay with *him,* and with wee Liam. I can't leave them, Dickie.'

'What about Kate and Laura? Can't one of *them* come with me?'

Kate and Laura are my two big sisters. They're twins but they're not identical like Joey and Hughie Deeney.

'Naw, son. Sure aren't the girls workin' overtime the day. We need the money, son, what with your da gettin' so little work at the docks. And anyway, Dickie, won't Mr Kelly be with ye, and your wee friend Charlie? You'll be all right, son. Just you go on out to the van, now. Charlie and his father are waitin' for ye. You'll be at the College in no time. Just tell them up there that your father or me couldn't come. You can fill us all in later about the meetin'. Go on now, son, and we'll see ye when ye come back. They're waitin' for ye out there in the van.'

There was no way I was going to a meeting in the College with Mr Kelly and his one-eyed son, Bap, with some people maybe pointing at us and whispering about who Mr Kelly was. About his IRA connections. And about why I was there with them, and not with my da or my ma, or at least one of my big sisters. Naw, no way.

'What was it ye wanted to say to me, Ma?'

'It doesn't matter now, Dickie. It'll keep till ye get back. Hurry up now, son.'

I turned and ran out into the yard, through the back gate and into the lane. My ma shouted after me, but I didn't heed her I was in such a hurry. Our Liam was there playing marbles with somebody from his class at school. I nearly fell over them. Liam was now in the gang as well, even though he was only seven. You have to be eight before you can join, but I'd promised him last year, after he'd got better from the shock when the cops raided our house looking for guns. But up to now I didn't allow him to go on raids, or anything like that. I didn't want my wee brother to get hurt or go mental like he did before.

'Where are ye goin', Dickie?' Liam shouted after me.

I didn't stop to explain. I ran on up the lane towards Creggan Road. But he came after me fast, still shouting. I had to stop. He was out of breath. He pulled at my arm, wanting to tell me something.

'What is it, Liam? I'm in a wile hurry. Can it not wait till I get back?'

'Did my ma not say to ye, Dickie?'

'Say what, Liam?'

'About Uncle Jimmy.'

'What about him?'

'He's back, Dickie, back up in our attic again.'

'He couldn't be, Liam,' I said quickly, my heart sinking. 'Sure he's over the border in Donegal.'

20

'Naw, Dickie, he's back. Honest. And I heard my ma sayin' that he wanted to see ye, and that he had something for ye.'

'Did *you* see him, Liam?'

'Naw, Dickie, I didn't.'

'Okay. Thanks, Liam. Thanks for telling me,' I said as I rushed on.

I couldn't believe what he'd just told me. He mustn't have got it right. Uncle Jimmy back? Naw, that couldn't be true. And back in our house? In the attic bedroom? That's what Liam had said. Now *I* was out of breath after listening to that. He'd stopped me in my tracks all right with that news.

Uncle Jimmy hadn't lived with us for about nine months. I'd hoped I'd never see him again, even if he was my ma's brother. He's an IRA man. And the last time he stayed with us, there was a lot of terrible bother. I was glad to see the back of him when he left. But for now, I had to get him out of my mind, because I had a very important meeting to get to.

I ran on, towards Creggan Road. I knew the way to the College myself. I could get there in about half an hour and be in time for the meeting. I didn't need anybody with me, especially not Bap Kelly or his da. On the way up the lane, I passed Cecil Colhoun's back gate. It was open and Cecil was in the back yard helping his ma to do some work. They saw me. But before I could shout hello to Cecil his ma had pulled him away. I felt sad: Cecil used to be one of my best friends in the gang, but he wasn't in it now and he never even comes out to play with us anymore. His ma doesn't allow him. His da was killed last year by the IRA. He was a B-Special and B-Specials help the police to catch IRA men.

At the top of the lane, I turned left down Creggan Road. But before passing the Terrace, I glanced to my left. The twin Deeneys, and now Danny Doherty as well, were still kicking the marrows about like madmen. To my surprise, Eva appeared from her doorway and joined in the game. Kevin Doherty didn't take part. He just stood there and laughed at them. Kevin sweated a lot, so he didn't run about much.

Constable Johnston had gone from the barracks window. He wouldn't have been too pleased if he'd stayed there looking down at his daughter playing in the street with my crowd. But for now I wasn't really concerned too much about any of this, even though the gang were annoying me a bit with their carry-on. I had other things on my mind. The meeting at the College was in less than an hour. I might even get there before Mr Kelly and Bap, because their van was still sitting outside our door. My ma mustn't have come out yet to tell Mr Kelly about me being away. Or maybe she just forgot because she was so throughother about everything. And especially now, if it was true that Uncle Jimmy was back.

CHAPTER 2

Miracle At The Gasyard

My da came home drunk one night last year and wrecked the house, looking for a gun under the floorboards in the bathroom. It was like a nightmare at the time, but it really did happen and I never forget about it, even when Mr Philson is giving me hassle at school, or when I'm planning raids for the gang, or trying to get enough money to buy gobstoppers for our Liam to stop him blabbing to my ma and da about what I'm up to. It's not just the nightmare thing that I can't get out of my mind, it's nearly everything my da does these days that's annoying me. But for now, I'd have to try and get him out of my mind.

When I reached the crossroads on Creggan Hill, I knew there were different ways I could get to the College. I began to run, my boots clattering loudly on the footpath as I headed as fast as I could down the hill. I began to sweat. If I was late, I'd be the laughing stock of the place when I walked in. Everybody would stare at me. The priest on the platform talking to the people would stop in the middle of his speech when he heard the door of the Big Study opening with a long, noisy creak. He would be very annoyed. Some people would laugh and snigger, especially a couple of the boys from my class in St Eugene's. And in between the giggling, there would be others, like Bap Kelly, who might be embarrassed for me as they watched Dickie McCauley, the Rosemount gang leader and the son of a drunk, struggling to make his way along the centre aisle to an empty seat at the back.

Naw, I wasn't going to let that happen. Being late, I mean. Not if I could help it. Even as I was running alongside the railings of the Cathedral and across the Little Diamond past the slaughterhouse where Danny Doherty's da had been killed by a cow – before Danny was even born – my mind was working hard. I needed a plan that would get me to the College before eleven o'clock.

Halfway down Bogside Street, on the footpath outside his front door, I spotted Bap Kelly's rattly old bike with the loose mudguards. It would do the job. Two of his wee brothers were standing there. They knew me. I shouted to them that I was borrowing the bike for a while. They didn't say a word, just watched me with their mouths open wide as I hopped on the saddle and went like mad down the street. Within a minute, I reached Lecky Road and pedalled as fast as I could towards the gasyard. That's where you turn left up the big brae to get to the College. You couldn't cycle it; the hill is too steep. As I jumped off the bike to begin the heavy push, a horrible thought struck me like a bolt from the blue. I'd forgotten the envelope with the letter in it. It was behind the clock on the mantelpiece in the living room. And I knew off by heart what was in that letter; I'd read it often enough. One page congratulating me on passing the exam, the important exam number on it that I was supposed to bring with me this morning, and the other stating that I had been granted the scholarship. And at the bottom of that page, in large black print, it said that this document must be signed by my da or ma and brought to the meeting. How could I have left it behind me? I felt stupid.

What was I to do? I reckoned it must be after half past ten and I was ten minutes away from the College, but now it would take me another half-hour or more to get home and then back to this spot again. Here I was, standing close to the gasyard, annoyed and frustrated. Annoyed with my ma, annoyed with my da and annoyed with myself for having forgotten the letter, and for having wasted so much time. But even with all the frustration

I felt, my brain was telling me that there could be a solution to this problem if I would only let my mind settle. So I did. And that's when a brilliant thought struck me. Kevin Doherty always prayed when bad things were happening around him, or when he needed something special. Well, I needed something special now. I needed a miracle to happen. I said a quick prayer and thought of what Kevin often said, that God helps those who help themselves. That's when an idea came to me. It was mad. But it was the only thing that I could think of.

I quickly jumped on Bap's bike and cycled as fast as I could, back the way I'd come, over Lecky Road, up Bogside Street, past the slaughterhouse and straight up the path towards the Cathedral. Father Mooney would be there. He was the priest-in-charge. He would know what to do. He knew everything.

I banged the knocker very loudly at the Parochial House. A woman came to the door, shushing me to be quiet. She looked angry. Before she could say anything, I shouted, 'I'm lookin' for Father Mooney. I need to see him right away. It's wile important.'

'Calm down, son,' said the woman. 'And anyway, ye can't see him, because he's not here.'

'Where is he?' I shouted again. 'I have to see him.'

'Don't be cheeky with me, son. If ye tell me what it's all about, maybe I can help ye.'

This woman was wasting time. It must be nearly twenty to eleven.

'You can't help me, Missus,' I said, trying to appear calmer. 'Where is Father Mooney? I really have to see him.'

'I told ye, son. Ye can't. He's over in the chapel hearing Confessions and he won't be free until twelve o'clock. Ye can see him then if ye'd like tae wait.'

'I can't wait, Missus,' I shouted. 'I have to see him now.'

Without saying anything else, I ran off towards the chapel. I didn't look back at her. If it was twenty minutes to eleven, there was still time to do something about the College meeting.

Father Mooney would know what to do. Before I knew it, I was in the porch of the Cathedral blessing myself at the holy-water font. I walked quickly up the left-hand aisle. There were three Confession boxes. Father Mooney's was the middle one.

'What time is it?' I whispered to the man sitting outside Father Mooney's.

'Shush,' he said.

'Can I go in before ye?' I asked the man. 'I have to see Father Mooney right away. It's wile important.'

'Shush,' said the man again.

I kept quiet and waited for a chance to make my move. And when the door of the Confession box opened, I rushed from my seat past a wee woman who was coming out. Even before the Confession box door had banged behind me, I thumped the grill, hoping that Father Mooney would open it before he began hearing the Confession of whoever was on the other side.

'What's this?' he whispered loudly. 'Who are you? What's all the racket about?'

'It's me, Father. It's Dickie McCauley. I have something very important to say to ye, and it can't wait.'

I heard the priest taking two big deep breaths before he spoke. 'This is very unusual, Richard. Most inappropriate indeed.'

I whispered frantically, 'I need you to help me, Father. I need you to do something right away.'

'What is it, son?'

I had his attention. Maybe the first part of the miracle was working. I told him everything inside a minute: about my da being drunk, about my ma having to stay with him and Liam, about the twins' overtime in the factory and about the letter I'd left behind the clock on the mantelpiece. I even told him about borrowing Bap Kelly's bike. But most important of all, I told him that the meeting in the College was to start in about fifteen minutes.

Father Mooney knew that I had passed the exam, because he'd been up to our house the day after I got word and he'd given me sixpence. He was very pleased and he even asked me that same day if I'd like to become an altar boy. I said I would. So he told me there and then that he would inform my teacher, Mr Philson, before the end of the school year so that he could teach me the Latin responses.

'Richard, my son,' he said in an annoyed voice. 'I understand the dilemma you're in, but I don't think I can help you at this very minute. Can't you see I'm busy now? Hearing Confessions?'

'But, Father,' I pleaded, 'there's only one man left outside your box. Couldn't he go to Father Martin or Father Donohue? Please, Father. Please help me. The meetin's startin' soon. Sure you could ring the President of the College and get him to delay everything until I get there with my letter. Please, Father. Please help me.'

Father Mooney didn't speak for a few moments. I knew he was working things out in his mind. That's what I always did when I had a big problem to solve. I'd go quiet even if the gang were with me. They always knew to shut up when I was like that. They'd see my face scrunched up and my teeth tight together and my eyes half-closed. That's probably what Father Mooney was doing at this very minute. And that's why I'd shut up. To give him time to think.

Suddenly, Father Mooney spoke. 'Right, Richard,' he said, 'come with me.'

I knew he'd made a decision. Before I could say anything, he was out of the Confession box and hurrying down the aisle, me trailing after him. He'd told the man waiting at his box that he'd be back in five minutes. The miracle might be working. I'd know soon. I looked up at the big clock on the gallery wall. It was after a quarter to eleven. On the way down the aisle, he went over to Father Donohue's box. There was nobody waiting there for Confession. He pulled back the curtain and whispered something to him. Father Donohue came out immediately and followed us quickly out of the chapel and over towards the Parochial House.

Things were happening.

'Go youse on, Father John,' he shouted, throwing him the key of his big black car. 'Rosemount first, and then straight to the College. And you can put that wee bike in the boot. Richard here will fill you in on all the details. Hurry now, Father, I have things to see about. And, Richard . . .'

'Yes, Father?'

'I hope you're still willing to become an altar server,' he said with a big grin.

'I am, Father,' I replied breathlessly. 'I'd love to be an altar boy.'

'Good, good,' said Father Mooney before he rushed into the Parochial House.

Within seconds, we were out of the Cathedral grounds and speeding up Creggan Hill towards Rosemount. I'd never been in a car before. It was great. Not only that, but it was a priest's car. Father Mooney's. The miracle was coming together. I felt it in my bones, the same feeling I always got when plans I'd made for a gang raid or something began to work.

When I told Father Donohue what I needed and where I lived, he turned right, into the Terrace, and pulled up outside our house. The street was still a mess with bits of marrow, and birds were all over the place, pecking at the stuff and then flying away when Danny and Kevin and the Deeneys and Liam went chasing after them. I noticed Eva wasn't there. If I hadn't more important things to do now, I'd have stopped their stupid game right away. Instead, I rushed into the house, got the letter from the mantelpiece and shouted to my ma to write her name at the bottom of the second page. She was so shocked at seeing me again that she didn't speak. She just signed the letter and handed it back to me as I rushed out and back into the priest's car. I didn't give her time to ask what was up. And if she had asked, I wouldn't have had time to answer her.

By this time, half the street were out to see what was going on. The gang crowded around the car, looking into it, their big mouths hanging open. Like gawks. My ma looked the same as she stood watching from the door.

28

Father Donohue drove off, laughing, but I couldn't see anything funny about all this. Seagulls and pigeons were flying everywhere in front of the car. It was a crazy scene. I turned the handle to let the window down because I was so hot and sweaty. I could hear the gang shouting my name as they ran after us to the end of the Terrace. I soon closed it up again.

'You must have some influence with Father Mooney,' said Father Donohue, still laughing as we drove down past the Cathedral and turned right towards Bogside Street. 'It's not everybody he'll go to such bother for.'

'Aye, he knows me well, Father, and he knows my ma and my da and the twins and our Liam. Our Liam's seven, Father, but I allowed him into the gang because of what happened to him with the cops last year.'

I was so excited now I couldn't shut up. We were on our way.

'Talkin' about cops, Father,' I went on, 'do ye not think it's strange that Catholic cops go to Mass with their guns in their holsters?' I asked him that because I'd noticed one or two of them at the back of the chapel in their uniforms. In fact, I'd seen Constable Johnston and his wife – and Eva – kneeling at the back last Sunday, and him with the full outfit on him, gun and all.

Father Donohue wasn't laughing now. Instead, he began to cough and didn't finish coughing until he reached the end of Bogside Street and turned onto Lecky Road. His face had gone red, but he did speak.

'It's like this, Richard,' he said. 'Everybody chooses his own vocation in life. And they follow that vocation as they see fit. Some people become priests, some become teachers, some bankers, some policemen, and so on. And they all take their responsibilities very seriously.'

I noticed right away that he didn't say dockers or factory workers or street sweepers or binmen or breadmen or anything like that. But even though I had a few other questions for him before we reached the College, I let him talk on.

'So, with regard to the policemen, Richard, with their full

uniforms on, it's probably because they're going on duty immediately after Mass.'

Father Donohue took a deep breath when he'd finished speaking. But I wasn't finished yet, because he hadn't fully answered my question. And I knew by the look on the priest's face that he wasn't happy when I spoke again.

'About the guns, Father. Do you think they should bring guns into God's house? Sure couldn't they go to an earlier Mass in their ordinary clothes and then go home afterwards and put on their police outfits?' He didn't answer but started coughing again as if he didn't want me to say anything else.

'Well, here we are, Richard,' he said, still spluttering a bit, but looking relieved as he drove up the path towards the College. 'Father Mooney's instructions were that I should leave you here. You're to go inside, into the Big Study. That's what he told me. Now, I'll get your bike out of the boot and you can leave it round the corner. It'll be safe there. Okay, Richard?'

'Yes, Father. Thanks,' was all I could say.

I felt like an idiot, standing there with Bap Kelly's old bike as Father Donohue shouted, 'Good luck,' and drove off. Stupid, that's what I felt as well, because I should have asked him about Father Mooney's plan instead of talking in the car all the time about cops and guns and everything. Rubbish stuff. But then again, I was thinking, when *I* made a plan for my gang, I didn't always tell them what it was. I just ordered them all to follow instructions, like the instructions the priest had given me a minute ago. Anyway, Father Donohue probably didn't know what Father Mooney's plan was. But I'd soon find that out for myself. In about a minute or so.

When I left the bike at the gable wall, I went to the outside toilet block. I cleaned my face and fixed my hair with a bit of a comb that I always carried. Half of the teeth were missing, but it did the job.

Now it was crunch time. I walked up the steps into the building. The Big Study door was to my right as I entered. A large staircase went up from the entrance hall to God knows where. Probably classrooms. It was a big place. The biggest place I'd ever been in, probably even bigger than Gwyn's Institute in Brooke Park.

I listened outside the door before turning the handle. I could hear nothing. No voices from inside. Maybe it was soundproof. My heart was thumping. I had a lot of questions in my head. Like, had Father Mooney been able to make some special arrangement for me from the Parochial House? And, had he been able to get in touch with his friend the President? Would I open the door now and find everybody looking at me as I first feared? Would Dickie McCauley be exposed as a stupid gawk? Or would the miracle happen? The one I'd prayed for at the gasyard over half an hour ago.

I turned the handle of the big door. It creaked. I remembered Kevin Doherty's favourite prayer. I said it quickly into myself: 'Oh, Most Sacred Heart of Jesus, I place all my trust in Thee.'

I then pushed it open, just wide enough to slip in. I looked around the place. Not a being was there. I suddenly felt excited, because I had a good feeling about everything now. I took the envelope from my pocket. It was a bit crumpled, but that didn't matter. I was here. And I wasn't late for the meeting. In fact, not only was I not late, I was the first one there. Father Mooney was brilliant. He'd done it. A miracle had happened. I made my way to a seat at the back and settled myself down after all the excitement.

A short time later, when the boys and their mas and das began coming into the Big Study, none of them seemed to notice me. And a couple of minutes after that, when the place was packed, the priest came into the room. Everybody stood up. He then said a prayer, but before he began talking about the rules and regulations, he apologised for the earlier change of plan. This, he said, was due to unavoidable circumstances, but he hoped that everybody had enjoyed the tour of the College during the last half-hour.

So that's how Father Mooney had done it! Brilliant. I couldn't have organised it better myself. And I was able to hide down every time I saw Bap Kelly looking round, searching for me. I didn't want him to see me. I didn't want to have anything to do with him. For the same reason that I didn't want Uncle Jimmy back in our house. And that's just the way it is. They had their lives; I had mine. And even though I was feeling good at this very minute, there was a very bad worry creeping into the back of my mind. And it was this: if our Liam was right, if Uncle Jimmy was really back in Derry, and staying in our house, then there was big danger for the McCauley family again. Maybe worse danger than last year, when people died and when others got badly hurt. And why would he want to see *me* anyway? I'd have to think more about that one. But later. For now, I would concentrate on the priest's speech.

CHAPTER 3

Now It Was My Turn To Cry

When I got back to Rosemount Terrace, I saw a very strange sight. Something you could never have imagined. Danny Doherty, Kevin Doherty and the twin Deeneys were sweeping the street. As they went along, they lifted millions of pieces of marrows into tin buckets. Constable Johnston was standing in his doorway, watching them. Eva was beside him, grinning from ear to ear. It was embarrassing. But not for me. I just kept my head down as I passed him, but still high enough to notice Eva winking at me. That made me feel good. If her da had seen her he'd have been annoyed.

As I walked into the living room, my da got up from his armchair and came to me, his arms out, wanting to hug me. His eyes were bulging out of his sockets and they were red and watery. He threw his arms around me and pulled me close to his big fat belly. I felt ashamed for him, for the state he was in. I hated the rotten smell off him, of whiskey and Guinness and sweat. And when he spoke, his voice was hoarse, probably from all the singing last night, and all his shouting yesterday, about me getting into the College. I pushed back from him a bit and looked up at his face. In his tearful eyes I could see *his* shame, too, and his embarrassment. And sorrow. Sorrow for what he was doing to himself, to the rest of us. He couldn't help it. That's what my ma had told me, often.

'I'm sorry, Dickie,' he said. 'I know I should have been with ye the day at the College. I've no excuses, son, and I promise ye wan thing this day if I never promise ye anything else, and that's that I'm goin' to make it up to ye. To youse all. And soon.'

Now, it was my turn to cry.

'It's okay, Da,' I sobbed. 'It's okay, everything's okay. I got to the College all right, Da. Father Donohue took me there in the car and I was in time and everything. Father Mooney sorted it. And the meetin' was great and I handed the signed form to the College priest and I'll be starting there in September. I'll be nearly eleven then, Da.'

But what I didn't tell him was about the hassle I had all morning trying to get to the College on time. Or about praying for a miracle near the gasyard. Or about taking Bap Kelly's bike. Or about Father Mooney making a last-minute phone call to his friend the President. Or about me not seeing round the College with the rest of them. And I saw no point in telling him that when the College priest was taking the signed form from me, he had a very grim look on his face. A look that wasn't a bit pleased with me. A look that even scared me a wee bit, especially when he called me Mr McCauley, and when he hissed through his teeth at me that what had happened between Father Mooney and the President was definitely a one-off favour. And that there would be no more favours. Not while he had anything to do with College arrangements in the future. That from here on in I would have to look out for myself.

'Do you understand what I'm saying to you, Mr McCauley?'

'I do, Father,' I replied.

Naw, there was no need to tell my da anything else, especially about what the priest had said to me, because God only knows what he would have done about it. Some things were better left for me to deal with in my own way and in my own time.

'Aye, Dickie,' said my da as he interrupted my thoughts, 'you're a big boy now. So it's nearly eleven ye are? I almost forgot. Sure don't the weeks and the months fly in? Ye've grown up that fast, son.' And he hugged me again, tight. I caught sight of

34

my ma out of the corner of my eye. She must have been standing there, at the living-room door, listening to me and my da, for she had a tear in her eye, too. And when she saw me looking at her, she rushed forward and hugged me, too, saying that she was sorry about this morning. That she was glad everything went well at the College.

There we were, my da and ma and me, hugging each other in our living room. It had never happened before. And if our Kate or Laura had seen us, they'd have giggled their heads off and probably made some smart-alec remarks like 'how come we never get hugged like that?' But I was lapping it up at this very minute. It wasn't often that I was the centre of attention in the house, and for all the right reasons. It made me feel good. So good, in fact, that I thought this could be the right time to ask them about Uncle Jimmy. I pulled away from both of them as I spoke. And I had a very serious and concerned look on my face. Not a put-on job, but the Real McCoy.

'Is it true, Ma, that Uncle Jimmy is back? Is it true what Liam was sayin'? If it is, he shouldn't be here, Ma, not in our house, not up in the attic again, Ma.' I turned to my da. 'The police will get him, Da, and put him in jail, and youse, too. This isn't a good safe house for him. He should have stayed in Donegal anyway, or Dublin, or wherever.' There it was. Everything out. All the fears that were on my mind. And I'd hardly taken a breath when I was speaking. Now I had to take a deep breath because my heart was thumping.

When I'd finished, my da pulled away from me and went back towards his armchair. I heard him giving a big sigh, almost a grunt. Before he sat down, he stared straight at me and put his finger to his lips. He wanted me to say nothing more. It was as if he was afraid, but I knew by looking at him that what Liam had told me was true; my da wasn't pleased about it, either. It was my ma who spoke. And she had a firm look on her face.

'Aye, Dickie, your Uncle Jimmy's stayin' with us for a wee wile. He has some work to do in the town. But don't be worryin';

35

he'll only be here for a week or so and nobody will recognise him anyway.'

How could they be so stupid? How could they allow him to stay with us? That's what my face was showing. And my ma knew it. And how would people not recognise him? That was a silly thing to say.

'It'll be okay, Dickie. Don't worry,' she went on. 'He won't be goin' out durin' the day, just at night when it's dark. And if nobody says anythin' to anybody outside the house, sure who's to know he's here at all?'

'But *we* know, Ma. Me and Liam and probably Kate and Laura, as well as youse.'

'Aye, son. It's just the family, just us that knows, an' we'll be sayin' nothin' to anybody. Anyway, Dickie, he wants to see ye. He's all chuffed about ye gettin' into the College. And I think he has something for ye.'

Well, I didn't want anything off him, but maybe I was a wee bit curious about why he was back in Derry.

'Now,' my ma continued, 'I'll go and make youse all a nice cup of tea and ye can bring Uncle Jimmy's up to him.' She turned and went out to the kitchen without saying anything else, but I noticed that she'd given my da a sharp look. The kind of look she sometimes gave *me* if she wasn't pleased with what I was up to. I stared at my da, still with my annoyed face. He knew I wasn't happy about this, even if he was still half-drunk. He waved me over.

'Dickie, son,' he whispered loudly into my ear, 'ye probably know by now that I don't agree anymore with all this badness, with the shootin' and killin' and all, and the bother it brings to everybody. Naw, son, I don't agree with it wan bit, and . . .'

He stopped talking when he heard my ma coming back into the room.

'Dickie,' she said as she leaned against the doorpost, 'will ye go out to the street and bring Liam in? Tell him his tea and piece is ready.'

'Right, Ma,' I replied and headed for the hall. As I was opening the glass door, I heard my ma's angry voice.

'Barney, don't be talkin' to the wain about politics, and about things he doesn't understand. I heard ye there, whispering to Dickie. He's far too young to understand what's happenin' in this country. He'll know all about it in a few years when he's old enough. And another thing, Barney McCauley,' – her voice was getting louder, – 'it was me that invited our Jimmy back here, because he has unfinished business and I'm stickin' by him no matter what you think. So ye can just shut up and drink yourself to death for all I care, because it's you and the likes of ye that has done nothin' for Ireland.'

As I was closing the glass door very quietly behind me, not wanting my ma to know that I'd been listening, I was aware that I didn't hear my da saying anything back to her. But I could imagine his face. Not wanting to annoy her. And not agreeing with her, either.

My heart was thumping like mad as I walked down the street. My ears were still ringing with my ma's words. I'd never heard her as annoyed as that before. I was shocked. And very worried. And even though I'd known for a good while that my da wanted the British out of Ireland as well, it was only when he was badly drunk that he sang rebel songs and talked about Hitler coming to take over. When he wasn't drinking, he just listened to the war news on the wireless.

And my two sisters thought the same way as my ma and Uncle Jimmy. It just wasn't right. And it had me worried.

Liam and Danny and Kevin and the twin Deeneys were standing near the air-raid shelter. They stopped talking when they saw me. Liam shouted, 'Dickie, all the gang, except me and Eva, had to clear up the street. The cop made them do it. He saw them stealin' the marrows and makin' the whole mess in the Terrace. They were stupid, Dickie, gettin' caught.' When Liam was talking, the gang had their heads down as if they were ashamed.

'Shut up, Liam,' I said, 'and stop blabbin'. Your ma wants ye in now. Tell her I'll be home in a minute. I want to speak to the gang.'

'Bugger off,' shouted Liam as he walked away in a huff. 'You're not the boss of me if it's not a gang thing. And messing up the street wasn't a gang thing. So there.'

Danny and the twins laughed. Kevin didn't. He didn't like to hear Liam cursing.

One of the Deeney twins then spoke. 'Dickie . . .' he said.

I stared at him. I didn't know whether it was Joey or Hughie, because their faces were identical and their clothes were identical. I decided to take a chance.

'What is it, Joey?'

'I'm Hughie,' he said with a straight face. That's when I decided that I'd have to come up with something so that in future I'd be able to tell them apart.

'Okay,' I said, 'what is it, Hughie?'

But Danny began laughing at the mistake I'd made. And I didn't like people laughing at me, especially fat Danny Doherty, son of Mrs Fatso Lardo Doherty. I'd see to him later.

'Bugger off, Danny,' I shouted to him. Kevin's eyes began to rise. He thought there was going to be a big row. But there wasn't, because I'd given Danny one of my special looks that said *don't tangle with me at this second because you'll come off worst.* And Danny Doherty took the hint.

'How did we do the day, Dickie?' asked Hughie. 'At the barracks? Did we pass the test to get into the gang?'

'You're both in,' I said to the twins. 'Youse did great the day. I saw youse. And messin' up the street afterwards with the marrows was a great idea. Who thought of that?' I asked that question because I wanted to find out who was stupid enough to come up with the idea.

'It was me,' said Danny, all proud of himself.

'Well done,' I said to him, but he knew by the way I spoke and by the way I looked at him that I wasn't pleased. That the whole carry-on was one of the stupidest things you could do. And destroying good food into the bargain. He got the message. Danny Doherty was getting too big for his boots. And you don't get much bigger than Danny Doherty. I'd sort him out later. For now, I had too many important things on my mind. Mostly about Uncle Jimmy.

Danny Doherty and Kevin walked on up the Terrace. That gave me the chance I needed to talk to the Deeney twins. I had something very important to ask them. It was about an order to carry out a mission of great importance. And I knew by their faces that they were pleased when I told them what the mission was. Little did I know then that what I was asking them to do would shortly become part of my plan to get rid of Uncle Jimmy. That's the way my brain worked sometimes. Planning stuff in advance that just might come in useful.

CHAPTER 4

At That Second I Could Have Been Killed

'Is that you, Dickie?' It was my ma. She was in the kitchen. She'd turned round when she heard the glass door opening. 'Your piece and tea is out.'

'Thanks, Ma,' I said as I walked past her into the living room.

But she called after me. 'As soon as ye've eaten, I want ye to bring that wee snack on the table up to your uncle.'

At the mention of Uncle Jimmy, I looked over at my da. He shrugged his shoulders and I noticed, too, that his eyes went up a bit like Kevin Doherty's. Liam was sitting on the chair at the table.

'Dickie,' he whispered as he turned and came towards me, 'me ma says we're not to tell anybody that Uncle Jimmy's back. It's a secret, and we're not to breathe a word about him outside the house, 'cause if we do, we could all be in big trouble. But why is that, Dickie? And why would you and me end up in big trouble?'

I pushed him back over to the table and told him to sit down. My da's eyes were closed. He looked to be asleep.

'It's like this, Liam,' I whispered. 'That's just the way it is. Uncle Jimmy's stayin' here for a while, so don't be mentioning it to anybody. It would be like blabbin'. Okay, Liam?'

He said nothing for a second. Just looked at me. I still hadn't answered his questions and I saw the disappointment in his eyes. He still wanted answers.

'Naw, it's not okay, Dickie. Why is it such a big secret? Why is he here anyway?'

'Look, Liam,' I said to him with the kind of put-on voice that meant I was fed up talking about Uncle Jimmy. 'I can't explain it yet, but I'll tell ye everything later. You go on out now and remind the gang that we're meetin' in the air-raid shelter at six o'clock.'

'Will I tell Eva, too, Dickie?'

'Aye, Liam, the whole gang. Eva and all.'

When Liam left the room, my da whispered to me, 'Well done, son. I think ye have the wee lad well trained.' I couldn't believe that he'd been listening.

He laughed quietly when he spoke, but I didn't think it was funny. There was nothing funny about any of this. When he saw my serious face, he changed his tune.

'Aye, I think wee Liam will keep his mouth shut, Dickie. But ye never know with wains.'

My da stopped talking for a bit before he went on. But not before he reached down the side of the chair and picked up an open bottle of Guinness and began drinking. He then smacked his lips together before speaking again.

'Do ye understand what a safe house is, Dickie?'

'Aye, I do, Da,' I sighed. 'Bap Kelly explained it to me wan time when—'

'Aye, the Kellys, son. They wouldn't know what a safe house was if it bit them up the arse.'

He laughed out loud this time when he said that. I just let him ramble on about the Kellys and about safe houses, but my mind blocked out most of what he was saying. Instead, I was thinking now that if there was anybody in our house who might blab about Uncle Jimmy, it was my da, especially when he was drunk. Because he got really stupid when he was drunk. I was thinking, too, that Uncle Jimmy must know that. And my ma must know that. And Kate and Laura, too. But *as* for Kate and Laura, you'd imagine that they'd be well out of all this IRA stuff because of what happened last year to their boyfriends Joey and Peter. Naw, the twins just wanted to be in the thick of things. They were worse than mad. And they were probably even planning some sort of revenge on the cops for the killing of Joey and Peter. I definitely now knew that I was right to try and do something about all this.

My brain was already working on it when my ma came back into the room. My da stopped rambling on when he heard her.

'Right, son,' she said. 'Bring that wee snack up to your uncle now. It'll do him till he gets his dinner at half six.'

'Okay, Ma,' I said as I took the tray from her.

I walked slowly up the stairs, thinking hard. What would I say to him? And what did he want to see me about? I was on the landing now. My mind began to race. Another set of stairs to go. What if I just pleaded with him? To leave us in peace. To go to some proper safe house. What if I put on a cry-and-sob job, with tears and snotters? Or even shout and curse at him and tell him what I really thought of him? Or what if I go the whole hog, the quiet way, and tell him that killing is wrong? Like it said in the commandments. Fifth: thou shalt not kill. Wasn't that what the priests were always telling us from the pulpit when bad things like murder happened in Derry or in other parts of Ireland? But would Uncle Jimmy listen to me? Probably not. He'd told me before that when there was a war on, it was okay to kill people. Like the war between England and Germany and the war between the IRA and the British.

I was halfway up the attic stairs when I heard heavy snoring. He was sound asleep. Should I go on up and leave the tray there or head back down? Or should I make a deliberate loud noise, like a cough or a false sneeze that would waken him? I decided to go on up and leave the food with him and slip quietly out of the room again.

As I tiptoed silently into the attic bedroom, I almost dropped the tray, because of what I was seeing, and if I had dropped the tray, I was thinking at that second, I could have been killed.

Because there was Uncle Jimmy – although he did look differ-ent: his hair was dyed black and he had a beard and a moustache – propped up in the bed, half-under the blanket, eyes closed, snoring away, and with a gun in his hand! He could have shot me, what with the shock of waking up suddenly and stupid with sleep.

My heart was racing like mad, so I took a couple of very quiet, deep breaths. This was worse than the time last year my da had shown me the gun under the floorboards in the bathroom. This was definitely worse than any arguments I ever had in school with Mr Philson. I swallowed hard, quietly, and breathed very lightly. I had to make a decision, and that was to get out of this bedroom as quickly as possible. And as quietly as possible. And I had to think hard, too, about a couple of things. Should I leave the tray down and risk making a noise or should I back out slowly and take it with me? I decided to leave it.

That's when I got the next big shock, for when I was look-ing round the room to see where I should put the tray, my eyes nearly popped out of my head. There in the left corner, against the wall, were about ten rifles and a bag of bullets lying on the floor beside them. You could see into the bag. I stood there, half-paralysed with fear.

I took one last look at Uncle Jimmy lying in bed. Uncle Jim-my, the big-time captain in the IRA. That's what my da had called him to his face last year when they had an argument. A 'big-time captain'. I left the tray on a wee table and slipped out of the room. When he wakened, he would know right away that somebody had been here. Some IRA man that, I was thinking, being seen fast asleep with a gun in his hand. And when he heard who had left the tray, he'd be even more embarrassed that he'd been caught out by a ten-year-old wain. Aye, I was glad I left the tray. That would be me one-up on Uncle Jimmy. But as I was going down the stairs, I felt very, very scared.

When I got to the hall, I could see my ma in the kitchen, washing dishes. She was acting normal. Surely she couldn't know that the attic bedroom was full of weapons. She called out to me, 'Well, Dickie, did ye have a good chat with your Uncle Jimmy? He told me this morning that he had somethin' for ye. Was it somethin' nice, son?'

'Naw, Ma,' I said. 'I didn't get talkin' to him. He was sound asleep. I didn't want to waken him. And I just left the tray there. He can get the food when he wakes up.' I don't know how I got that out without exploding at her.

'That's okay, son,' she replied. 'Sure ye can talk to him later when he gets up. Why don't ye go out to play now?'

Before leaving the house, I looked into the living room. My da was sleeping. He had a Guinness bottle lying sideways in his hand. Empty. I looked at the clock on the mantelpiece. It was after two. I'd be starving by the time the girls got home from the factory but I didn't care. Just now, I wasn't a bit hungry. And food was the last thing I'd be worrying about for the rest of the day.

CHAPTER 5

A Mad, Crazy Sort Of Plan

Before closing the glass door behind me, I looked at my ma. I wanted to run back to her at that moment. To tell her what I'd seen. To plead with her. She was the one who could make all this go away. She was the one who could tell Uncle Jimmy to disappear. To take everything with him. And not come back. Ever. But it was useless. And I knew it. She wouldn't have listened. Not to me anyhow. She was too caught up thinking about Uncle Jimmy and the IRA and only half-thinking about me and Liam. There was no point talking to my da about it, either. I'd definitely have to sort all this out by myself. With some help!

I stood in the porch for the guts of five minutes. In shock. Trying to work out what I could do. Nothing sensible was coming to me. I was shaking. My heart was still thumping and I was breathing very fast. I needed to calm down, because some stupid thoughts were now running through my mind. Thoughts like slipping back into the house, going up the stairs and quietly taking the guns and bullets from under a sleeping Uncle Jimmy's nose and dumping them somewhere. Thoughts like me and Liam starting a very big screaming match in the house this evening when everybody's there, except Uncle Jimmy, and with us maybe threatening to run away from home if they didn't do as we asked. And even some mad thoughts about me going to Bap Kelly's da to ask him to contact the IRA and get the guns, *and* my uncle, to a proper safe house this very day. Aye, these were some of the stupid notions running through my brain at this minute. I felt helpless.

I looked up and down the Terrace. Danny and Kevin and Liam were playing ball at the air-raid shelter. By now, Liam would have told everybody about the meeting at six o'clock. Maybe I'd feel better by then. But for now, I didn't want to talk to anybody, so I just walked slowly up the footpath towards Creggan Road. I needed to be by myself. To have time to think. But that's when I remembered that I was to meet Eva Johnston at half two outside her school gate. She'd arranged it. She said she wanted to give me something. And before that, I had to check out something else with the Deeney twins.

Mrs Fatso Lardo Doherty, Danny's ma, was standing in her doorway with her big fat arms folded. She was alone, probably talking to herself.

'Hello, Dickie,' she said, pointing to her left as I passed her. 'The boys are down there playin', down that way, son.'

Mind your own business, you big fat nosey parker. Why don't ye go back into the house and get yourself a big feed? And stop bothering me.

'It's okay, Mrs Doherty. I have a wee message to do. I'll see them later.'

I walked on slowly, keeping my head down, not wanting any of the gang to come after me, not wanting anybody else to talk to me. I had too much on my mind at this minute for stupid talk. Out of the blue, I heard a whispering voice calling me. 'Dickie, Dickie.' I stopped for a second and listened. I was outside Cecil Colhoun's front door. He'd left the gang last September after his father was murdered. I nearly always slowed up as I was passing Cecil's house, hoping that he would be standing at the door. He never was. The voice was coming from the direction of the front sitting-room window. 'Dickie.' I heard it again. I stopped and walked backwards a wee bit and peered through the window. I saw a movement. It was Cecil. The window was open a bit.

'Dickie,' I heard him whisper again, 'take these.' He pushed a bunch of comics through the space. 'They're for you, and for Liam. I have to go now.' And he disappeared behind the curtains.

I could hardly believe it. It gave me a great feeling. Cecil talking to me again after all this time. It made me forget for a minute about Uncle Jimmy and the guns and stuff in the attic.

I shoved the comics up my jumper and waved a silent goodbye to him. I couldn't wait to show them to Liam, because I hadn't really bought many since Billy Burnside left the street.

Billy had been another of my best friends and always gave me loads of comics. He'd been next to me in the gang. Everybody liked him. But the gang hadn't been the same since my two friends left. We hadn't gone on any decent raids or kidnapped people or shocked anybody with the loose electric wire at Cnoc na Ros snooker hall. In fact, we'd done hardly anything.

I turned right at the top of the Terrace and down towards the girls' school. At this minute, I didn't feel in the form for meeting Eva because of everything that was happening in our house. But I had no choice. I couldn't very well have knocked at her door with some stupid excuse that I couldn't meet her. She'd have seen through that right away. Uncle Jimmy was spoiling everything. But I still wondered what Eva was going to give me.

I hurried on down the slope, tucking my jumper inside my belt to keep Cecil's comics from slipping out. I had about fifteen minutes to wait before Eva would come, so I dandered a bit further on towards the big, sloping field on the right. This was the North Street Bunch's territory and I hoped I wouldn't be spotted. It would look very bad for me if I was captured. I could imagine what people would say if that happened. About stupid Dickie McCauley getting himself caught by the new Rosemount gang. I'd be finished. Danny Doherty wouldn't let me live that one down. And Kevin Doherty wouldn't stop praying until I was let go.

Even though there was only a little danger here, I'd still stay alert and keep my eyes peeled. If the twin Deeneys were doing the job I'd asked them to do earlier, they'd be in far more danger than me. I'd ordered them to lie low and spy on the North Street Bunch, who were building a dam at the bottom of the field. I'd spotted a whole crowd of the enemy a few days earlier beginning to block up the stream that ran through the lower fields. They were using old planks of wood and sods. I remember at the time wishing that *I* had thought of it. Danny and Kevin and the twin Deeneys would have loved that plan. We could have made our own swimming pool. At this very moment, I was feeling a bit jealous of this North Street Bunch.

But now, before Eva came, I'd have to check if the Deeneys were on the job. I needn't have worried, for there they were, letting on to play football at the upper end of the field, tapping the ball to each other, now and again running after it down the slope for a bit, pretending they had miskicked it, but cleverly watching at the same time what was happening at the bottom of the field. Aye, these Deeney boys were good. They came running over when they spotted me.

'Dickie,' said Joey breathlessly. I knew before he said another word that it was Joey, and not Hughie. Because of his hair. I'd asked him earlier, over in the Terrace, if he'd comb it the opposite way to Hughie so that I could tell the difference. From right to left, I'd said, like girls do. And he had. I smiled to myself when I saw it. It really did make him look a wee bit different. But not much. Probably nobody else would notice. That would suit me.

'Hello, Joey. Hello, Hughie,' I replied, allowing them time to catch their breaths before they said anything else. 'Have youse completed the mission? Did any of them see youse watchin'?'

'Nobody saw us, Dickie,' said Hughie, full of excitement. 'And you were right: they're all down there makin' a swimming pool. The dam's nearly built. It looks smashin', Dickie.'

'Great work, boys,' I said, grinning at them.

'Thanks, Dickie,' said Joey.

'Youse have done well,' I went on. But even as I spoke, I could sense that a real good plan regarding Uncle Jimmy's removal from our house was also forming at the back of my mind. And I knew immediately that my earlier instinct about telling the Deeneys to carry out this mission was spot-on.

'What are we goin' to do next, Dickie?' This time it was Joey who spoke. 'Are we goin' to wreck the dam? We're up for it, Dickie. You just give us the word.'

'I know youse are ready, boys,' I said to them, 'but we've got to work this out very carefully. And don't worry. One way or the other, we'll sort that crowd out. Aye, we'll soon spoil their stupid games.'

'Great, Dickie,' said Hughie. 'We can't wait.'

And that's when I realised that I really would need their help. Without the Deeney twins, the plan that was building up in my mind about Uncle Jimmy wouldn't work. For it was a mad, crazy sort of plan that I was hatching. And I knew it wouldn't work with just me and Joey and Hughie. Danny and Kevin would have to be involved, too, even though I wouldn't let them know what the real plan was. And because it was a very dangerous plan, there was no way that I could allow Eva and our Liam to be involved. I'd have to find a way of keeping them out of it. From not even hearing about it.

'And listen,' I continued. 'There's something else I want to say to youse.'

'What is it, Dickie?' they said together.

'Well, it's like this,' I replied quickly. 'After what youse did the day, first at the barracks with the marrows, and now the spyin' job on the North Street Bunch, I have to tell youse that I'm pro-motin' the both of youse as the two deputy leaders of the gang. But say nothin' yet to anybody.'

They were speechless when they heard this. I knew they were delighted. But the way my mind was working now was that I needed right-hand men in the gang that I could trust, because ever since Billy and Cecil had left, things just hadn't been the same. Danny and Kevin had tried to fill in for them, but they were useless. They couldn't carry out orders properly and nothing important was getting done. So that's why I was coming out with this stuff now about promoting the twin Deeneys. Because their help was vital.

After praising them some more, I told them that I'd see them at six o'clock. In the air-raid shelter.

'Right, Dickie,' said Joey. 'Wee Liam told us about the meetin' a while ago. We'll be there.'

They ran off like two greyhounds towards Rosemount Terrace, probably to meet up with Danny, Kevin and Liam. I said a wee prayer that they wouldn't blab about anything. There was too much at stake. And I hadn't time at this minute to be working on the plan that was still only about a quarter of a plan. You needed peace and quiet for that. I decided to do some very serious thinking after my meeting with Eva at the girls' school.

CHAPTER 6

Eva's Gift To Gawk-Mouth

'Why were the twins in such a wile hurry?' laughed Eva. 'Is somebody after them?' She was standing at the school gate, waiting on me. I hadn't seen her at first because she was behind the pillar.

I shrugged her question off, as I didn't want her to ask me what we'd been up to. That made me feel a bit guilty, because after all, she *was* a gang member. But her da was a cop; and that meant any plan, or even part of a plan involving Uncle Jimmy, shouldn't be mentioned in any way in Eva's presence. In fact, it could be a matter of life and death if she accidentally let some information slip in her house. You could do that without thinking.

So I just said, 'What's that you have?'

It was something inside a paper bag that she was holding.

'It's a book, Dickie. It's a present for you.'

She was smiling at me. I didn't know what to say at first. I was shocked. Nobody had ever given me a present before, except Uncle Jimmy, and all his were second-hand stuff like jigsaw puzzles with parts missing and old Ludo and Tiddlywinks games that he'd picked up on his travels.

As Eva handed me the present, I stammered out a thanks that couldn't have sounded like thanks, because I wasn't used to this sort of situation. And I looked around me quickly at the same time, hoping that nobody would see what was happening: I was feeling a bit shy. I was glad that nobody was about. But I was even more glad that the twin Deeneys had gone, because it's all right for people to know when the likes of Billy or Cecil sometimes give you comics, but it's definitely *not* all right to be seen getting something from a girl.

'Are ye not goin' to take it out of the bag, Dickie?' she laughed.

'Aye, aw aye, Eva. Thanks, Eva,' I said with a half-gawky look that you sometimes see on Danny or Kevin's faces. I gave a couple of quick coughs and then took a deep breath as I opened the bag and took the book out. My mouth opened even further when I saw it. It was *Kidnapped* by Robert Louis Stevenson. I had read it before, about a million times. And I hated it. And Mr Philson even made us read it in school nearly every day as well.

I slowly took the stupid look off my face and gave a big, false, surprised kind of smile to Eva.

'Wow,' I said as I opened the front cover. 'It's lovely, Eva.'

Inside the cover, Eva had written her name after FROM and my name after TO. And then XX and OO below that.

And as I was about to ask her what the XX and OO were all about, I spotted somebody out of the corner of my eye, coming from the Rosemount Terrace direction, pushing a bike and heading our way. It was Bap Kelly. I wasn't sure whether he'd seen me. Or Eva. I didn't want him to see us. And I definitely didn't want to see him. Everything about him annoyed me. Eva looked a bit surprised and a wee bit shocked when I pushed her back behind the pillar. And then I nodded to her to shush. But it was too late. I heard him shouting my name.

'Dickie, is that you, Dickie? The twin Deeneys told me you were down here.'

My heart sank. At that moment, I could have killed Joey and Hughie, even though I knew that they'd done nothing wrong. All they did was probably just answer Bap's question when he'd asked them if they knew where I was. Now I had to make *my* move. I looked at Eva, whispering shush once more, before I stepped back from the gateway onto the front path. She was puzzled.

'What's up, Dickie?' she said before Bap reached us. 'Who's that shoutin'?'

'It's only Bap Kelly,' I whispered. 'I'll get rid of him. You stay there. Don't let him see ye.'

But I'd just made another stupid mistake with Eva.

'What are ye talkin' about?' she suddenly hissed with annoyance. 'Who do you think ye are anyway, shushin' and shovin' me like that? And I'll see anybody I want to see. Do ye hear me?'

In a flash, she was away. Her eyes were blazing, and she left me standing there on the footpath as she pushed me back and charged her way up the street. She didn't even look at Bap Kelly as she passed him. But he looked at her, even taking the time to turn his head and stare open-mouthed after her as she strode angrily away. Now I hated Bap Kelly even more than before. Nearly as much as I hated Uncle Jimmy. Bap Kelly had no right to be here, up in Rosemount again, annoying me, and spoiling my day altogether. He'd pay for this. As he came alongside me, pushing his old rattly bike, I gave him one of my special looks. Looks that were nearly always followed by a hot rasper of a spit from the back of my throat and straight into an eye. Bap Kelly was a goner. One way or the other.

He looked at the book in my hand. The stupid *Kidnapped* book. I shoved it up my jumper as he spoke. Now I was bulging even more and wishing that I'd gone home earlier with the comics.

'Were you givin' the cop's daughter a present, Dickie? The book, I mean. Did she not like it? Is that why she went off in a huff? I'm not surprised; it's a rotten story anyway.'

I ignored his stupid questions.

'What do ye want, Kelly?' I shouted as I watched Eva heading fast towards Rosemount Terrace.

'It's about the bike, Dickie, the wan ye borrowed this mornin' to go to the meetin' in the College.'

'I didn't go to the meetin' on your stupid bike,' I shouted. 'I went in the priest's car.'

For a second or two, he was lost for words. And he looked puzzled. 'Our Joe said you took it from the street. He said you were in a wile hurry and that you were sweatin' like a pig. Sure ye could have come in our van. My da waited for ye for nearly half an hour. Then your Liam came out and told us ye were away. Did your ma not tell ye, Dickie, that ye were gettin' a lift with us? My da was wile annoyed with youse all, because we just got there in time ourselves. And then when we didn't see ye in the Big Study, we thought that something had happened to ye. Or maybe that you weren't goin' to bother goin' to the College at all.'

'Shut up,' I shouted. 'Will ye just shut up, Kelly? Shut your bake and keep it shut. Have ye just come up here to Rosemount to annoy me? And mind your own business from now on, about where I go, who I go with, or how I get there. Because it's none of your business what I do. Now, what was it that ye wanted?'

I thought for a second that he was going to turn away without saying anything else. But knowing Bap Kelly as I do, you can be sure there's always something else he has to tell you. And there was. As he spoke, I could see the sun glinting off his glass eye. That annoyed me, too, because I think he sometimes did that deliberately to try to put people off their stride if they were getting the better of him.

'Naw. It's like this, Dickie,' he said. 'I just came up to tell ye that the bike's yours if ye want it. Sure ye know I hardly ever use it anyway because of the bad eye and all, and nobody else in our house wants it. My da says I can give it to you if ye want it. He was thinkin', too, that it might come in handy for ye, for goin' to the College. It would save ye a lot of money on bus fares. What do ye think, Dickie? It's yours if ye want it.'

Not for the first time, Bap Kelly had stopped me in my tracks. There I was a minute ago threatening in my mind to blind him for life, shouting and roaring at him for annoying me and wanting him to disappear. Forever. Aye, there I was, jumping in headfirst when I should have been calm and not showing myself

54

up. Not only in front of Bap but in front of Eva earlier. But Bap had taken me by surprise when he'd appeared, and made me act the way I did with Eva. And now this surprise with the bike. Something I would never have expected. But something that I'd always wanted. Nobody in our street owned a bike. Not even Cecil, or Billy when *he* lived there, and certainly not Danny or Kevin. And I don't even remember my da having a bike. Eva's da had one, but that didn't count because it was an RUC bike, so it didn't really belong to him.

Once more, I stared at Bap. But this time I wasn't angry, even though I was still a bit annoyed over Eva leaving the way she did, and about how stupid I'd been. In the way I'd handled things, I mean. But the anger had left me, and now the annoyance of everything else was leaving me as I stared down at the bike. Crock and all that it was, it was still a bike, and it was mine for the taking.

'If ye don't want it, I'll have it,' I said without looking up. 'But only if ye really don't want it.'

'It's all yours, Dickie,' said Bap and he pushed the bike towards me. And as he did, his coat sleeve went up his arm a bit. Deliberate, like. It was show-off time. He knew it, and I knew it, and he knew that I knew it. But I didn't care, because it was the bike I was thinking of most. But it was hard not to notice the new strap-watch on his wrist. As he deliberately flaunted it again and again in front of me, I knew that I had at least to mention that I'd seen it. And, like his glass eye, it, too, glinted in the sunlight as he finally stretched his arm out some more and handed the bike over to me.

'That's a nice watch you've got, Bap,' I said without being enthusiastic about it. And as I spoke, I was turning away from him with the bike and intending to go on about the rest of my business without any further conversation.

'Aye, it's a beaut, Dickie,' he replied, stopping me in my tracks. 'My da got it for me for passin' the College exam. He gave it to me this mornin' in the van when we were goin' up to

55

the meetin'. Did you get anything, Dickie? I mean, for passin' the exam?'

'Naw, Bap,' I said calmly. 'I got nothin' yet. I've hardly been in the house since the meetin', but I hear whispers about different things.'

Bap knew I was lying, covering up, but he said nothing more about it, or even about his strap-watch. That was finished with and Bap was satisfied. But what he did say next rocked me back on my heels, leaving me speechless for a minute.

'Isn't it great about your Uncle Jimmy being back, Dickie? After all this time. I hear he was up in Dublin seein' people and organising stuff. My da says that things'll begin to happen again soon. It's been too quiet, Dickie. That's what my da said. Too quiet.'

I was glad I was more than half-turned away from Bap as he spoke, for he would surely have seen my big mouth hanging open with shock if I'd been facing him. The shock of Uncle Jimmy organising stuff. And about things happening soon. About it being too quiet. But I wasn't going to let myself down. Not to Kelly, and not to anyone else – ever. I was too cute for that. I'd learned a long time ago that you could give yourself away badly and weaken your own position if you showed surprise or fear or shock or even too much joy at what people said.

So I controlled myself within seconds as I moved slowly back round to face him. I'd already quietly done the big deep breath thing, and the long, quiet sigh. But even though my face would look normal as I replied to Bap, my insides were turning over, churning, and tight as a drum at the same time. In fact, I felt as if I was about to explode. Instead, I gave a half-smile as I spoke.

'Aye, Bap, it's great,' I said quietly, now changing from the smiley look to the serious stare. 'But I have to warn ye not to say a word about this to anybody.'

I looked from side to side as I whispered to him, giving him the impression that there was always the chance that our conversation could be overheard, even by some passer-by across the road.

'Naw, Dickie. Ye don't have to warn me about stuff like this. You know me. I don't blab to anybody about anything. It's too dangerous, Dickie, but I just had to say to ye about it, about everybody being delighted that Jimmy's back. And about your Kate and Laura, too. About them goin' for special training in Donegal when they get their holidays from the factory in August. My da says they'll be perfect for doin' jobs that men can't do as easy. The cops won't suspect girls as much, Dickie, that's what my da said. And my ma, too.'

'Now, you remember, Bap, not a word,' I hissed at him through gritted teeth as I turned away quickly so that he wouldn't see the changing expression on my face. I felt sick. I was weak at the knees. My heart was racing. I had to get away this very second, away from the situation I was in. Away from Bap Kelly. I was about to burst with the tension.

'I'll see ye later, Dickie,' he shouted after me as I quickly headed off, pushing the rattling bike in front of me. I didn't care about seeing him later, or what he thought about me not saying cheerio, or about me not thanking him for the bike. It was what he'd said about Uncle Jimmy and then about Kate and Laura that was running round my head now. Especially about them training in Donegal. In August. I thought I was about to die with the shock of it. So I *was* right. The twins were really mad. And stupid. Now *they* could be in the firing line as well. And maybe it was just because they wanted revenge. Things were definitely getting a lot worse for the McCauleys by the minute. And out of control. That's what I was thinking. Unless something was done about it. And quick.

CHAPTER 7

About The Guns And Ammunition

I needed time to think. I needed to be by myself. I'd have to go somewhere quiet and then try and work out how to stop things happening. Bad things. But first, I had to get home. The comics and the book inside my jumper were annoying me. I'd leave them in my room, maybe under the bed or under the pillow. I deliberately went down the back lane. I didn't want to meet Eva or any of the gang in the Terrace. Especially not Eva because of what had happened at the school gate, and because I didn't know yet what I should say to her. I didn't have time to work that one out yet. But Eva was the least of my problems. For now.

I left the bike in the back yard before I went into the house. Nobody was in the kitchen. So far so good. The living-room door was closed. As I passed it, I could hear the muffled sound of music coming from the wireless. The sitting-room door was open. I looked at the clock on the mantelpiece. It was three o'clock. I took my shoes off and began walking up the stairs. Quiet, like. On the landing I listened intently for any noise in the attic. Nothing. Uncle Jimmy was keeping very quiet, too. That suited me. I went into the bedroom, took the comics and the book from under my jumper and pushed them under my pillow. They'd be safe enough there. I'd share the comics with Liam later. Maybe I would even give him my old tattered *Kidnapped*. It was time that he was reading proper books anyway. I placed my shoes quietly on the floor. I sat on the bed. I'd just stay here for a while. This was as quiet a place as any at the moment to try to gather my thoughts about everything. The news from Bap Kelly about our Kate and Laura was annoying me very badly. Nearly as much as the whole Uncle Jimmy carry-on up in the attic. My heart was still thumping.

I hadn't even begun to think things out when I heard the toilet flushing and the bathroom door opening. Almost at the same time. It might be Liam. It wasn't. It was my worst nightmare. Uncle Jimmy. Now standing there in the landing in his stupid disguise, looking in at me.

'Hello, Dickie,' he said. 'The very man I wanted to talk to. It's been a while since I saw ye last.' He came into the room, looking around it as if he'd never been here before. That was the first time I noticed that he had crafty eyes. And they seemed to flit from place to place without really settling on anything in particular. He was fully dressed. The last time I'd seen him he was in bed, asleep, in a sort of nightshirt and stripey pyjama trousers. And with a gun in his hand.

'Is that a new book ye've got there, son?' he asked, looking past me.

I turned around. *Kidnapped* was sticking out from beneath the pillow.

'Aye, Uncle Jimmy, it's a new book. I got it the day.'

'That's nice,' he said. 'Was it a present?'

I didn't answer. Just tried to change the subject.

'I was up at the College this morning, Uncle Jimmy. It was an important meeting.'

'Aye, I heard that, son. And congratulations on gettin' the exam. You're a bright boy, Dickie. You'll do well.'

I didn't want his praise, or his nosiness. I didn't even want him in the room, talking to me. I hated him. And I didn't say thanks. I couldn't. I think he noticed that something wasn't right.

'Is everything okay, Dickie? You look a wee bit out of sorts.'

'I'm a bit tired, that's all, Uncle Jimmy. I've been on the go all day.'

'Why don't ye lie down for a while, son, for a wee rest? Here,' he said, 'I'll take that wee book out from under your pillow. It'll be more comfortable. Oh! And comics, too!' he added.

That's when he laughed, holding the comics in his hand.

'Do ye remember, Dickie, you used to get the comics from the cop's son? Seems a long time ago now.' He chuckled when he said that. A nasty sort of chuckle. But he didn't ask me where I'd got this lot. If he had, I would have lied, because he would have said nasty things about Cecil's dead da.

'This is a nice book, Dickie. *Kidnapped*, and it's new. Not like the old one I gave ye some time back, eh?'

He opened the front cover. I knew he was reading what Eva had written. The TO and FROM thing. Now I was in for another slagging.

'Well, isn't that nice, Dickie, gettin' a present from your wee friend? And I heard she was in your gang as well. I'm glad youse are good friends. She's a lively girl, son.'

I couldn't believe what I was hearing. I stared up at him, just to check that he wasn't being sarcastic. That he wasn't warning me, or mocking me the way he did when he heard last year that I was friendly with Sergeant Burnside's son, Billy. I was left almost speechless, except for, 'Aye, she's in the gang, Uncle Jimmy.' And I knew by his expression and the way he spoke that he meant what he said. There was no scorn in his voice like the last time. And no sign of a threat. It was puzzling.

'I think I'll lie down now, Uncle Jimmy, and get a wee rest.'

I said that to get rid of him. I didn't want to talk to him anymore. I didn't even want to look at him.

'Okay, Dickie,' he said as he was leaving the room. 'I'll see ye later on when you're rested. And I've got something for ye, too. Eva's not the only one who can dole out presents. Oh, and here's your book. I nearly had it away with me.' He laughed as he said that. But I didn't take him on. I just took it from him and lay back on the bed and began closing my eyes. He gave me another look, a bit of a questioning look, I thought, before he turned and left. Probably because I hadn't mentioned his disguise. I was glad when he closed the door behind him.

In the quiet of the room, I closed my eyes tight. I was exhausted, all right, but I didn't want to sleep. Not at this moment anyhow. I had too much on my mind. Maybe this was the quiet time I needed to think things through, to try to work stuff out. Even to work more on the plan that had been in my mind earlier. The plan for everything that was bad in my life to go away.

I closed my eyes even tighter and began to get rid of the thoughts for now that might interfere with what was really important. Thoughts of Eva and the way she was angry with me. Thoughts of Bap Kelly and the different ways he annoys me. Thoughts of the gang meeting at six o'clock and what I might be saying to the rest of them about stupid missions. And thoughts of the bike sitting in the back yard. My bike. Even if it was a bit of a crock. I closed my eyes even tighter and began to let another part of my mind take over.

Now I could think straight about what mattered. About Uncle Jimmy. About dangerous Uncle Jimmy. About the guns and ammunition. About my mad twin sisters planning to train for the Movement. About my stupid ma for allowing all this in our house. And about my stupid da for being a drunkard nearly all the time. And about what could happen if there was a cop raid on our house this very day. And it was this last thought that really frightened me, because you could be executed if you were got with guns. You heard that sort of stuff on the wireless sometimes and you could read about it in newspapers.

One Sunday last year, I was reading about two men, two foreign Secret Service agents who were caught in a rubber boat somewhere near the coast of Scotland. They'd got there in a German seaplane. They were captured by the police after they were spotted by some railway men. I remember writing their names down in a jotter a whole lot of times because of the funny spellings. One man was called Karl Drucke. He was a thirty-five-year-old German. The other man was called Werner Waelti and

61

he was from Switzerland. I think he was about twenty-five. They were both fighting for Hitler. Anyway, from what I remember, they were caught with guns and secret wireless stuff, and emergency rations and German sausages. They were executed a couple of days after they were captured. Killed for being spies. Shot through the heart.

Well, now I was thinking that everybody in our house could be in the same boat as that, except for me and Liam. They could all be hanged, or even shot, because the British could say they were spies. Fighting against the British, they would say, because the RUC and the B-Specials were British. So what would be the difference between what happened to Karl Drucke and Werner Waelti and what could happen to the McCauleys? No difference, I was thinking at this minute. So something would have to be done about it before anything serious really happened.

After about ten minutes, a good plan was taking shape in my head. That's when I must have fallen asleep, satisfied that things were working out. About what I should do.

***

I woke with a start. It was my ma calling me. I jumped off the bed, put on my shoes and went down the stairs quickly. She heard me.'

'Hello, Dickie. Is that you? I wasn't sure if ye were in the house or not.'

'Aye, Ma. I was up in the bedroom.' I didn't tell her I'd been asleep. You could smell the dinner cooking. My da was sitting in his armchair, as usual, listening to the wireless. Liam was at the table, doing his homework. He never asked for help with it. With sums or reading. He was smart. Smarter than I was at his age. I looked at the clock. Nearly five o'clock. I must have slept for a couple of hours. I felt well rested. And good, too, because I now had a plan to deal with everything.

CHAPTER 8

The Best Present I Ever Got

'Dickie.' It was my ma calling me from the kitchen. I got up from the chair and left my comic on the table. My da just looked at me without saying anything, and Liam didn't even lift his head. It was almost as if I didn't exist. But they'd all know soon that I did.

'Aye, Ma, I'm here,' I said as I went into the kitchen.

'Will ye bring this wee cup of tea up to Uncle Jimmy and tell him to come down for his dinner at half six?'

My first reaction was to refuse, to make some sort of excuse, because I didn't want to see Uncle Jimmy again, not just now anyhow. And I didn't want him to be asking me any more questions. But then, I thought, maybe I should go up to the attic again, because I could check if the guns and other stuff were still there. It was better to see the lay of the land than act blindly when the time came.

I looked up at my ma as she handed me the cup. I could see she was tired. She was always tired. If she just minded her own business, her own family business, and didn't get caught up in any carry-on with Uncle Jimmy, she'd look okay. Aye, and maybe my da wouldn't drink as much then, either. Minding her own business would definitely be a very good idea. For all of us.

'And tell him there's no more food goin' up to him. If he wants anything from now on, he can slip down himself, when the coast's clear. You tell him that, son.'

63

'Okay, Ma,' I said. 'I'll tell him.'

'Oh, and don't forget, Dickie, when you're up there, Uncle Jimmy has somethin' for ye. He told me about it earlier.'

'Aye, ye were sayin' to me about it before, Ma, but he was sleepin' the last time I was up there.' I didn't tell her that I'd already spoken to him.

When I went into the attic room, Uncle Jimmy was sitting on the edge of the bed, reading a book. He looked up when he heard me, but not before I'd taken a split-second glance around the room. He didn't spot that. Stupid Uncle Jimmy, again. The guns were still there, on the floor, but this time under an old blanket. With the bag of bullets beside them now closed up.

'My ma sent this up, Uncle Jimmy,' I said as if butter wouldn't melt in my mouth. I'd decided to play him at his own game. Dickie McCauley style. I'd reckoned earlier that there would be no point in confronting him about what he was at. No point in pleading with him, either. Things had gone too far with Uncle Jimmy. In the danger game. He had his way of dealing with it. But I had my way, too, as he would find out soon enough.

'Well, well, well,' he said. 'If it isn't the wee genius again. And did ye get a sleep, son?' He left the book on the bed and reached for the cup of tea.

'Aye, Uncle Jimmy, I slept for a while. I feel better now.'

'Ye look better, too, Dickie. That's good, that's good.'

'That's a great disguise ye have, Uncle Jimmy,' I said deliberately, half-hoping that he might let slip some information which would be useful. 'You'd never know it was you.'

'That's the idea, son. I don't want to take any chances when I'm in Derry. With the cops, I mean, even though they have nothin' on me. It's better to be safe than sorry. You know what I mean, Dickie.'

'Aye, it's better to be safe than sorry,' I repeated after him, my mind half on another question. 'And will ye be stayin' long, Uncle Jimmy?'

'Not sure yet, not sure yet, son,' he said. 'And now, before

I take the tea, there's some things here I want to give you. I picked them up in Dublin a few days ago. Thought you might like them.'

He reached under the bed as he was speaking and brought out a large parcel. 'For you,' he said, handing it to me, 'for doin' so well at school and gettin' the College exam. Open it up, son. It won't bite you.'

He'd said that last bit because my first reaction was not to take the present, not to take anything from him, ever again. It would be like taking blood money. Like Judas taking the thirty pieces of silver. But I took the parcel with a big smile on my face. A fake-surprise smile. I was playing the game rightly so far.

'What is it, Uncle Jimmy?' I said with false excitement. 'What did ye get me?'

'Open it up, son, and ye'll soon find out.'

I tore open the parcel as if I couldn't wait to see what was inside. And I put on a very big surprised look when I saw what was there. Under different circumstances, I would have been really pleased and excited, but all I felt was a cold shiver running through me. And that wasn't just because of the guns and stuff that were lying on the floor a few feet away from me. It was also the fear I felt because of the hold my Uncle Jimmy seemed to have over my ma and the twins. And because of the terrible danger we were all in. But fearful and all as I felt, I was still playing his game. And he didn't know it yet.

I kept the amazed look on my face when I held the present up in front of me. A brand-new leather schoolbag with a brass buckle.

'Now look inside the bag, Dickie,' he said with a big grin on his face. 'Just a few other wee things that you'll need.'

I opened the clasp. Inside was a geometry set in a special case, loads of jotters and exercise books, a fountain pen and different colours of ink in bottles and a set of spare nibs. It was like an Aladdin's cave in there with treasures that I could only have dreamed of. That's when a stupid thought went through my mind. A very stupid thought. If only Bap Kelly could see this. He'd have swapped half a dozen strap-watches for what I'd just got. And the thing was, and nobody would believe this if they could read my mind, I had no intention, ever, of keeping this stuff. But I held the right expression on my face with even bigger smiles than before. All part of the plan. All part of the game.

'Thanks, Uncle Jimmy,' I said with a false breathless excitement in my voice. 'This is the best present I ever got.' And it was, even though I didn't want it.

'It's my pleasure, Dickie. Aye, my pleasure, son. And I'm proud of ye. And I couldn't wait to give it to ye. It was burnin' a hole in that parcel since I brought it home.'

I didn't know what he meant by that, about it burning a hole, but I wasn't one bit pleased about the 'brought it home' part. This wasn't *his* home. This was the McCauley home. But I kept smiling.

'Now, Dickie, take the lot with ye downstairs and show it off to everybody this evening. Okay, son?'

'Aye, Uncle Jimmy. I will,' I said as I began to back out of the room with the bag in my hand.

'Oh, by the way, Dickie,' he said suddenly. And I noticed his voice had changed when he spoke. 'C'mere a wee minute, son.'

I walked towards him again. And this time he held my free hand, very tight. I felt a bit tense but I still kept the smile.

'Aye, Uncle Jimmy. What is it?'

'Was it you that brought the tea up earlier this afternoon?'

My heart began to race.

'Aye, it was me. My ma told me to bring it up to ye, but you were sleepin' so I put the tray there for ye, on the wee table. I hope it wasn't cold when ye woke up, Uncle Jimmy.'

'Aw, that doesn't matter, son. About the tea, I mean. I just wanted to thank ye for that. You're a good boy, Dickie, saving your ma from climbing all them stairs.'

I tried keeping the smile on my face as he spoke, but it was beginning to wear a bit thin, and I hoped he didn't notice. I was doing my best to keep up the act.

I tried to pull my hand away as he was telling me that I was a good boy, but he held it even tighter as he went on. 'Just wan other wee thing, Dickie. Ye didn't by any chance notice anything unusual when ye came in here? When I was sleeping, I mean? Earlier on in the day? Anything out of the ordinary?'

'Naw, Uncle Jimmy. Just your disguise,' I said, keeping my voice steady. 'That's the only thing I thought was out of the ordinary. If I hadn't known it was you in the bed, I wouldn't have recognised ye.'

I knew immediately that what I was saying was stupid stuff, but it was the only thing I could think of at this moment. And I knew as well what he was getting at. He was really trying to find out if I'd seen the revolver in his hand, or the guns and ammunition at the other side of the room.

'Are ye sure that's all ye seen, son?' he said as he pulled me even closer and stared straight into my eyes. He was glaring at me intently, with the same kind of grim look that the priest at the College had given me this morning.

Now I felt a bit scared. But I didn't show it. I wasn't going to give in at this stage. But my smile had gone a bit. And he noticed.

'Are ye okay, son?' he said. 'Is there anything botherin' ye, Dickie?'

I took a quiet deep breath. 'Naw, Uncle Jimmy. I'm okay, but you're holdin' my hand wile tight. You're hurtin' me!'

He wasn't really hurting me, but I said that to distract him. It worked. He let my hand go.

Then *he* took a deep breath. And then another. He sat further back on the bed.

'Sorry, Dickie, sorry. I didn't mean to hurt ye. It's just that things are a bit tense with me at the minute. You know what I mean, the way things are, ye can't be too careful. Sorry if I hurt ye, Dickie.'

'That's okay, Uncle Jimmy, and thanks for the great presents.

They're brilliant. Thanks, thanks a lot.'

That seemed to relax him right away, me saying thanks all the time and talking again about something different. I was off the hook.

But Uncle Jimmy wasn't. And the difference was that he didn't know that he wasn't off the hook. How could he? Sure he didn't even know he was on the hook in the first place. But it wouldn't be long before he did know. And him believing that I hadn't seen the guns and ammunition was another one-up for me. All part of the plan. But if the plan didn't work, I was the one who would be in very big trouble. But that's the chance you take when you're a gang leader.

I looked back at him as I was leaving the bedroom. He was reading his book again. I'd been dismissed! Halfway down the attic stairs I shouted up to him that his dinner would be ready at half six. 'And from now on,' I called out with a false laugh, 'my ma says you're to come down for your own food.'

I knew he heard me, but he didn't answer. I didn't care. I had done what my ma asked. Before going back down to the front hall, I went into my own bedroom and shoved the schoolbag and everything else under my bed. Far away under. Out of sight. And out of mind. For now. Blood money or bribes wouldn't stop me from doing what I now had to do.

CHAPTER 9

A Sudden Tension In The Air

As I walked towards the air-raid shelter, I was wondering if Eva would turn up for the meeting. I'd be surprised if she did, the way she'd stomped off earlier. I got the impression then that she'd never speak to me again. I'd soon find out.

She wasn't there. The rest of them had assembled, as ordered, and were standing around the upturned tea chest that my da had got for us from the All-Cash Stores last year. Danny Doherty had already lit the two candles. He had taken on that job from the very beginning. Kevin Doherty's eyes were glinting behind his jamjars. He looked worried. But Kevin always looked like that before a meeting. In case there was a raid or something being planned. He liked dangerous stuff, but his hands were never far from his rosary, like now, for his right hand was in his pocket, probably fingering the beads.

But Danny was quiet. Too quiet for my liking. He seemed different. Something was up. And he was soon to let me know what, when he suddenly shouted, 'What's this about attackin' the North Street Bunch? When was this arranged?'

There was a sudden tension in the air.

'Are ye speakin' to *me*, Danny?' I said quietly, trying to calm things down. I had enough on my plate now without wanting to confront him. But I might have to.

'Aye, I'm speakin' to you, McCauley, and I want answers.'

I glared at him and said nothing; I knew he had more to

get off his chest. But I noticed, too, that Kevin looked scared. He knew that trouble could be brewing. Danny must have said something to him before the meeting.

'Not only that,' Danny went on in an even louder voice, 'but ye had Joey and Hughie spyin' for ye the day and they're only new in the gang. Could *we* not have done the spyin'? Me and Kevin. Why did ye pick them to do it and not us?'

He'd got what he wanted to say out in the open. To make a big issue of things. That's what Danny often did. Just to get attention.

'Are ye finished?' I asked him.

'For now,' he said.

Before I spoke, I turned quickly to the twin Deeneys and gave them a wink. They would now know what I was about. They were smart.

'Shut up, Danny,' I said with a very firm voice. Like when I gave commands. 'Are ye stupid or what? Did ye not know that this was just another test for Joey and Hughie?' I lied. 'To qualify them to get into the gang,' I went on.

Stuff was just coming out of my mouth. But I now knew what I was definitely going to say next, and it should do the trick. But before I could say it, Liam had butted in. 'Aye, shut up, fat Danny, are ye stupid or what? Don't ye know that new gang members have to do two tests now? Sure Dickie told us that last week. Are ye deaf as well as stupid?'

Wee Liam was piling it on, lying for me, backing me up, and I was proud of him. But Danny wasn't finished yet.

'Naw, you shut up, Liam. You're only a wain and ye know nothin'. And anyway, *you* didn't have to do any tests to get into the gang. Dickie just said the word and you were in. Same as Eva. And what I'm sayin' is right. The Deeneys there done the test. Wan test and they were in. Proggin' the marrows from the barracks. So all this stuff about second tests is a load of rubbish. And just made-up.'

Now Danny really was goading me. He already knew that

Liam was in the gang because of what happened to him last year with the cops. Getting injured and badly shocked and all. That was enough of a test for anybody. And Eva was in the gang because I said so. And because I was the leader. So I just told Danny to shove off out of it if he wasn't happy.

Kevin began to say something, but Danny interrupted him. 'Naw, you shove off, McCauley. I've as much right to be in this air-raid shelter as you. Just because you're goin' to the College you think you're smart, but you're not smart at all. And anyway, after Billy Burnside and Cecil Colhoun left the gang, you should've had us, me and Kevin, doin' the spyin' and things. Doin' important stuff.'

I looked over at the Deeneys, and at Kevin and Liam. The Deeneys had straight faces on them. Giving nothing away. They knew I was in control. And they knew where they stood. Kevin's eyes were still halfway up into his skull and Liam was grinning from ear to ear.

Danny's outbursts were playing right into my hands. I couldn't have planned it better, because what he was saying about spying, about him and Kevin doing the spying, was exactly what I already had in mind for them. As part of the bigger plan to get the McCauley family out of trouble. But I had to play all this out as if Danny had won the argument, just to give him the satisfaction and keep him on board. I had to play it another way, too, because I couldn't afford to have my authority undermined.

Everybody was looking at me to see what would happen next. How I would treat Danny's outbursts. His accusations. His demands. Before I spoke, I took the usual two or three very quiet, deep breaths. You could have heard a pin drop in the air-raid shelter. I knew by their hushed silence that they were expecting Danny's comeuppance inside the next thirty seconds. I waited for about ten seconds before I spoke.

'C'mere, Danny,' I said quietly, ushering him towards me at the same time with my hand. At first, he stood his ground, but then, for some reason that I was glad of, he took two steps forward. His

71

defiance was weakening. I continued, my hand still out and my forefinger pointing straight at his face. 'There's just three things I want to say to you, Danny Doherty. One, Billy Burnside and Cecil Colhoun left the gang because they were forced to. And it wasn't of their makin'. Now, off your own bat, you can walk out that door if ye want to. Ye can leave the gang if ye want to. It'll be your choice. Nobody's forcin' ye to go and nobody's forcin' ye to stay. It's up to you what ye do. But if ye do stay, ye follow orders from here on in.'

Danny was breathing heavy, staring at me. And still defiant. But not as much as before, because when he spoke, his voice was lighter, not shouting. 'I'll do what I want to do, McCauley,' he said, gasping a bit with the excitement of everything.

Kevin began to speak again, trying to calm things down. 'Look, boys, why don't youse—'

'Shut up, Kevin,' I hissed. 'Not now.'

I turned back to Danny and continued. 'Two, Joey and Hughie Deeney are in the gang to stay, because they're two very important members.'

When I was saying that, I turned to the twins. They looked pleased. They knew what I meant.

'They've done their two tests and passed with flyin' colours,' I said. 'And you, Danny, you never had to do even wan test to be in the gang. But if ye leave now, ye won't get back in unless *you* do two tests as well.'

Kevin Doherty now had the beads held high in front of him. You could hear them rattling. His hands were shaking. But he was quiet except for his very heavy breathing. The twin Deeneys were staring straight at Danny. Liam was still grinning.

I could sense that Danny's mind was working overtime. You could see it in his eyes. You could read what he was thinking. That if he walked out now, he'd never get back in. Because he'd never pass the tests. And he knew it. Before he spoke again, his eyes narrowed.

'And what's the third thing, McCauley? You said there were

three things. What else has smart-boy McCauley dreamed up? And if—'

It must have been when Kevin saw my jaw tightening, and my eyes half-closing at Danny's insults that he decided quickly to interrupt him again. And maybe it was just as well for both of us that he did, because a very large dangerous spit was forming inside my mouth. One that could knock him stone-dead and shut him up forever. And one that could blow all my plans apart. I held back the spit. Kevin's prayers were answered.

I sighed silently in relief as Kevin started again. 'May the Holy God in Heaven look down on us this minute and take pity on our plight. May the—'

'That's enough, Kevin,' I said quickly, because I knew it was now time to sort this out. To sort it out once and for all. To sort Danny Doherty out. The way *I* wanted him to be sorted. So that we would both be winners and walk away satisfied.

'The third thing is this, Danny,' I said.

Ye have a big mouth on ye, nearly as big as your big fat stomach.
'You're in this gang because I need ye.'

You're more than useless at times when it comes to taking orders.
'You're a valuable gang member and we couldn't do without you.'

I asked the twin Deeneys to do the spyin', Danny, because you and Kevin would have blown the job. Youse would have been spotted right away. Useless gits. The two of youse.

'So what I'm sayin' now, Danny, is this. I want you and Kevin to take charge of the spyin' job on the North Street Bunch. And when the dam is finished, youse report back to me. And then we'll fix a time to wreck it. That'll show them who's boss in this area. Okay, Danny?'

He didn't say anything right away. It was as if what I was saying to him hadn't fully sunk in.

'Right . . . right . . . Okay, Dickie.'

The penny was gradually dropping. That not only was he still in the gang but he was being given another mission to carry out.

'And, Danny . . .'

'What?'

'Youse are to take Eva and Liam with youse on the spyin' mission.'

I could see by Danny's face that he was pleased. In fact, he was more than pleased. He was delighted and excited, and nearly back to the old Danny who used to take orders without question. And Kevin's eyeballs were back to normal behind the jam-jars as well. I even breathed a sigh of relief myself.

'Sounds good to me, Dickie,' said Danny, smiling from ear to ear as if he'd won a prize. But he still couldn't let it rest. He had to get his last spoke in about the twin Deeneys. As if he was getting his own back. As if he was now the big boy in charge. But I let him off with it because it suited me.

'But what about Joey and Hughie?' he said excitedly – as if he really cared. 'What'll they do now if they have no spyin' to do?'

'Don't you worry about that, Danny,' I told him quickly. 'I'll find somethin' else for them to do when youse are spyin'. Okay, boys?'

I'd turned to the twin Deeneys as I spoke. They just nodded at me, then smiled. They knew they were part of a bigger plan, but nobody else knew. And if Uncle Jimmy had a sixth sense, I was thinking now, or if he had any sense at all, he should be using it, because things were working out much better in my mind now. About what I should do. Aye, Uncle Jimmy should be a worried man. His days in our house could be numbered. Very shortly.

I called to Liam to blow out the candle as we were turning to leave the air-raid shelter. That's when I noticed Eva standing just inside the door with a football in her hand. I hadn't heard her coming in, probably because of Danny shouting most of the time. But I wondered how long she'd been there, how much she'd heard. As Liam was blowing out the candle, the others were heading out the door. He followed them but was back in a couple of seconds to tell me to hurry up because the dinner would be ready. You could hear the rest of them shouting outside. Eva was still standing there at the door of the air-raid shelter, waiting for me to pass. And as I made to go out the door, I felt her hand touching mine for a few seconds. I didn't pull away, because it felt nice, but I was hoping that nobody saw us. And I was glad, too, that she wasn't huffing with me anymore. Before we walked into the Terrace, she whispered, 'Good one, Dickie. Ye played a good one there. I heard most of what went on.' With that she was gone, bouncing the ball in front of her, then kicking it from foot to foot the rest of the way up the street. She was good, all right.

I called quietly to the twin Deeneys to come back for a minute. I'd some instructions for them that I didn't want anybody else to hear. But before I could speak, Hughie handed me a paper poke. 'Here, Dickie,' he said. 'We meant to give you these gobstoppers earlier but we forgot.' I took them off him and said thanks.

'Listen, boys,' I then whispered to them. 'All I can tell youse at this stage is that we have something bigger on than an attack on a stupid dam. Just youse two, and me. So say nothin' to anybody. I'll give youse more details later, but wan thing's for sure, our plan will go into action on the same night that Danny and Kevin are wreckin' the dam. That way, if anything goes wrong, we can say that we were down at the dam as well. Like an alibi.'

I'd never seen the twins so excited. After Joey whispering, 'Okay, Dickie,' and with a big happy grin from Hughie, the two of them turned and were halfway up the street before I could take a deep breath. But as I watched them running off, there were a couple of things that I couldn't get out of my mind. Things that had been bothering me, even during all the fuss in the air-raid shelter. Two niggly things, in fact. Two puzzles. Why, I began to think now, was Uncle Jimmy so pleased today about me being friendly with Eva Johnston, a cop's daughter, when last year he was warning me against being friends with Billy Burnside, a cop's son? It didn't make sense. It was a real conundrum. And how did Danny Doherty know about the plan to attack the North Street Bunch, and about Joey and Hughie doing the spying? The only explanation I could come up with was that he might have seen me with the twin Deeneys earlier. Looking down at the dam. That was it. And then he added two and two together. Danny might be stupid but he could still count to four. Sometimes. As for the Uncle Jimmy conundrum, I still had a lot of thinking to do on that one.

CHAPTER 10

Shenanigans: I Knew What It Meant

I could smell the dinner as I got closer to the house. Sausages and bacon. My favourite. And I wouldn't choke on them, even if it was Uncle Jimmy who'd bought them. But when I went in, my ma said the meal wasn't ready yet. 'Maybe another ten minutes or so,' she said. 'It would have been ready in time if your da in there had peeled the spuds for me. Some chance of that.'

She laughed when she said that last part, but it wasn't a real laugh. It was a fed-up sort of laugh. I looked into the living room to see if Liam was there. He wasn't. Just my da with his ear to the wireless as usual. He told me to sit down and listen. That I might learn something. It was just the usual stuff. Some man talking about the war again. I didn't want to say that I wasn't interested in what Hitler was up to in Europe or England, because I was more interested in what was going on at home. About the IRA and their war. And about what I was planning for Uncle Jimmy. I sat down anyway to please him. The man on the wireless was spouting away about the Germans attacking Russia in a place . . . I think he called it Sebastopol, or something like that. And then he went on about the RAF dropping bombs on German shipping docks and aerodromes. The worst part was when he announced that a woman and her two sons were killed in their house in East Anglia in England by a German bomb. It made me sad thinking about it.

When the man on the wireless stopped talking and some music came on, my da reached back and turned the sound down. I knew he had something else to say to me.

'Where'd ye get the bike, Dickie? I saw it in the yard when I was out for coal. It looks a bit of a wreck.'

'Bap Kelly gave it to me, Da. I could get it fixed sometime and use it to go to the College in September.'

'That's a good idea, Dickie. That wee Kelly boy's a good friend of yours. But I'm not too keen on his da. With the things he gets up to.'

I didn't put him off his notion about Bap but I nodded my head in agreement when he spoke about Mr Kelly.

'Where's Kate and Laura?' I asked him. 'Are they not in from the factory yet?'

'Aye, son, they're in the front sittin' room, talkin' to that eejit of an uncle of yours. They'd be better off gallivanting out the town than gettin' mixed up with shenanigans like that.'

There it was again. Shenanigans. I knew what it meant. It covered everything that I was worried about.

'Why is he really here, Da? In Derry, I mean? In our house?'

'Dunno, son. You know as much as I do, but I'll tell ye wan thing, he's not here for the good of his health, or anybody else's health for that matter.'

I knew exactly what my da meant but I pretended I didn't. I just wanted more information if my da had it.

'I heard he was only goin' out at night, Da. So why the disguise? And he told me the day, too, that the cops had nothin' on him. It doesn't make any sense. The disguise, I mean.'

'I really don't know, son. Maybe if ye ask your ma she'll be able to tell ye, for she tells me nothin'.'

That was a good idea. Maybe I would ask my ma if I got the chance. She was bound to have more information than my da, seeing she was the one that allowed him and the guns and stuff into the house in the first place. But I still got the impression that my da knew more than he was telling me.

That's when I decided to slip out to the hall, to the front sitting-room door, because my da had reached back to the wireless again and turned up the music. That was his way of telling me that our conversation was finished. I gave him a nod as I left, but he didn't wave back or anything. He just stared in front of him. Blank, like. I sat on the bottom stair. If anybody asked why, I'd pretend I was there to shout up to Liam when the dinner was ready. But I was really there to listen. To try to hear something about when Uncle Jimmy would be leaving the house this evening. At what time. And how long he'd be away. These pieces of information would be vital if my plan was to work.

I could hear the murmuring of voices from the sitting room. The door was a wee bit open because of the broken lock. First, Uncle Jimmy's voice, then Kate's and Laura's butting in, sometimes at the same time. Like in an argument. Uncle Jimmy seemed to be doing most of the talking, but it wasn't loud. I'd have to get closer to the door. But that could create a problem for me, because my ma was still in the kitchen and she'd spot me standing there, listening. It could blow everything. But I wasn't stumped yet. I had an idea. I rushed upstairs into our bedroom. Liam was sitting on the floor, reading a comic. He didn't seem to notice that I was there. I reached under the bed and took out a box. It was Tiddlywinks. I went downstairs quickly, sat on the floor with my back to the wall next to the open door of the sitting room. I very quietly opened the box and set up the game. Now if my ma or anybody else spotted me, they'd take no special notice. I listened intently.

'The thing is, girls,' I heard Uncle Jimmy saying, 'youse just don't have any experience yet. But youse'll soon learn.'

'But, Jimmy,' said Kate, 'could we not even go out with ye the night? We wouldn't get in the way.'

'It's not that simple, Kate,' said Uncle Jimmy. 'The powers that be wouldn't accept youse yet. Youse have to be vetted and all, and signed up. Oaths and things. And then youse have to be trained properly. It takes time. Weeks. Youse can't rush into things like this. Everything has to be done properly. Youse are young, and there's plenty of time. So probably August would be best. And timing is very important for everything. This war's goin' to go on for a long while yet, you mark my words, girls. There's a good bit to go before we clear this lot out of the North. Now, as youse know, I have to go out on some business the night, and the next two nights after that, so maybe we'll get a chance later to talk some more. Okay, girls?'

That was all I heard, because my ma was shouting that the dinner was ready. I gathered up the game and rushed up the stairs as quietly as I could. They didn't spot me, but I could hear the girls arguing with Uncle Jimmy as they left the sitting room. They weren't happy. I heard him shushing them. And that was it. For now. I'd got some information, not enough yet, but it was a start.

Liam didn't notice me, even as I was putting the Tiddlywinks back under the bed. He was still reading the comic. He reminded me of me when I was his age. But he was as cute as a fox, too, especially the way he'd backed me up against Danny Doherty. And lying, into the bargain. I shook him by the arm.

'What is it, Dickie?' he asked as he looked up at me.

'Your dinner's ready, Liam.'

'Thanks, Dickie. I'll be down with you in a wee minute. And, Dickie . . .'

'What?'

'Thanks as well for allowing me to help in the spyin' mission on the North Street Bunch. We'll soon take care of that crowd, Dickie.'

'Aye, we will, Liam. But you be careful. Don't depend too much on Danny and Kevin. And keep your head down.'

'Don't worry about me, Dickie, I can handle myself. I'm nearly eight, ye know, and I'll look after Eva as well.'

'Thanks, Liam.'

'And, Dickie . . .'

'What?'

'I saw ye holdin' hands with Eva in the air-raid shelter. But no worries,' he said with a cheeky grin, 'I won't tell anybody.'

I was a bit shocked. And a wee bit taken aback. But not much. Because it was only Liam. I could handle him. I fingered the bag of gobstoppers in my pocket. I didn't need one for him now but I'd have to keep them handy in case he was tempted to blab. Blabbing about Eva holding my hand wouldn't be a big crime. Not like blabbing about a life and death situation. But I was certainly worried about the grin he had on his face. Liam was getting more devious. And crafty. He might try to use this information against me if he wanted something special. I'd have to watch him more carefully. But for now, I had something else to see about.

I told Liam not to go downstairs yet but to wait for me because I had to go to the toilet. He went back to his comic, but the grin was still on his face.

'Okay, Dickie,' he said.

I didn't go to the bathroom. Instead, I slipped as quietly as I could up the attic stairs and had a quick look. The rifles were still there under the old blanket, the bag of bullets sitting beside them. I turned quickly and headed back down, into the bathroom. I pulled the chain, for effect. Flushing the toilet like that sometimes came in handy. But before the meal, there was something else I had to do. And I definitely didn't want Liam spying on me this time. I'd spotted Eva through the window. She seemed to be alone, just kicking the ball against the barracks wall.

'Liam,' I said, 'you go on into the bathroom now. Go to the toilet and then get washed for the dinner. I'll wait for ye down in the hall.'

As soon as he left the room, I went flat on my belly and reached as far as I could under the bed. I pulled out Uncle Jimmy's parcel with the stuff inside it that he'd brought me. I took the tin box with the geometry set from the bag and shoved it quickly into my pocket. Within seconds, I was down the stairs and out into the street. Eva was still there. I ran up to her.

'I have something for ye, Eva. A wee present . . . just to thank you for the wan ye gave me. I hope ye like it,' I said breathlessly.

She stopped kicking the ball and turned towards me, staring at the box in my hand.

'What is it, Dickie?' she said, surprised as I handed it to her.

'Open it and see,' I said as I walked away, shouting to her that I'd see her later.

But before I had taken five steps, she called out, 'Dickie . . .'

I turned and stared at her, knowing something was up. Her head was down and she looked sad.

'What is it, Eva?'

I walked back towards her.

'It's nothing,' she said.

'What's nothin'?' I asked. 'What do ye mean it's nothin'?'

'I'll tell ye later.'

'Tell me now. I'm not goin' till ye tell me.'

She lifted her head and looked straight at me.

'It's my da,' she whispered. 'He wants to send my ma and me and wee John to Dublin until the war's over. He says it's not safe here.'

My heart was racing as I listened to what she was saying. I felt shocked.

'But my ma doesn't want to go and she doesn't want us to go, either.'

I didn't know what to say. All I could think was that I might never see her again. And I couldn't even imagine what it would be like in the Terrace without Eva. She's my best friend. Now I felt sick at the thought of her leaving.

She went on. 'And he said that John would get into a special school in Dublin, with the Christian Brothers, because there's nothin' in Derry for the likes of him.'

That's when things began to sink into my thick skull. So that's why her wee brother didn't go to St Eugene's and that's why he never came out to play, either. Liam had asked me about him a couple of times, but I never had an answer. And nobody ever asked Eva about him. Now I knew.

'Wee John's backward, Dickie. He was born like that. He just stays in the house with my ma.'

I didn't want to hear any more, because my heart was thumping as I listened to her. But I had to say something.

'When are ye leavin', Eva?' I asked her in a croaky voice. There was a lump rising in my throat. I wasn't able to say anything at this very second. And I didn't want to cry. At least not here in the middle of the street. She looked at me again, the way she does when she gets very determined about something. She was breathing heavily as she replied.

'I'm not, Dickie, I'm not goin'. My ma and John can go to Dublin if they like, but I'm stayin' in Derry.'

Now I stared at her again – puzzled, like – and thinking hard. Wondering just how she'd manage to do that.

That's when she looked again at the box I'd given her. It was as if she was seeing it for the first time.

'What's this, Dickie?' she asked.

'Open it and see,' I said to her again as I walked away, shouting to her as well that I'd see her soon.

I'd already shut the glass door behind me when Liam was coming down the stairs. I felt my knees trembling as I wiped a big tear from my eye. Liam didn't look at me. I was glad, because he would have spotted that I was very upset. And I didn't want to talk about what had just happened in the street. I felt rotten for Eva. And I felt rotten for myself as well.

I took two big deep breaths as we turned towards the living room together. For now, I'd have to try and forget about what Eva had just told me and get over the shock of it, because I had a feeling that more bother was around the corner.

We went into the living room together. Everybody except my ma was sitting at the table. My da was in his usual seat and Uncle Jimmy sat between Kate and Laura. Everybody had big faces on them. But before we sat down with the rest of them, Liam stopped dead in his tracks when he saw Uncle Jimmy, then began to back out of the room stiffly. He didn't know who it was. He didn't like strangers in the house, especially not since a crowd of cops poured in through our front and back doors last September. Naw, Liam hadn't fully got over that. I'd stepped back with Liam, and when we were almost out in the hall, I whispered, 'It's okay, Liam. It's only Uncle Jimmy in disguise.'

Liam's tension eased a bit, but he kept staring into the room. I felt stupid. I should have warned him, or somebody should have warned him.

'But why . . . why?' he stammered.

And before he asked anything, I told him again that everything was okay. That it was just a bit of fun. But he kept staring, still a bit anxious. He couldn't understand what was happening. How could he? He was still only seven. I could hardly understand what was happening myself. And not just because the whole thing was ridiculous but because it was stupid, and dangerous. All in one. Now I was determined more than ever to sort it all out. But for the moment, I would stay calm and stick to the plan in mind. For everybody's sake, except Uncle Jimmy's. Reluctantly, Liam sat down beside me at the table. And kept staring at Uncle Jimmy.

'Right, everybody, tuck in,' said my ma as she brought in the last two plates, my da's and her own. 'Doesn't this look good? Bacon and sausage and spuds. Sure ye wouldn't think there was a war on the way we're eatin',' she continued as she put the plates down. She looked at Uncle Jimmy as she spoke. I was glad that she didn't say 'thanks to Uncle Jimmy, here,' because that would really have made my da very angry.

'I hear ye were up at the College the day, Dickie,' said Laura, 'and ye got there on a bicycle and in the priest's car as well. You do it in style, Dickie, but you'll have to explain that wan to me sometime. And are ye all signed up now and ready to go?'

I gritted my teeth, wondering at the same time how she knew about me on Bap Kelly's bike, and feeling annoyed, too, at the way she was making light of the terrible morning I'd had. I could have shouted at her that not only did I go by bike and car but I could have gone in Bap Kelly's da's stupid old van if I'd wanted to. But I didn't. Didn't shout at her, I mean. I just said, 'Aye, Laura, everything's sorted.'

It suddenly crossed my mind as I was speaking that if Kate and Laura were going to join the IRA in August, and if my ma was involved in some way, too, and if my da got caught up in some sort of crossfire with the whole carry-on, there might never be a College for me, because the whole family could be dead soon, or in jail, or on the run, maybe even living in some safe house. And then what would happen to me and Liam? We wouldn't be allowed to stay in Rosemount Terrace. Officials would come and put us in a home, or someplace where we'd have no freedom. It would be like the end of the world. With no family, and no friends, and no gang.

'That's great, Dickie,' said Kate, interrupting my thoughts. 'And I hear Uncle Jimmy got ye everything ye need to start with. Bag and books and all. Aren't you the lucky boy?'

I nodded as if I was agreeing with her but I didn't smile or anything, because at the same time as she was speaking, I saw my da looking over at her, then at Uncle Jimmy, and then at my ma. His face was getting a bit angry looking, but he didn't shout out as he normally did when Uncle Jimmy was being praised. I hadn't told him about the stuff that Uncle Jimmy had given me, because I knew that it would have made him mad.

Once he cleared his mouth of food, my da spoke quietly and calmly. 'Aye, we're all proud of our Dickie, and I can tell youse all now that I'll soon have his new school uniform for him, and his old bike will look as good as new by the time I'm finished with it.'

'Thanks, Da,' I said as I smiled over at him. I didn't want to say just now that I didn't want a school uniform, or even need a school uniform, because the College priest had told us this morning that it wasn't necessary, that people had a choice to wear one, or wear their own clothes if they wished. He'd mentioned the war and all, and the difficulty in buying things like that. But I said nothing about this, because I knew anyway that there was no chance ever of my da buying me a uniform, or even fixing my bike. I'd heard all his promises before, but it sounded good anyway, him saying it in front of everybody, especially Uncle Jimmy.

We were finishing off our meal when there was a loud knocking at the glass door. Liam was the first off his chair to answer it, my mother shouting after him, 'Liam, don't let anybody in.'

He didn't seem to hear her, because he rushed on into the hall, and before you could say Jack Robinson, Mrs Fatso Lardo Doherty, and her fat son, Danny, who now thought he was second in command of the gang, were practically in the living room. Mrs Doherty leaned against the doorframe and folded her big fat arms. Danny stood in front of her to hide her big belly. Probably on her orders.

'Hello, Kitty, Barney, everybody,' she said as she looked at us. 'I was just passin' and I thought I'd call in to see youse and congratulate wee Dickie there about gettin' into the College. Isn't it just great, Kitty, that somebody from our street got that exam? And I heard, too, that wee Cecil Colhoun and Billy Burnside are goin' to Foyle College. They got their exams as well. Isn't it a pity, too, that they're not all goin' to the same College, them being the great friends they used to be and all.'

I thought she was never going to shut up, but she suddenly stopped when my ma got up and walked towards her and attempted to guide her into the sitting room.

'Aye, it's great, Mrs Doherty,' she said, reaching for her arm. 'Will we go on into the other room and have a wee natter about everything and leave these wans to finish their meal?'

I knew what my ma was up to. She didn't want Mrs Doherty to have any contact with Uncle Jimmy, or at least with the man in our house who wasn't supposed to look like Uncle Jimmy but was supposed to look like a total stranger. This should be good, my ma trying to move a big fat nosey woman who didn't want to be moved. And big fat Danny as well. Aye, Mrs Doherty was nosey, all right. Everybody in the world knew that. And for once, I wanted her to stay where she was and ask awkward questions. Maybe me and Liam, and even my da, would get some of the answers we were looking for.

As I expected, Mrs Doherty didn't heed my ma. She stood her ground and began talking very loudly.

'It's just that wee Danny here was out the back on Friday night before he went to bed and he saw your visitor there,' pointing her eyes towards Uncle Jimmy, 'walkin' down the lane and then goin' in your gate. I was tellin' Danny that youse must have somebody stayin' with youse.'

It was obvious right away that Mrs Fatso Lardo didn't recognise Uncle Jimmy.

Now it was my ma's turn to stop her in her tracks. She obviously hadn't thought this one through, about who she would say this 'stranger' was if he was spotted, or why he was here, and how long he'd be staying with us. And by the looks of things, Mrs Fatso Lardo had no intention of moving until she got some answers. And an answer she would have to get, and pretty quickly, otherwise there would be a lot more questions asked in the street, gossip questions that would create even more gossip, and even more questions. That's what I was thinking anyhow. And that's what my da must have been thinking, too, because out of the blue, and to everybody's surprise, he spoke out. In fact, what he did say saved the day. For now.

'Aye, Mrs Doherty, this is my brother Joe. He's livin' in Dublin now; workin' there for years. And he's up for a wee visit to Derry to see us all, maybe for three or four days.'

I could feel the relief all round the table and the pride on my ma's face for my da as she stood there helplessly in front of Mrs Doherty and Danny.

'It's nice to meet ye, Joe. And how long have ye been livin' in Dublin? Isn't it strange that we never met before this?'

Obviously, Mrs Doherty wasn't finished yet, because you could see by the way she was now leaning her big fat upper arm and shoulder against the doorframe that she had a lot more questions to ask.

Uncle Jimmy coughed to clear his throat as if he was about to reply, but my da cut in again as quick as a flash.

'Ah, sure, Mrs Doherty, hasn't he been in Dublin half a lifetime? Doin' big work up there by the sound of things. Sure they couldn't do without him now. Isn't that right, Joe?'

As my da was speaking, he was looking over at Uncle Jimmy and grinning. The biggest grin I'd ever seen on his face. Liam began to snigger. I gave him a dig in the ribs, not hard, but he wouldn't stop. That made me giggle as well, watching Liam, and I was glad he was finding the situation funny now, since he'd been a wee bit scared a while ago when he first saw Uncle Jimmy in disguise. Him not knowing then that it was Uncle Jimmy.

At this point, my ma was making another move to get Mrs Doherty and Danny out of the way by saying that she'd make her a wee cup of tea and they could take it in the other room. But I knew by the way she was standing there that she still wasn't going to budge until she got more information. It would take a bigger woman than my ma to move Mrs Fatso Lardo. Now fat Danny was grinning, even when his ma began to speak again. I think he saw the predicament my ma was in.

'And what line of work are ye at in Dublin, Joe? And is there much talk about the war there?'

I knew at this stage that my da would have to stop talking for Uncle Jimmy and that Uncle Jimmy would have to start talking for himself, because it was beginning to look as if Uncle Jimmy couldn't speak at all. Obviously, my da felt the same, so he just shut up, and with a gawky kind of smile on his big red face, he looked over deliberately at Uncle Jimmy. Me and Liam and Danny were still giggling. Liam was about to explode, but I noticed that Kate and Laura looked very tense. They were probably thinking now that the game was up. My ma had gone very pale and looked even more nervous than the girls. We all waited, all of us staring at Uncle Jimmy now as he spoke. And it was worth the wait, because it was a strange type of accent we heard coming from his mouth. It was like what ye might hear on Raidió Éireann, in a play or something. And he shouted out as well.

'Do you see you, Mrs whatever your name is, and the likes of you, youse are nothin' but lousy oul' nosey bitches. With nothin' better to do than hang about the street all day gossipin' about other people. And I'd thank ye for now for your enquiries if I was the type to thole ye, but I'm not the type to thole ye, so just turn that big arse of yours round and get it out of this house, right this very minute, along with your big fat son.'

Me and Liam exploded, but Danny's face dropped a mile. He looked badly shocked at Uncle Jimmy's outburst. Kate and Laura just sat there looking dazed. My da opened a bottle of Guinness he just happened to have in his pocket and had half of it swallowed before Mrs Doherty and Danny were back in the street. We could hear my ma apologising as she was closing the glass door behind her.

***

Very little was said after the dinner. It was as if nothing exciting had happened. Or nothing unusual. And I was none the wiser about Uncle Jimmy's plans. About where he'd be going later and what time he'd be leaving. But at least Liam was a bit happier, not just because he now knew who this 'stranger' was but because he enjoyed the funny side of what had happened when Mrs Doherty appeared.

When he went up the stairs to read some more comics, I took the opportunity to slip out of the house without anybody noticing. I was about to organise something that hopefully might answer the questions I'd been asking myself earlier. About Uncle Jimmy. About where he'd be going tonight. And how long he'd be away. I needed to know. Timing was very important, he'd said to Kate and Laura earlier. Well, timing's very important to me, too, Uncle Jimmy. And now was the time as well for Danny and Kevin to earn their place in the gang. With a real mission.

CHAPTER 11

What's The Mission? When Does It Start?

I knocked at Dohertys' door. Mrs Fatso Lardo answered. She glared at me.

'What do you want?' she growled, 'I don't think my Danny should speak to youse McCauleys anymore after the insults we got the day from that uncle of yours.'

'My ma sent me up, Mrs Doherty,' I lied. 'She couldn't get up herself just now, but she'll see ye later. She's very, very embarrassed about what happened. Uncle Joe's drunk, ye see, and my da, he's drunk too. They've been drinkin' all day, Mrs Doherty, and Uncle Joe didn't know what he was sayin', or who he was sayin' it to . . . to a good friend of my ma's. That's what she told him, Mrs Doherty, that you were her best friend and that he should go and apologise to ye.'

'Well, your Uncle Joe's no gentleman, drink or no drink. I can tell ye that. Because no gentleman would treat a lady like that, or anybody else for that matter. He's a disgrace, son, that's what he is, a bloody disgrace, for insulting me the way he did, and shoutin' at me the way he did. Your da would never do that, drink or no drink.'

'I'm sorry about all that, Mrs Doherty. I'm sure it won't happen again, because my ma's been bargin' away at him since ye left. I was just sent up to apologise to ye.'

I tried to look sorry to Mrs Fatso Lardo, to look the part, but I wasn't one bit sorry. She deserved all she got, even if it was from my stupid Uncle Jimmy, who I probably hated more than she did. And anyway, she shouldn't have pushed her way into our house the way she did. If she hadn't, she wouldn't have been insulted. So really, it was all her own fault.

'Well, you just tell your mother that I'm not a happy woman. I mean, I just went down out of courtesy to welcome the man, and look what I got for my trouble. Insults, nothin' but bloody insults, and I'm still shakin' with the shock of it all.'

I didn't notice she was shaking in any way. If she had been, it would have been more of a wobble.

'I'll tell her how ye feel, Mrs Doherty, and she'll probably call up to see you tomorrow to apologise by herself.' I was glad I said probably.

I think by this stage Mrs Fatso Lardo's mood was beginning to melt, because she'd got a lot quieter in the last half-minute, but if I had to apologise to her once more, I'd probably vomit all over her front porch.

'Is Danny in, Mrs Doherty?' I said quickly in case she would go on and on about insults and stuff. 'I just want to apologise to him as well. He must have felt it, too, the things that were said to youse.'

'Aye, you're right, Dickie. He's very hurt. Not so much for himself but for me. But hold on, son, and I'll get him for you. You're a good boy, Dickie McCauley, ten times the man of that uncle of yours.'

I had her. Eating out of the palm of my hand she was. Now for Danny. I didn't have to wait long. He just appeared suddenly from behind his ma. He must've been there all the time, listening. Danny Doherty was sneaky like that, but his sneakiness came in handy sometimes. And it could come in handy again tonight, because I had a wee sneaky job for him.

'Thanks, Dickie,' he said as he came towards me. 'I heard what ye said to my ma. Your Uncle Joe's not a nice man, even if he was drunk. I don't like him, Dickie. I'd rather have your Uncle Jimmy, but he's away now, isn't he, on the run? A wanted man, Dickie.'

Danny Doherty was a sickener. And he was wrong about my Uncle Jimmy. Even though I wished he was right, about being on the run or being a wanted man. But he did this sometimes, to try to make himself a big man. He'd stick the knife in even after I'd done him a favour. But I'd let him off this time, because this very evening, Danny Doherty would hopefully be doing *me* the favour, even if he thought it was the other way about. That's one of the things I liked about him. He was stupid. Most of the time. And that suited me. He just didn't know any better.

'Danny,' I said to him after his ma had gone back into the house, 'ye know the way I appointed ye to take charge of the spyin' mission on the North Street Bunch?' He nodded.

'Well, I was wonderin' if youse would take on another spyin' mission, even before youse do that wan, startin' the night. Just you and Kevin, I mean. Youse would have to promise to tell nobody about it. Ever. It would be a secret for life. The most important mission youse would ever do.'

Danny got very excited. Even more excited than earlier in the air-raid shelter.

'Will I get Kevin?' he whispered, looking around him to make sure nobody was listening.

'Naw, Danny,' I replied. 'When I tell ye what ye have to do, you can explain everything to him. Okay?'

'Okay, Dickie. What's the mission? When does it start?'

'It could be a three-night mission, Danny, and you and Kevin might have to stay up very late each night, without your ma knowin', and without Kevin's ma and da finding out. Are ye game, Danny? If not, say so now and I'll abandon the mission.'

I'd said that last bit to make sure he'd do it. That was the Danny I knew. Threaten to take something away from him and he grabs hold of it, even if he doesn't know what it is yet.

'Aye, I'm ready for it, Dickie, and I'll make sure Kevin is as well. Give me the details now.'

'It's like this, Danny. Your ma said that you saw my Uncle Joe out in the back lane last night.'

'Aye, that's right, Dickie, I did.'

'And what time was that, Danny?'

'About half ten, Dickie.'

'And did he see ye, Danny?'

'Naw, I hid behind our gate when I saw him. Then he went in through your back, so I guessed then that he was a friend or a relative of your ma or da. And I told my ma about him this mornin', and that's why she, well, the two of us, went down to your house. To find out, if ye know what I mean.'

'I know what ye mean, Danny.'

'So what do ye want me and Kevin to do, Dickie?'

'Well, first, you'll have to lie in wait for him to leave our house tonight. Probably about the same time. But I'll tip youse off. I want youse then to follow him and find out where he goes and who he sees.'

Danny was getting even more excited now, so I caught him by the arm and looked dead straight into his eyes. To calm him.

'Danny,' I whispered, 'this could be a matter of life and death. Are ye sure youse are up for it?' And I meant what I said.

'Definitely, Dickie,' he said hoarsely. His eyes were beginning to bulge. Not as much as Kevin's did when he was afraid of something, but big enough for me to know that he felt that this was the most important and dangerous mission of his life. And the most exciting.

'Now, remember, Danny,' I warned him, 'if he spots youse, just abandon everything and clear. Vamoose. Skedaddle. As fast as youse can. Do you hear what I'm sayin', Danny?'

'I do, Dickie, but he'll never spot us. I'll make sure of that.'

Danny seemed calmer now. And up for the plan.

'Right,' I said quietly now. 'But if he does happen to catch youse, by surprise, I mean, don't give the game away. Don't tell him anything about my part in it. Just tell him it's a stupid prank or something.'

'We won't, Dickie. I promise. We won't blab.'

Not for a second did fat Danny seem to wonder why they

were to follow Uncle Jimmy – or Uncle Joe, as he thought – not once did it cross his mind to ask me why. He would just follow orders. That's Danny for you. But I knew in my heart that they could pull it off, because really, there was nothing difficult about this mission. Following somebody was easy.

'Right,' I whispered as I was leaving. 'I'll tip youse off when Uncle . . . when Uncle Joe is leavin'.'

I'd nearly said Uncle Jimmy. That could have blown everything. Danny didn't catch on.

'Okay, Dickie,' he said, 'I'll go up the street now and fill Kevin in on the details.'

As I still had some time to spare I went for a walk to Brooke Park. For a bit of peace and quiet. I sat on a bench and gazed blankly over the city below. At the church spires and houses and shops. But I couldn't help thinking all the time about the plan. And I prayed that it would work.

I headed for home after that. I'd just go about my business in the house. Nobody would suspect that I was watching out for Uncle Jimmy. I might even play stupid Ludo or Tiddlywinks on the hall floor with Liam. We would be allowed to stay up late anyhow because it was Saturday night. Aye, sitting in the hall like that would be a good idea, because I'd know in advance when he was leaving. I'd hear him preparing, and that would give me time to warn Danny and Kevin. I didn't have to involve Joey and Hughie Deeney tonight, because as far as I was concerned, this was only a dry run. But if things worked out tonight as planned, and the dam at the bottom of the field was finished by tomorrow, then the bigger plan would go into operation tomorrow night. Aye, tomorrow night the whole gang could be involved, but only the Deeney twins and me would know what was really happening. The big plan would be happening. The very dangerous plan. About the guns and stuff. And even if the dam wasn't completed, I'd think of another tactic to divert attention. But one way or the other, the guns would definitely be gone. And they'd be well out of the reach of Uncle Jimmy.

These were all the things that were going around in my head as I went into the house. Inside, things looked normal. I glanced at the clock in the front sitting room. Nearly half past eight. Hopefully, plenty of time yet before Uncle Jimmy left. And by this time, Danny would already have informed Kevin Doherty about the plan. I could imagine Kevin's reaction as he listened to it. But I was certain that he'd go for it. Even Kevin loved dangerous adventures. And if they were caught, he wouldn't blab, either. That was the strange thing about Kevin: he could be as good as the rest of us when it suited.

My ma and the twins were in the kitchen, washing the dishes and chatting away as usual. I could see into the living room. There was no sign of Liam. Maybe he was upstairs. And there was no sign of Uncle Jimmy, either. I hoped he hadn't left already. If he had, my plan was scuppered. And I'd look a right fool to Danny and Kevin.

I went into the living room. My da was back in his armchair. Three empty Guinness bottles were on the floor at his feet and a nearly full one in his hand.

'Where's Uncle Jimmy, Da?' I whispered. I didn't want my ma or the twins to hear me. He lifted his head slowly and stared at me. His face was blotchy pink and his eyes were red. He didn't reply but he pointed his finger up towards the ceiling.

I went out to the hall again and deliberately shouted up the stairs to Liam to bring down the games. I wanted my ma and the twins to see us playing there, in the hall, so that they wouldn't suspect anything. About me, I mean. Checking up on Uncle Jimmy's movements.

'What are ye shoutin' about, Dickie?'

'I'm lookin' for Liam, Ma, to bring down the Ludo and Tiddlywinks from the bedroom. He said earlier that he wanted to play some games,' I lied.

'Well, he's not up there, Dickie. He must have forgot about ye, because he left the house a while ago. He said he was goin' up the street to play with Danny and Kevin.'

95

My heart gave a jump. Then it sank. This wasn't supposed to happen. The stupid wee fart could ruin everything.

'That's okay, Ma,' I said without looking anxious or panicky. 'Sure I'll just go on out and join them. We can play the games later.'

She went back into the kitchen. I heard her saying to Kate and Laura that I was very good to wee Liam. I heard the twins laughing as I was closing the glass door behind me. I didn't care about them laughing at me anymore. I had more important things to worry about.

I stood there in the porch, juking up and down Rosemount Terrace. I couldn't see anybody, except Mrs Doherty standing at Cecil Colhoun's house. She must be gossiping with Mrs Colhoun, I thought. Probably telling her about being insulted by the big, bad Joe McCauley. The man that didn't exist. But where was Liam? And more important than that, where were Danny and Kevin? I strolled up the footpath with my hands in my pockets – casual, like. As if I hadn't a care in the world.

'Hello, Mrs Doherty. Hello, Mrs Colhoun,' I said with a forced smile.

'Oh, hello, Dickie,' replied Mrs Fatso Lardo. Mrs Colhoun didn't say anything to me. In fact, she turned her head away – deliberately. She hadn't spoken to me or any of the McCauley family since her B-man husband was shot dead.

'Did ye see our Liam anywhere?' I asked.

'Liam? Aye. Liam's up in our house with Danny and Kevin and Eva Johnston. He just went up there about ten minutes ago. I told him to go in and play with the rest of them.'

With that, she turned away and continued her gossip.

'As I was sayin', Mrs Colhoun, that man Joe McCauley's nothin' but an ignorant brute, the way he . . .'

I didn't want to hear any more, so I hurried on. I had other things to deal with. Right now. More important things. Like getting Danny and Kevin away from Eva and Liam and then me getting back to my own house quickly in case Uncle Jimmy left. Nothing was straightforward this day and I was beginning to feel very tired. But I couldn't let things slip now. There was too much at stake.

I took a deep breath and walked into Dohertys' house. They were all sitting round a table, staring at a thousand pieces of a jigsaw puzzle. What a waste of time and effort, I thought. The best jigsaws had about three hundred pieces. But it wasn't the time to say that. Danny looked over at me and shrugged. It was the kind of shrug you give when you're in a situation that you can do nothing about. The look on Kevin's face was enough. He didn't need to shrug. But my guess was that Mrs Doherty had arranged this wee get-together. She did that sometimes when she thought her Danny was bored. But her timing was wrong. Danny was anything but bored. He was raring to go. To get on with the mission. So was Kevin. I'd have to do something about it. And quick.

'Danny,' I lied with a knowing wink to him that nobody else saw, 'I was talkin' to your ma outside and she wants ye to go a wee message over to Deeneys' shop for her. She said Kevin could go with you to keep ye company.'

Without saying anything, Danny and Kevin left the room. For the next couple of minutes or so, to avoid Eva and Liam suspecting that anything out of the ordinary was going on, I stayed with them and helped put about ten more pieces of the jigsaw puzzle in place. I then said I had to go but that I'd be back as soon as I could. As Liam kept searching for another suitable jigsaw piece, Eva looked at me strangely, a slightly annoyed and puzzled look on her face. She guessed something was up. Eva wasn't stupid. Before I reached the glass door on my way out of Dohertys', she was behind me, pulling at my arm.

'What's happening, Dickie?' she whispered. 'I know some-thing's happening. What is it?'

I could barely look her in the eye. I felt ashamed. For lying to her. And I knew by her expression that she was hurt. Hurt that she was being made little of. That she was being lied to. And that she wasn't involved in the action. But I saw something else, too, in her eyes. Disappointment. With me. With Dickie McCauley, who was supposed to be her best friend. And especially after what she'd revealed to me earlier about her da wanting to send her away. That's what I read in her eyes. But I couldn't tell her about anything that was happening. Especially not her, a cop's daughter, because Eva might accidentally say something about it to her da. Naw, I was definitely right about not involving her in any of this – except maybe in the stupid raid on the North Street Bunch's dam – that would be okay because that was just a diversionary tactic.

But Eva needed some sort of an explanation. I couldn't just walk away and say nothing. I'd have to say something, even if it wasn't the truth.

'Look, Eva,' I said. 'What is happening is top-secret, senior gang-member stuff. And besides that, girls wouldn't be allowed to do it because it's too dangerous.'

I couldn't believe the rubbish that was coming out of my mouth, but at this minute, my brain wasn't working right and I couldn't think of anything else to say except, 'And Liam's too young to be involved as well, so it would be great if you would stay with him doing the jigsaw for another wee while.'

I pushed on out before she could say anything else or ask me questions that I couldn't answer. I felt as if I had betrayed her very badly. As if I had slapped her, or pushed her the same as I'd done earlier at the school gate. When this was all over, I didn't know how I was ever going to make it up to her. But I'd think of something. I couldn't allow Eva Johnston to leave Derry, hating me. I liked her too much.

CHAPTER 12

Da, Youse Could All Be Hanged

I went the long way back to my house. I did this for two reasons: one, to avoid any awkward questions from Mrs Fatso Lardo, who was still out gossiping, and two, to check up on Danny and Kevin. I needn't have worried on the second score, because as soon as I reached the end of the Terrace and turned right, there they were, the two boyos, down on their hunkers, playing a game of marbles on the footpath. A clever ruse if ever there was one. I gave them a quick nod of praise and headed on, and round to the right, into the back lane. What I had to do next was get back home and check on the situation with Uncle Jimmy.

When I went into the house, nobody seemed to be downstairs except my da. He was dozing in his chair, an empty Guinness bottle in his hand and five other empties scattered on the floor beside him. The wireless was still on low, playing music. I went quietly back out to the hall and listened. I could hear nothing. I pushed the sitting-room door open, but there was nobody there, either. I listened more intently then because I thought I heard voices from upstairs. I slipped up quietly to the landing and clearly heard Uncle Jimmy and my ma talking in the attic. I wondered where the twins could be, because I could see in through the open door of their bedroom and it was empty. That's when I heard chatter again from the attic – and then laughter. This time, I recognised Kate and Laura's voices. You couldn't mistake them. But I wasn't able to make out anything that was being said. All the voices were muffled. I went into my own bedroom and deliberately kept the door open a wee bit so that anybody passing wouldn't see in, but open wide enough for me to hear if anything might be said out in the landing. Within minutes, I heard footsteps on the attic stairs and the voices of my ma and the twins. They all seemed to be speaking at the same time, so I could hardly make out anything that they were saying except for stuff like 'it'll be well worth it' and 'they deserve all they git'.

I had no way, at this moment, of knowing the exact time. If Uncle Jimmy didn't make his move soon, I might have to abandon tonight's mission. But I needn't have worried. Five minutes later, I heard him coming down the attic stairs onto the landing and then into the bathroom. Within a short time, he was on his way downstairs. I quietly moved out of my room to the landing and listened.

'I'm away,' I heard him shouting to my ma and the girls. 'I'm away out the back.'

I rushed down the stairs as quick as I could, out the glass door in a flash and up the Terrace past Mrs Fatso Lardo and Mrs Colhoun. Both of them gave me a strange look because I was going like the hammers of hell. Danny and Kevin heard me coming, for they were standing waiting just round the corner. Kevin's hand was in his pocket, fingering his beads, and you could see the sweat on his forehead. And he hadn't even done anything yet! Danny looked a bit tense.

'This is it,' I whispered. 'He's left the house, by the back lane.'

All three of us quickly went round the corner, back into Rosemount Terrace, and hid ourselves in the porch of the first house. We kept juking out, looking up towards Creggan Road. But seconds later, when there was no sign of Uncle Jimmy, I ordered Danny to go up round the corner again and look. He came back a short time later and said that there was nobody there. That my Uncle Joe must have gone another way.

I felt stupid. And I felt foolish. And I didn't like feeling stupid or foolish, especially in front of Danny and Kevin. So I leapt into action.

'Follow me,' I ordered, 'down the back way into Warke's Lane. He must have gone that way.'

Why I had assumed that Uncle Jimmy would simply come up the back lane into Creggan Road and then head down the hill towards the Cathedral direction I'll never know. Probably because if *I* had been meeting people, it would have been downtown. Stupid me.

We ran as fast as we could but when we reached the bottom of our lane and looked both ways, to the right and the left, there was no sign of Uncle Jimmy.

'Come on,' I hissed breathlessly. 'Up this way.'

I steered Danny and Kevin towards Park Avenue, where the big Rosemount Shirt Factory is. If he'd gone that way, we were bound to see him. But again, there was no sign of him.

'What about Brooke Park?' suggested Danny. 'He might have gone down that way.'

'Okay,' I said, 'let's head there.'

But again, we couldn't see him. There was not one person in the park, as far as our eyes could see. I was baffled. And disappointed. I knew then that I should have followed Uncle Jimmy myself, out the back gate. At least that way, I'd have seen which direction he'd gone. But the more I thought of it now, the more puzzled I became, because there was no way that we should have missed him, for we were only seconds behind him. Naw, no way. There must be another explanation. But I had no answer. For now, I would have to abandon tonight's mission. There was no point in continuing with it if the person you were supposed to be following has completely disappeared.

'Right, boys,' I said as we walked back to Rosemount Terrace. 'Tonight's mission is off. The plan'll have to be changed.'

That's when I saw Danny Doherty smirking. I wasn't a bit pleased. And just as I was about to blame both of them for messing things up with the Uncle Jimmy mission, I immediately thought better of it. I might need Danny later, so I didn't want another big row, even though I could see by his face that he was raring to have a go at me. He was obviously still simmering after the last bust-up in the air-raid shelter. He began spluttering something under his breath as I walked quickly away.

But Kevin came running after me. 'Dickie,' he whispered breathlessly, 'don't you worry about Danny. He's just a bit annoyed that we missed your Uncle Joe.'

I stared at Kevin, pleased at what I was hearing. And standing up for his friend as well. I felt relieved.

'Thanks, Kevin.'

'And, Dickie . . .'

'What, Kevin?'

'I'll make sure that Danny and me'll keep watchin' for your Uncle Joe. And if we see him, we'll follow him and report back to you.'

'Great, Kevin,' I said. And that's the way I left them, going on down the Terrace with Danny shouting stuff after me which I didn't heed. I had more important things to do at this minute.

I banged at Dohertys' front-room window. Within seconds, Liam and Eva appeared at the door.

'What's up, Dickie?' said Liam.

'Nothin's up, Liam. My ma wants ye home.'

I said nothing to Eva, just gave her another apologetic look. She stared at me, puzzled at the state of me. And puzzled, too, at Danny Doherty up the Terrace, still ranting and raving and waving his fist. Liam didn't notice. He just ran on home. As I was about to follow him, Eva called me.

'Dickie,' she said quietly, 'thanks for the geometry set. It's fantastic.'

I could see by her eyes that she meant it. At last, something good was happening for Dickie McCauley. I walked slowly the rest of the way down the street, disappointed about the plan not working, but happy at the same time. Because of Eva Johnston. And I prayed to God that she'd be able to stay in Derry.

I had one more thing to do before I went to bed. I needed to check if the guns and ammunition were still in the attic. Liam was already in the living room with my ma and da and the twins. I went upstairs. Very quickly and very quietly. I stopped on the landing and listened. They were all talking downstairs, and laughing at times. As if they hadn't a worry in the world.

I went up the attic stairs and into Uncle Jimmy's bedroom. The rifles and the bag of bullets were still there under the old blanket. There was no sign of the revolver. But there was a small brown suitcase sitting on the floor behind the rifles. I hadn't seen it before. I pulled it out and opened the snap-lock. I could hardly believe what I was looking at. In fact, it took my breath away when I saw what was in the case. It was packed full with money. Twenty-pound notes, ten-pound notes, five-pound notes and ten-shilling notes. There must have been hundreds and hundreds of pounds there. I closed the lid quickly and snapped the lock shut. My heart was racing as I placed the case back carefully, hoping that I had left no clue that it had been disturbed. I quietly left the attic and slipped down the stairs into my own bedroom. I sat on the edge of the bed, trying to get to grips with what I had discovered. I found that difficult because there must be more money in that case than in the whole of Derry. Except maybe for banks. I couldn't even begin to imagine why Uncle Jimmy had this money, or where he'd got it. It was a real mystery.

'Dickie.' It was my ma shouting up to me. 'Dickie, do ye hear me?'

I went out to the landing. 'Aye, Ma, I'm here.'

'Come down now, son. Your piece and milk is on the table. Ye must be starving. It's after ten o'clock and youse should be in your beds.'

'I'll be there in a minute, Ma.'

I walked slowly down the stairs, thinking very hard about everything. Especially about the dosh in the wee brown suitcase. Liam passed me on his way up. I told him that there was a whole pile of new comics under the pillow. His eyes lit up. In the hall, Kate and Laura nearly bumped into me on their way out. They didn't say anything, either, but they were all dressed up and you could smell perfume off them.

'Where's Kate and Laura away, Ma?' I asked when they'd banged the front door behind them.

'What, son, what did ye say?' my ma asked as she was coming out of the living room to the kitchen with some cups and plates. She looked tired.

'Kate and Laura, Ma, they're away out.'

'Aye, Dickie, they've gone to a factory dance in the Corinthian.'

A yucky pastime, as far as I was concerned. I went into the living room and sat down to take my food and drink. My da was still asleep in the armchair, snoring soundly. When I was halfway through the meal, my ma shouted in to me to leave my dirty dishes in the sink when I was finished. She said she was going to bed.

'What about my da?' I called out to her as she headed for the stairs.

'Aw, him. As soon as he wakens, he'll come up, son. Don't you worry about him. Now, you get up yourself as soon as ye finish that.'

'I will, Ma,' I shouted to her, but I don't think she heard me.

I was so tired that I could hardly finish the bread and milk. But I didn't want to go up to bed yet, tired and all as I was, because I had a lot of things to work out in my head, and you wouldn't be able to do that in the bedroom with Liam probably yapping away half the night about the comics he was reading.

After I left the cup and plate out in the kitchen sink, I went back into the living room. It seemed strange to be the last one down the stairs except for my da. Usually he stayed up chatting to my ma for a good while after we all went to bed. I looked at him and felt a wee bit sad. His face was very red and his nose was purple with spots on it. Ugly, like. He wasn't snoring now, but you knew by the look of him that he was still sound asleep. And as I was staring at him, and even though I felt a terrible sadness about him drinking so much, I knew that I loved him. Because he was my da. Liam loved him, too. But I don't think anybody else in the house loved him. Not the way we did anyway. I then did something that I'd never done before. I climbed up on the arm of his chair and leaned my head against his shoulder. He moved over a wee bit as if he was making room for me. I hated the smell of Guinness off him. It was rotten, but I still snuggled even closer to him because it made me feel good being with him. He was the only big person in the house who thought the same way as I did about nearly everything and it made me feel safe being close to him like this.

As I lay there against the warmth of his body and as I listened to his strong, steady breathing, I began to whisper stuff to him, even though I knew he couldn't hear me.

'Da,' I said, and I looked up at his closed eyes. 'Da,' I repeated, half-hoping that he'd waken, but at the same time, I didn't want him to waken. In a sense, I didn't want him to hear me. But in another sense, I did, because he was smart and he might be able to tell me what to do about everything that was bothering me.

Before fully realising it, I was chatting to him about all that had happened since this morning. Except the bit about Eva having to leave. I didn't really want to talk about that. He already knew about the College stuff so I went on and on about the rest of my day. About what was in my mind.

'I've been tryin' to find out, Da, about Uncle Jimmy. About why he's here, and in disguise, even if the police aren't after him. And why is my ma allowin' the twins to go to Donegal in August to train for the IRA? Can you not stop them goin'? It's all annoyin' me, Da, especially the rifles and everything upstairs in the attic. If the police raid the house, we'll all be arrested and taken away. Youse could all be hanged, or shot, like those two German spies last year.'

I felt my heart thumping as I was saying these things, because they were all very, very serious, and nobody in our house seemed worried. I took a deep breath to calm myself before going on.

'And that's why I was doin' a lot of plannin' the day, Da, with the gang. I was plannin' to get rid of the guns, to shift them.'

I was in full flow now, telling him about the plan. I just had to talk about it, because it was a good plan, if only Uncle Jimmy hadn't disappeared the way he did.

'The thing is, Da, about the plan, what I was goin' to do was this: when I found out how long Uncle Jimmy was goin' to be away this evening, I had another plan then for Hughie and Joey Deeney to help me move the rifles and stuff tomorrow night when he'd be out of the house. Because he told my ma and the twins that he was goin' out for the next few evenings to see about things. Tonight would have been the dry run, Da, to give me the chance, ye see, to know if we would've had enough time to get rid of everything before he came back. And it could work, because it's very late now and he's not back yet, so we would have plenty of time tomorrow night, Da. Twenty minutes would do it, Da, if he does the same thing. Twenty minutes. That's about all I would have needed. But to be sure, I'd lined up Danny and Kevin tonight to follow Uncle Jimmy so that I'd know for certain how far away he'd be. But they lost him.'

I rattled on about tomorrow night's plan then, about how me and the twin Deeneys would sneak the rifles and ammunition out of our house when it was dark and then the Deeneys would jump over the barracks wall. I'd hand the stuff over to them, and they'd bury everything deep under the soft clay in Sergeant McBride's wee garden plot.

'But I wouldn't touch the suitcase of money, Da. And there's hundreds and hundreds of pounds in it,' I whispered. 'Money's not like weapons, Da. It can't kill you.'

I'd said that last bit in a loud whisper.

As I snuggled even more closely to my da, my eyes were already half-closed. I could hardly stay awake. But I was feeling better now because I'd got nearly everything out that was bothering me, even if he didn't hear a word I'd said. And when he put his arm tight around me just at that second, I felt really safe. And away deep down, I felt a tingle of excitement, too, because maybe this plan for tomorrow night could still go ahead. With just me and Hughie and Joey and nobody else. Aye, I'd let the boys know the details tomorrow. But then again, I was thinking, maybe I should sleep on it and . . .

***

'Da, waken up, will ye, for God's sake, and let that wain get up to his bed. It's nearly two in the mornin'.'

I'd woken up suddenly. Kate and Laura were standing there. For a second or two, I didn't know where I was or what was happening. Until my da began pushing me off the chair and mumbling something to me about going on up.

Kate and Laura were still giving out to him as I was climbing the stairs. I was stiff and numb, and a bit cold. But I knew I'd soon warm up when I got into bed beside Liam. I could still hear them arguing downstairs as I snuggled under the warm blankets. I'd be able to sleep longer in the morning because it was Sunday.

CHAPTER 13

It's You And Me, Dickie, Against The Rest

My da went to ten o'clock Mass with us. With me and Liam. He'd never done that before. He always went with my ma and the twins to the twelve Mass. But he stayed at the back of the Cathedral. We had to go on up the middle aisle and into our own class groups. The teachers were directing boys and girls from different schools into their usual seats. Liam pushed his way into a row where his best friends were before his teacher could order him where to go. Liam was like that. Thran at times. Just did his own thing. Mr Philson glared at me as usual as I moved into a place beside one of the boys from Marlborough Road. You would think that he would be calm and gentle and kind in the chapel, but he was just the same as he was in school. Thick. And bad tempered. I knew he hated me. But I didn't care. I would only have him for another week. As I sat there waiting for Mass to begin, I wondered what Philson would say on Monday when he heard from Father Mooney that I was one of the boys to be trained as an altar boy. He'd probably explode, because he'd find it hard to stick. First, having to teach me the Latin responses, I mean. And then afterwards, when I was trained, watching me up on the altar assisting priests. Naw, it would do his head in completely. I was looking forward to that, because I had as much right to be an altar boy as anybody else, even if Philson didn't think so.

During this Mass, I wanted to concentrate on the movements of the altar servers so that I could learn the routine ahead of the others. But I was distracted because of last night. My mind was still flitting about everywhere with the stuff about Uncle Jimmy and guns, and the money in the suitcase, and plans not working out. And, of course, about Eva Johnston.

When Mass was finished and we were walking down the aisle, I glanced over at the girls' side. I saw Eva, and she saw me, but then she put her head down as if she didn't want to be spotted looking at me. Especially in the chapel. I looked for my da, but he was gone from the back seat. Probably standing outside waiting for us. He wasn't. He was heading towards the wee gate into Creggan Street, looking back now and again to see if we were following him. Liam caught my hand, pulling me, then dug his nails into me because he didn't want me to stop and talk to anybody. He did that sometimes when he was in a hurry. And he was in a hurry now. I could sense that he wanted to tell me something. In private.

My da was waiting for us outside the gate and I knew by the look of him, too, that *he* wanted to tell me something as well. He put his hand in his pocket and pulled out a coin. A sixpence. He gave it to Liam and said, 'Would ye run up to the shop, son, and get me a Sunday paper? If there's change, ye can get some sweeties for you and Dickie. Okay, Liam? Will ye manage that, son? We'll wait for ye here.' Liam was a wee bit hesitant because he'd never gone a message before by himself. But then he went, proud as punch, and with a cheeky look on his face. But there was more to all this than met the eye, and I knew that when my da now turned to me and spoke. Getting rid of Liam was his plan so that he would have me by myself.

'Before Liam comes back, Dickie,' he said, 'there's somethin' I want to say to ye.'

'What is it, Da?'

'About last night, son, when ye were sittin' with me in the livin' room and talkin' about everything that was botherin' ye, about your Uncle Jimmy and about the IRA and about the rifles upstairs, and about Kate and Laura, and . . .'

As my da was speaking, I felt myself going weak. I couldn't believe what I was hearing. I stared up at him as he went on. How could I have been so stupid, I thought, mouthing everything off like I did, thinking he was totally fast asleep and not able to hear me? I'd just wanted to let it all out, to take the pressure off my skull so that I could think better. But I'd blabbed. That's what I'd done. And I'd blabbed without realising it. But then I remembered, too, that last night, I'd half-wished that my da could really hear me. That he would turn round to me when I was finished speaking and tell me not to worry. That he'd handle everything. Well, part of my wish was coming true now, all right.

My legs were shaking and my stomach was heaving. With nerves. I took a deep breath, then another before I spoke. It was more of a hoarse whisper when it came out, but strangely, as I talked, I felt a bit relieved, too, because my da didn't look angry, or annoyed, or anything like that. In fact, he looked pleased. As if he was proud.

'Da,' I said, 'I didn't know ye heard me last night. I thought ye were sound asleep. I was just gettin' stuff off my chest.'

He put his hand on my shoulder, and spoke. 'It's okay, Dickie. Nothin' I hear anymore surprises me. It's what we're goin' to do about it, son. What do ye think? It's you and me, Dickie, against the rest.'

I could smell last night's Guinness off him as he leaned forward to me.

I didn't answer him. How could I? What could he do about it all? Nothing, I was thinking, because everybody and everything would be against him. My ma, the twins and Uncle Jimmy wouldn't allow him to do anything. They'd laugh at him, and threaten him. That's just the way it was. I could have lied now, and said, *Aye, Da, we'll sort them all out. We'll solve everything together. You and me, Da.* But I didn't lie to him. It wouldn't have been fair or honest. So I just looked up at him. At his big purple face, red eyes and spotted nose. And he knew by my expression that there was nothing me and him could do about it. But that's why he'd come to Mass with us. Stuff must have been in his mind half the night. All the things I'd said to him. And then when he woke, he probably got the mad notion that he could help in some way. And I wondered as I looked at him if *he* hadn't been able to concentrate on the Mass as well because of everything that was running around in *his* mind. But as he looked back at me and hesitated before he spoke again, I knew by his expression that he himself now knew that we could do nothing. At least not together.

'You go on home now, son. Take wee Liam with ye and give the newspaper to your ma. I have a couple of wee messages to do down the town.'

'Okay, Da,' I replied, my heart still thumping but relieved at the same time that I hadn't agreed to some stupid plan with him. Something so stupid that it could only lead to more bother – and more danger.

As I watched him going down the street towards the town, I felt very sad for him. And sad for me, too. And for our Liam. Things seemed so hopeless at this very minute.

'Where's my da?' asked Liam when he crossed the street with the newspaper and two lollipops.

'He has somethin' important to do down the town, Liam,' I lied. 'He said he'd see us in a wee while.'

Liam said nothing.

As we sauntered up Creggan Street towards the crossroads, I took a quick look back. My da was out of sight, but I guessed where he was going. To some pub that opened its door on a Sunday, to a secret knock. To people 'in the know'. He'd told us about that one time when he came home drunk one Sunday evening. But nobody laughed except him, because there was nothing funny about it, or about him making my ma cry, or funny about him shouting and singing and roaring like a bull in the street, or showing us all up in front of the neighbours. But my worry at this minute was that he might come home this evening, mad drunk, and start shouting all over the place about how he and Dickie were going to sort everything out. With Uncle Jimmy and guns and stuff.

We trudged slowly on up the hill. Liam didn't speak at all on the way. Just kept sucking his lollipop. That gave me time to think about some things. Things about Eva Johnston, and getting Danny Doherty back in line. Before we reached Rosemount Terrace, just before the barracks, Liam threw away the lollipop stick and turned to me.

'Dickie . . .'

'What, Liam?'

'Why did Uncle Jimmy go into Eva Johnston's house last night? I didn't think that he liked policemen.'

'What? What are ye sayin', Liam?'

'About Uncle Jimmy, Dickie. He came out our back gate last night and went in through Johnstons' yard. And then on into their house. I saw him, Dickie. Honest.'

'What are ye talkin' about, Liam? That's stupid talk. And dangerous. It couldn't have happened. Sure ye couldn't have seen him. Sure you were in Dohertys' house, doin' a jigsaw puzzle with Eva. You're makin' this up, Liam.'

'I am not, true as God, Dickie,' he shouted. 'I'm tellin' ye the truth. And don't be callin' me a liar, Dickie. I definitely saw him. It was when Eva said she had to go to the toilet in Dohertys'. I just went out to their back yard to pass the time. I juked out the gate. That's when I saw him. And when he went into Johnstons', I slipped down the lane, followed him, like. And then he went in their back door.'

'Shush, Liam,' I whispered, looking around me, 'there's no need to shout.'

'There is a need to shout, Dickie,' he roared at me, 'when ye don't believe me. And I don't want to talk about it anymore.'

And with that outburst, he grabbed the Sunday newspaper out of my hand and in a rage began tearing it to bits.

'Okay, Liam,' I said quietly – and fearfully – trying to catch my breath. 'I do believe ye. Honest, Liam, I do believe ye.'

And I did now, because I'd looked at his face, and into his eyes. Liam was definitely telling the truth.

But how *could* this be true? I thought. It was unreal. Why would Uncle Jimmy be going into a cop's house? That's the question Liam had asked me in the first place. It didn't make sense. My mind went into overdrive, and so did my heart. Uncle Jimmy? Was he a traitor of some sort? An informer? A renegade? A blabber? A major big-time blabber? The sort of blabber that gets executed by his own side?

I put out my two hands to help Liam off the grass, but he pushed me away. He was still crying and he was angry and huffy. And disappointed with his big brother. Dickie McCauley had let him down for the first time ever. And I felt rotten. Now I had three people to make up to: Danny Doherty, Eva Johnston and Liam. Life was getting more and more difficult for me by the minute. And I was running out of ideas about how to sort things out.

CHAPTER 14

Liam's Big Surprise

It must have been nearly half eleven when we left the park. Liam was walking ten steps behind me, and each time I stopped and looked back at him, he stopped, too. He didn't want to be with me. He was still too annoyed with me for not believing him. Before I reached the air-raid shelter in Rosemount Terrace, I knew I had to make things right with him. And I couldn't let him go near the house yet because of the state he was in. He looked terrible from the crying. He was sweaty looking and flustered; he had a runny nose and a dirty face. Questions would be asked in the house, and I wasn't in any mood to be answering questions. Especially about what had got him into this state in the first place. Because if I did tell the truth, then everything would be out in the open. About Uncle Jimmy, maybe being an informer, a renegade, a traitor. Naw, that wouldn't be good. I'd have to be very careful. I wanted Uncle Jimmy out of our lives, but not the way I was thinking that it could happen if word of this got out. But then again, it was a very useful piece of information to have. One that I might be able to use if everything else failed.

My ma and Kate and Laura would be leaving shortly to go to twelve o'clock Mass. Because of that, I decided it wouldn't be a good idea to go near the house yet. I mean, for Liam to go near the house. For now, I had to think of something to keep him from being seen by my ma or Kate and Laura. They'd kill me if they thought I had done something to him.

I stopped behind the air-raid shelter and beckoned Liam to come forward while at the same time I was keeping a lookout up the street in case they would come this way to go to Mass. But Liam wouldn't budge. He still kept his distance. I could be in big trouble if I didn't sort this out right now, because if he took the notion, he could slip right past me and on up to the house. That way, the game would be up. I definitely had to think of something. Right now.

'Liam,' I said with a big smile on my face, 'I've got a great surprise for ye up in the house.'

He stared at me. He didn't believe me. I didn't believe me, either, because as far as I knew at this second, I had no surprise for him. Never mind a great one. But my mouth kept saying things that I hoped would get him on my side without my brain working out what.

'Something you've always wanted, Liam. Something very valuable.'

Now I was talking total rubbish, but the words were out of my mouth before I could even think what I might give him. And if I did think of something, it would have to be really different from anything that I'd ever given him before.

Now Liam spoke. He was interested. At least this was a first step. 'What is it, Dickie? What's the surprise?'

'You'll see when we get up to the house, Liam.'

'I want to know now, Dickie.'

'I can't tell ye that. Sure it wouldn't be a surprise if I told ye before ye see it. That'd be stupid.'

He looked at me again, this time with no huff on his face. I had him. For now. He walked forward slowly. As he did, I turned round and saw my ma and the twins heading for Mass up the Terrace towards Creggan Road. They hadn't seen us. I walked slowly up the street, thinking hard. Liam followed me.

As soon as we reached the front door, Liam asked me again about his big surprise. 'Where is it, Dickie?'

'It's upstairs,' I said with my brain working overtime. 'Come on upstairs and I'll show ye.'

Liam was really excited. But I was in a stupid dilemma. And I could only blame myself. What could I give him? Comics? No, he'd seen them all. One of the games? No, he knew he could use those anytime. A book, an old one that Uncle Jimmy had given me? No, definitely not, he'd throw it back at my face and go into a rage. *Kidnapped*, the new book that Eva had given me? No, because he'd tell everybody about it, including Eva, and that would be a very big mistake. For me. What, then? The poke of gobstoppers in my pocket? Definitely not. He wouldn't think there was anything great about that. So what could I give him? Time was running out. We were halfway up the stairs when an idea for the great surprise struck me. And it was an even bigger surprise to me when it did strike. Because it was a mad idea. And one that could get us both into very serious trouble. But in my mind, it was a done deal. I had no choice. I could think of nothing else.

'Right, Liam,' I said. 'You go into the bathroom for a few minutes and get a good wash. And when ye come out I'll have the surprise for ye.'

'Great, Dickie,' he said excitedly. 'I can't wait.'

As soon as he closed the door behind him, I rushed up the attic stairs and into Uncle Jimmy's bedroom. Everything was still there, the guns and all, and the brown suitcase. I opened the case quickly and took out a red ten-shilling note. Within seconds, I was back down, sitting on the bed and casually appearing to read a comic as he was coming out of the bathroom. I felt strangely calm, even after what I'd just done. I'd stolen money. A lot of money. And I'd never done anything like that before. This could be a mortal sin. But I still felt calm . . . as if I hadn't done anything wrong. It was strange. I didn't feel guilty. Maybe that was because of the relief I felt that I now had the surprise for Liam. He came into the room.

'Well, Dickie,' he asked, 'what have ye got for me?'

'This is something that ye've never had before, Liam, something very valuable. But before I give it to ye, ye have to promise

116

on oath that ye'll not tell anybody about it, about who gave it to ye, or why.'

'Honest to God, Dickie, I won't,' said Liam, breathless with excitement. 'I won't say a word to anybody. I promise, Dickie, on my oath. What is it, Dickie?'

'And, Liam,' I said, staring straight at his eyes, 'if anybody does happen to find out that ye have this, ye'll have to tell a lie and say that ye found it in the street. Okay, Liam?'

'Okay, Dickie. I could tell a lie about it if I had to. That's a promise. No bother to me, Dickie. I could easily lie.'

When he said that, a terrible thought struck me. What if he was telling a lie about seeing Uncle Jimmy going into the cop's house. Naw, he couldn't have been lying. I'd have seen it in his eyes. And I knew when people were lying. Because I knew how to lie, too. You had to sometimes, to survive.

'This is it, Liam, your surprise.' I opened my hand with the ten-shilling note in it and passed it to him. He looked at it in wonderment at first, then in total amazement.

'Gosh,' he gasped, 'a real ten-bob note. Is it real, Dickie?'

'Aye, it's real money, Liam, and it's yours.'

I then told him that I would take him downtown some day, maybe to Littlewoods or Bennett's, or Woolworth's or Edmiston's. He could buy a real football or something else that he liked.

'Gee, thanks, Dickie, this is brilliant. I'll buy ye something, too, when we're down the town.'

'Maybe after we get the school holidays next week, Liam, we'll go down then. But in the meantime, I want ye to hide the money.'

'Okay, Dickie. How about under the mattress?'

'Aye,' I said, 'under the mattress would be good.'

And that's where Liam put the ten-shilling note before we went down the stairs to eat. I knew in my heart I'd done a mad thing. And a bad thing. But I had no choice. However, there was one thing that I was pleased about, and that was that Liam hadn't asked where I'd got the ten bob from.

They had left the wireless on in the living room. Some man was talking about the war again. Something about German planes over in England, attacking places called the Midlands and East Anglia. He said it ended twelve months of freedom from night-time bombing.

I was fed up listening to news about people being bombed. It was cruel. But if you were in the living room when it was on and my da was there, he would shush you to keep quiet. He wanted to hear about everything that was happening. I think he wanted the Germans to win. Just because it was the British they were fighting. But he didn't have to shush me when a man called Lord Haw-Haw was speaking from Germany. He had a strange voice, very posh. My da told me that Lord Haw-Haw was an Irishman, and a friend of Hitler's. His real name was William Joyce. I liked listening to the way he talked because his voice was funny and snobby, but not when he told us all to surrender. Because I would never surrender to anybody. I'd fight to the death. My da told me, too, that William Joyce fought for the British in Ireland over twenty years ago. For the Black and Tans. Against the IRA. Now, sometimes, he was on the wireless, telling people to fight against the British. Sure wasn't that what the IRA were doing? It didn't make sense to me. And it made Lord Haw-Haw a traitor. The same way as Uncle Jimmy might be a traitor if what Liam had told me was true. Siding with the enemy. An IRA man siding with a cop could make him a traitor. The whole thing was giving me a headache thinking about it.

But it got me thinking about something else, too. If Uncle Jimmy really was a traitor working for the British, maybe that's where the money in the brown suitcase came from. Maybe that was his pay. And if it was, then the ten bob that I took from it to keep the peace with Liam wasn't really stealing. Because it was traitor money. And if it *wasn't* stealing, I was thinking at this very second, then maybe I should take some more. Because if it got me off the hook with Liam five minutes ago, and kept the peace and got him out of the state he was in, it was bound to be useful for keeping the peace from time to time with Danny Doherty, too, because he seemed to be the one I had the most bother with. And as well as that, I might be able to slip some of it into my ma's purse now and again when she has no money. She'll just think it's a miracle or something. And I could put some in the poor box at the chapel and some into the box in school for the black babies.

I began to feel good about this plan. So when the notion was on me, and because Liam was now content enough sitting at the table finishing his piece and reading a comic, I turned the wireless off because of the stupid war news and headed straight for the stairs to the attic. This was as good a time as any to do what I was going to do, because Uncle Jimmy wasn't in the house. I'd heard my ma telling the twins this morning that he hadn't even come home last night. And my ma and the twins wouldn't be back for another hour.

I don't think Liam took much notice of me as I was leaving the room, but I shouted to him anyway to go out to play in the street when he was finished eating. He didn't look up, but I knew he heard me. And I didn't want to be disturbed for a while. I had an important job to do. I slipped up the stairs. When I reached the attic bedroom, I was out of breath and my heart was racing. Now I had to decide if I was going to go through with this mission or not. Some wee doubts kept niggling away at me, at the back of my mind. But I felt at the same time that there was no going back.

Out of curiosity, I decided to count Uncle Jimmy's money before taking any more of it. I pulled out the suitcase and pressed the snap-lock open. The money was in neat bundles. I took each bundle out, one at a time, the twenty-pound notes first, and began to count. I had the job done in less than half an hour. Altogether, there was one thousand nine hundred and ninety-nine pounds and ten shillings. And the ten-shilling note under our mattress would have made it two thousand pounds. That's when a smart idea struck me. With so much money there, so many notes, Uncle Jimmy, or whoever owned it, would never miss the ten shillings that I'd already taken out of that bundle. And if they didn't miss that, I was thinking excitedly, they wouldn't miss a pound note, either, or a five-pound note, or even a ten-pound note and a twenty-pound note, out of the other bundles.

I did a quick count in my head. I'd be able to take thirty-six pounds and ten shillings now, this very minute, probably without anybody noticing that it was away. And if it was counted by somebody after I took my lot out, somebody who was told it was two thousand quid, they'd just think that whoever put it there in the first place must have made a mistake in each bundle. Some people were stupid like that. So that's what I decided to do. Take the thirty-six pounds and ten shillings. It would never be missed. And it wouldn't be stealing. And it wouldn't be a sin, because it was traitor money. I would put all of it to good use. Like Robin Hood of Sherwood Forest. He took from the rich and gave to the poor. And he was a hero. But I didn't feel like a hero yet. I just felt excited about what I was doing. And a bit nervous. I counted out the money that I was taking and put it into my pocket. I had more dosh on me now than my da or the twins would earn in three months. It was a fortune, but nothing compared with what was still left in the suitcase. Within a minute I had put all the rest back, in their neat bundles. As if they'd never been disturbed.

Just then, like a bolt of lightning, it struck me. About how stupid I was. About what I'd just done. About taking the money. Especially the twenty-pound note and the ten-pound note and even the five-pound note. But not so much about the quid note or the ten-bob note. Stupid, stupid, I thought, you can't get much more stupid than this, Dickie McCauley. How in a million years could I have expected to get away with going into a shop and trying to buy something with big notes like that? Just to get the change in wee notes and coins. The shopkeeper would have called the cops. I'd have been a borstal case after that. And ruined for life. And it was mad as well to think that I could have slipped any of it, either, into my ma's apron pocket, except maybe a ten-bob note or a few coins. She wasn't stupid. She'd have asked big questions that I couldn't answer. And she would have been pointing the finger at me.

Without any further hesitation, I took the money out of my pocket and put it back in the brown suitcase. It only took a minute altogether to put each note in its proper bundle. I was back to square one. Strangely, I felt better. And not a bit guilty. Because I knew that it was traitor money. And I didn't feel guilty, either, about the ten bob I'd given Liam, because he was the one who discovered that Uncle Jimmy was a traitor. Now, besides the other things that were still bothering me, I'd have to think of some way of keeping Danny Doherty happy. I walked slowly down the attic stairs again to my bedroom. Just to sit there in the quiet. To give my head time to think properly after all the excitement.

That's when I heard my ma and the twins coming back into the house from Mass. As I listened to them chattering and laughing I wondered what they could be so happy about. Especially as they now probably knew what Uncle Jimmy had stashed away upstairs. How could you be happy about the likes of that? I'd have to play them at their own game and find out more. About what Uncle Jimmy was really up to, and why he hadn't come home last night.

CHAPTER 15

Secrets, Liam, I'm Sick Of Secrets

I stuck my head out of the bedroom window and looked up and down the street. Liam was there, talking to Danny and Kevin. I called to him. He came right away. He knew it was important by the sound of my voice.

'Liam,' I said quietly to him when he came into the bedroom, 'I want to ask ye if you'll do something wile important.'

'Aye, I will, Dickie. What is it?'

I went out of the room before answering him, to check that there was nobody coming up the stairs.

'Sit down on the bed, Liam,' I whispered when I came back in. 'Do ye remember a while ago ye told me that Uncle Jimmy went into the cop's house in disguise, in through the back?'

'Aye, Dickie, I saw him. Sure I told ye I saw him.'

'I know ye did, Liam, and I believe ye. And I'm sorry for not believing ye earlier.'

'So what are ye saying to me now, Dickie?' he said, looking a bit apprehensive. As if I was going to start into him again.

'Naw, naw, Liam,' I reassured him immediately, 'there's nothin' to worry about there.'

He seemed to relax when I said that, so I continued, 'It's just all this secret stuff that's buggin' me, Liam. I mean, there's a lot of things we should know about, and nobody's tellin' us.'

'What do ye mean, Dickie?'

'Secrets, Liam, I'm sick of secrets in this house.'

'What secrets are ye talkin' about, Dickie?'

Liam looked at me with his big eyes. Eyes with questions in them. Intelligent eyes. But I had to be careful about how I would say things to him. I didn't want to shock him. But I had only a few minutes to put my plan to him before we were called downstairs.

'Secrets, first of all, Liam, about Uncle Jimmy. What secrets do ye know already about Uncle Jimmy?'

He looked at me, a bit puzzled at first, but once he spoke, I knew he wasn't afraid the way he used to be. Liam had grown up a lot in the past nine or ten months, especially since I allowed him to join the gang.

'I know he's some sort of a big-time captain in the IRA, Dickie, and I think he might be on the run from the cops. And I think that's why he's disguised. And as well as that, Dickie, I think it was Uncle Jimmy's gun the cops were lookin' for when they broke in here last year and wrecked the place. And I'm nearly sure, as well, that it was him and them two other boys, Kate and Laura's boyfriends, that burned the B-men's hut over in Thompson's Field round about the same time.'

Liam had hardly taken a breath when he was telling me this. But he wasn't finished yet.

'And I didn't say anything to anybody about Uncle Jimmy goin' into Eva's, because that could be blabbin', Dickie. Not until this morning. I had to get it off my chest, Dickie, but just to you. That's not blabbin', Dickie, sure it's not? And ye believe me now, don't ye, that I was tellin' ye the truth?'

'Aye, Liam, I do believe ye. And what ye told me was not blabbin'. This is wan of the things I'm talkin' about. Wan of the secrets, Liam, that nobody's tellin' us about, when we have every right to know. It's not blabbin' when it's a matter of life and death.'

'Aye, Dickie, you're right. We should be told everything in case there's danger. And if there's danger, Dickie, we should know what the danger is so that we can do somethin' about it. You're right about the secrets, Dickie, we should know about them.'

I stared in amazement at Liam as he went on. He was beginning to sound a lot like somebody I know very well. Me.

Before I spoke again, I let my mind race on with the things that were going through it. At this very minute, here I was, up in the bedroom with Liam, planning to use him in about five minutes to find out stuff from my ma, and the twins, about Uncle Jimmy, about the guns and the ammunition, and the suitcase of money, and maybe about why he went into a cop's house. About him maybe being a traitor. Aye, here I was, thinking that it might be the most difficult thing in the world to get Liam to help me with the plan, and wondering would he be up for it. And he was proving by the second that he was. But first, I had to be totally honest with him, or at least as honest as I could be just now, because I had some secrets of my own that I didn't want people to know about.

'Liam,' I said, 'would ye really do something wile important for me, for us, Liam?'

'Aye, I will, Dickie. Didn't I say I would? What is it?'

'Well, when my ma calls us downstairs, and after we have eaten, I'm goin' to start askin' questions. Like the questions we have just been talkin' about. About Uncle Jimmy. Why is he back in our house? Why is he in disguise? Why did he go into the cop's house? Things like that, Liam. And as soon as I start the questions, will you cut in and say that ye want to know, too, because it sounds dangerous? And danger makes ye feel sick. And if ye like, Liam, you can pretend to be sick, even vomit if ye can. Do you know what I'm sayin', Liam?'

'Aye, Dickie, I do.' And he laughed when he said it. 'I've seen ye myself with the snotters flyin' out of ye, and the vomit and the tears. You're good at it, Dickie. Do ye think I could be good at it, too, Dickie?'

'Aye, Liam, ye'd be perfect. Probably better than me.' And I meant it.

'I'm glad ye said that, Dickie, because I think I caught ye out a wee while ago.'

'What do ye mean, Liam?'

'In the park, and before we went into the park, when I told ye about Uncle Jimmy.'

'What are ye talkin' about, Liam?'

'The sweatin', Dickie, and the runny nose, and the dirty face and the tears, and the angry face, and tearing the newspaper, and the huffs, and the stayin' ten feet behind ye on the way home. All for your benefit, Dickie. All bluff. And I got ten bob out of it as well. For all the trouble I went to. What do ye think, Dickie? Did I definitely pass the test?' And he laughed when he said the last part.

I was gobsmacked. All I could do just then was stare at him. In total silence. For about thirty seconds. With my mouth beginning to open. Again. That's when I burst out laughing. And he did the same. When it had fully dawned on me what he'd done, I walked towards him with my arms outstretched, to hug him. He hugged me as well. And we danced round the room, laughing until we could hardly laugh anymore. I pushed him back from me and looked straight into his eyes again before I spoke.

'Liam,' I said, 'you're nothin' but a wee fart.'

'Dickie,' he replied immediately, 'you're nothin' but a big fart.'

The two of us went into more fits of laughter until we were out of breath. To catch Dickie McCauley out like that was definitely a one-up for him. If anybody else in the gang had done it to me – except for Eva – they'd have got a back-of-the-throat rasper-job from me, straight into an eye. And that would have been that. Now I knew Liam was definitely ready. And I knew something else, too, at that split second. Something that could get rid of the guns and ammunition without me having to lay a hand on them, or needing Joey or Hughie to help. For a great plan had just struck me. The best plan ever. Aye, this could do the trick, all right. It was definitely worth a try anyway. I decided to go for it.

'Liam,' I then whispered, 'there's somethin' else I have to tell ye about, something that I have to show ye, I mean, before we go downstairs. Because ye have the right to know, and it's all goin' to come out anyway when we tackle them about everything.'

'What is it, Dickie?'

With that, I nodded to Liam to follow me. We went out to the landing. I put my finger to my lips. He nodded. We listened for movement from downstairs. There was none. Only laughter and loud talking. I signalled for Liam to follow me again. Up the attic stairs. On tiptoes, scrunching our faces with each creak we heard. When we reached Uncle Jimmy's room, I took a couple of deep breaths, for I felt at that second that I had to prepare Liam for what he was about to see. Because a terrible thought had struck me. What if, when I showed him the rifles and the ammunition, he broke down and went into hysterics? Or what if he froze and went into a trance of fear, like going mental? What would I do then? I'd be the worst in the world for putting him in this position, and the whole plan would be ruined. Nobody would forgive me. Especially me. And I would deserve all I got.

'Liam,' I whispered as I turned round to him, 'I need ye to be very, very brave right now, because I'm goin' to show ye somethin' that could frighten ye. Somethin' that could scare ye very, very badly.'

'What is it, Dickie? Is it somethin' dangerous? I like dangerous stuff.'

I stared at him again, shocked at what he was saying about danger but pleased at the same time, because the pressure was off me a wee bit now.

'Aye, Liam, it is about dangerous stuff. It's about guns and ammunition. Do ye know what ammunition is, Liam?'

'I do, Dickie. It's bullets and stuff, like shells and things. Ye read about it sometimes in the comics, and ye hear it on the news, on the wireless.'

'You're right, Liam,' I said, relieved that he didn't look to be in a panic about this. 'But I'm goin' to show ye the real thing now, and I don't want ye to be frightened. Stuff like this would frighten Danny and Kevin.'

'But not Cecil or Billy, Dickie. It wouldn't frighten them, because Cecil's da had a rifle, before the IRA shot him, and Billy's da would have a revolver in his holster in the house, and he would see loads of guns in the barracks if he ever went to visit him. And Eva, too, Dickie. Her da's a cop as well, so she would know about guns. Naw, Dickie, I'm not afraid. Not anymore. I'm like you, Dickie.'

'Great, Liam, I'm glad.'

I decided to waste no more time, because my ma would be calling us down any second. But as I took the blanket off the rifles and ammunition, I watched Liam's face for any sign of fear. It was just the opposite. His eyes lit up in wonder when he saw the guns. I could sense the excitement in him.

'God,' he said, 'they're brilliant. Who owns them, Dickie? Are they Uncle Jimmy's? Are they IRA rifles? And is that ammunition in the bag?'

'Aye, Liam,' I replied as calmly as I could. 'It's ammunition, all right, and the rifles belong to the IRA. They're all a big danger, Liam, and we've got to get rid of them. Will ye help me to get them out of the house, Liam? Are ye game?'

Not for a second did he hesitate. 'Aye, Dickie. I'm game, all right. You and me'll get rid of them okay, because it's wile dangerous havin' them here.'

His eyes were sparkling as he spoke, and I knew immediately that he was up for it. But I had something else to say to him. Something very important.

'Great, Liam. But there's another thing, too,' I said quietly.

'What is it, Dickie?'

'It's when we go downstairs, Liam. We might be able to find out everything else that's goin' on. Secrets, I mean, Liam, stupid secrets.'

'Okay, Dickie,' he said with the same enthusiasm. 'We'll find out the secrets, too, because secrets can be dangerous as well. But not as dangerous as guns. Isn't that right, Dickie?'

My heart was thumping as I nodded to him, thinking of what

he had just said. He was right. Secrets could be very dangerous, too. But did he fully understand what he was saying? I mean, he wasn't even eight years old. And would he be able to carry out the plan I had hatched? Was I asking too much of him? That's what I was thinking at this very second. The whole thing could blow up in my face if it didn't work. But if it did work, it would solve a lot of problems. And keep us all safe.

Before I had time to put the blanket back over the rifles, Liam had reached out his hand. He began to lightly touch the barrels with the tips of his fingers. He was trembling, and maybe even a wee bit afraid, but I didn't stop him, because I remembered just then the fear that I had felt last year when my da asked me to touch a revolver. And I'd gotten over that.

As he pulled his hand back from the guns, he turned to me and asked, 'What's in the suitcase, Dickie? Is it more ammunition?'

I didn't want to lie to him, because it could spoil things if I did. So I just told him.

'It's full of money, Liam. It must belong to the IRA, too, but I'm not sure.'

'I don't believe ye. Open it up, Dickie, I want to see it.'

I hesitated for a split second before I released the catch and lifted the lid. This time, he didn't say a thing, just put his hands in and touched the bundles of money, staring at them in disbelief. That's when I thought I heard a noise coming from downstairs.

'Shush, Liam,' I whispered, 'shut the lid now, quick, and put the case back where it was. And put that blanket over the rifles.'

I went to the bedroom door and listened to make sure nobody was coming up.

'Okay, Dickie,' I heard him saying, 'the job's done.'

I looked back over my shoulder before we left the bedroom. Everything was in order. Nothing looked disturbed.

When we went down the attic stairs and back into our bedroom, I had another brainwave. One that could make things better between me and Danny, and between me and Eva.

'Liam,' I whispered, 'there's wan more big favour I want ye to do for me. And then a wee favour after that.'

'Aye, Dickie. What are they?'

'Well, first of all, as ye know, last night I had a bit of a row with Danny, and then I sort of fell out with Eva over something else.'

He looked at me with a big grin on his face. A cheeky grin. He was mocking me. The wee fart knows nearly everything. But I didn't care, because I now knew he wasn't afraid. And, like me, he was ready for what we were going to do downstairs.

'This one's an easy favour, Liam, and there's no danger in it. It's about that ten shillings I gave ye a while ago.'

'Aye, what about it, Dickie? Do ye want it back?'

'Naw, Liam. But I was thinkin' that it would be a great idea if the whole gang could go to the pictures, and maybe have a plate of chips each afterwards in Harley's. Danny and Kevin have never been to the pictures, so that would be a great surprise for them.'

'No problem, Dickie. And what about Eva? Would she go, too, Dickie?'

When he said that he had another big grin on his face.

'Aye. Eva, too, Liam, and the twin Deeneys.'

But as I spoke, I got a sinking feeling that Eva might be away in Dublin at that stage, along with her wee brother.

'And what about Cecil and Billy?' he asked quickly. 'Couldn't they come as well? Sure they used to be in the gang.'

'That's a great idea, Liam. I never thought of them. Good thinkin', Liam. I'll ask Cecil to let Billy know.'

'And how much would all that cost, Dickie, the pictures and the chips? For everybody? Would I have enough?'

I had already worked that one out as he was asking. Fourpence each for the pictures and fourpence each for chips. Altogether for nine of us – including Eva – seventy-two pence; that's six shillings.

'The whole thing would cost six bob, Liam, and ye'd have four left.'

'Sounds okay to me, Dickie. Do ye want the money now?'

'Naw, later, Liam. I'll let ye know.'

'And what's the other favour, Dickie?'

'Aw, aye, Liam, the second favour. Would you have time to go round the gang in a wee while and let them all know that there's a meetin' in the air-raid shelter tonight at seven o'clock? And I'll be able to tell them then about the pictures and the chips. But keep that part under your hat till then, won't ye, Liam?'

'Right, Dickie, I will. Don't worry. Are we goin' downstairs now?'

'Okay, Liam, let's go.'

We went out as far as the landing. I was intending to keep Liam talking about ordinary stuff until my ma would call us, because I was thinking that he might be worried about going down to the living room. But it was me that was the nervous one. And a bit tense, too, because of what was about to happen. Liam was as cool as a cucumber. As we began our way down, he tugged my sleeve and whispered, 'Don't worry, Dickie, I'm up for it.' Then, suddenly, he sat on the top stair. 'You go on, Dickie. I'll be down in a minute. And don't worry. We're goin' to get rid of all the guns and stuff. Trust me.'

I said nothing, but my excitement was rising. I reached the front hall. This was it. It was now or never.

CHAPTER 16

Please Don't Allow Him To Stay, Ma

'Ah, there ye are, Dickie. I was just goin' to shout up for youse. The tea's ready. Is Liam not there?'

'Aye, Ma. He's comin' now.'

She was walking from the kitchen into the living room with a big plate of bread pieces. But I didn't feel hungry, even though I must have been. It was the nerves.

Then, without warning, Liam came thumping down the stairs. Fast. And roaring and squealing at the same time,

'Ma, Ma,' he shouted at the top of his voice. He rushed past me towards my ma and threw his arms round her as she turned. She looked afraid for him. I must have looked shocked, but *I* wasn't acting the way he was. The twins jumped up from their seats, very worried looking. He was brilliant. He was in his element, and he looked the part. His eyes were standing out in his head, tears were running down his face and a snotter was coming out of his left nostril.

'What is it, Liam?' my ma cried out over the noise. 'Did Dickie hurt ye?'

I was annoyed for a second when she said that, and then angry as she looked at me. As usual, I was getting the blame. But I didn't care this time, because the game was on. And as Liam squealed more, his eyes became wild looking. He was brilliant. Away ahead of me. He must have decided off his own bat that the best plan would be for him to do the early shouting. And

131

that I would follow up with the questions.

'Guns, Ma,' wailed Liam. 'Hundreds of guns, up in the attic, Ma, in Uncle Jimmy's room. Don't let the cops come, Ma. Get rid of them now, Ma. Please, please, please. I'm scared, Ma.'

As Liam did his act, I took quick sneaky glances from my ma's face to the twins' faces. To get their reactions. I'd know by their expressions if they knew about the guns. They did. They knew, all right. But it didn't stop them from looking scared as well. Very scared. For Liam. They'd seen him going mental before, but this time they didn't know that it wasn't real. He was still playing the game really well, and it got even better when he now began to moan, and sob, and then scream out again. Liam had seen their faces, too, because he soon followed up with a sort of a quieter whimpering, sobby cry as he slowly fell to his knees holding on to my ma's legs at the same time. As if he had no energy left. His head was almost on the floor.

'Get the guns out, get the guns out. Please, please, please, Ma,' he sniffled. 'Get them away, away now, Ma. Please.'

'Kate, Laura,' my ma suddenly shouted, 'get all that stuff out of the house. Now. Right now. Do youse hear me? I don't care what Jimmy says, or anybody else says. That's it. We're not goin' through all this oul' carry-on again with this wain.'

My heart was leaping in my chest. Things were beginning to happen. The plan was working. And as Kate and Laura rushed out of the room and up the stairs, I played my part as well. I stood there, speechless, as if I was in shock. As if I couldn't move. As if I was affected by the state that Liam was supposed to be in. But it wasn't all an act on my part, because I was trembling too. A real trembling. With the excitement of what was happening. Liam had pulled it off in one brilliant stroke. Inside seconds, he was getting things done. But he still kept the act up. Still moaned as my ma was lifting him. And as she was comforting him, he looked up at her, his face a mess with tears and snotters.

'Everything's goin' to be all right now, son,' she said as she pulled him tighter to her. Over and over again she said it. 'The guns are goin' and everything's goin' to be all right. Don't worry anymore, son.'

But Liam was far from finished. He had more up his sleeve.

'But what about Uncle Jimmy, Ma?' he squealed. 'He can't stay. He can't stay. Don't allow him to stay, Ma. Please, please, Ma.'

'It's okay, Liam. I'll see to everything. Don't you worry, son. Everything's goin' to be all right.'

'But it's not, Ma,' sobbed Liam, 'it's not. Somethin' bad is goin' to happen. I saw Uncle Jimmy . . . last night, Ma . . . goin' into the cop's house . . . through the back way.'

'Shush, shush, son,' she said quietly, looking around her as if hoping that nobody else had heard what Liam was saying. She needn't have worried on that score. For now. Because the twins were still upstairs. But I suspected immediately that she knew something about this, too.

Liam began to squeal louder again, for effect, in case this part wasn't hitting home. His act was getting even better. And I didn't have to say a word or do anything to help him. Not yet anyway. The wee fart was doing it all by himself. And I felt very proud of him, not scared for him anymore, because from now on, I knew that Liam would be able to look out for himself. In the street. At school. Doing most gang things, and even outwitting big people when he needed to.

As my ma kept comforting Liam – as *she* thought – and saying things to calm him, I took the opportunity of leaving the room and going out to the kitchen. I shouted to her that I was getting Liam a drink of water, but she didn't hear me. But what I was really up to was spying on the twins, because I'd heard them seconds earlier thundering down the attic stairs.

As I was filling a cup with water from the tap, they passed me like a flash. I don't think they even noticed me. Kate had the rifles under her arm, still wrapped up in the old blanket, and Laura was carrying the bag of bullets. I saw no sign of the brown suitcase. Maybe they'd come back for it. And they were in such a hurry they didn't even shut the back door after them.

I looked out the kitchen window to see what was happening next. I thought they'd go straight out through the gate into the lane and head off somewhere with the stuff. But they didn't. Kate opened the coalhouse door and the two of them slipped inside. Soon I heard them shovelling coal, and I knew right away what they were up to. They were burying the guns. Stupid, I thought. How stupid could they be? Sure if the cops raided the place, wouldn't that be one of the first places they'd look? I felt like running out and telling them that, but I didn't, because they wouldn't have listened to me. I stood there, looking out the window for the next five minutes, listening to the noise of the shovelling.

Then I went back into the living room. Liam was still being held by my ma. Very tightly. I could see one side of his wee face staring at me. The other side was tucked against her. He was continuing to moan and sob, and sniffle, but at the same time, he was able to give me a wink. How crafty was that, I thought.

That's when I heard the twins coming back into the house, banging the kitchen door behind them. You could hear them washing their hands and talking excitedly to each other. Within a minute they were back in the living room.

'How is he, Ma?' whispered Kate as they came in. 'Is he okay?' We've hid the stuff under the coal in the meantime. When Jimmy comes back, he can shift it out altogether.'

'He'll be okay now, girls,' my ma whispered back as she began to rock Liam from side to side. 'He'll be okay in a wee minute.'

But it wasn't to be okay for my ma or the twins. And Liam knew it *shouldn't* be okay for them, because he'd heard where the guns were as well, and *he* knew it was stupid, too. Act II was about to begin. And I sensed it before they knew it. He suddenly pulled away from my ma and began to squeal and moan and whimper again, and in a big crying voice he told them to get the guns out of the coalhouse. 'Now, now, now,' he shouted. He then ran towards my da's big armchair and darted behind it as if he was hiding. I could hardly believe what I was seeing and hearing. It was a great move.

134

But I couldn't stand there like a gawk anymore. I knew that it was now my turn to play my part as well. So, first, I ran forward, shouting, 'Liam, Liam, it's goin' to be okay, everything's goin' to be all right. They're goin' to get rid of everything.'

But Liam kept going strong behind the chair, the sobbing and the moaning as loud as ever.

'Ma,' I shouted back, putting on a sort of a cry myself, 'don't let our Liam go mental again. Please, please. Sort everything out now. I'll take the guns away if youse like. I'll take them over to Thompson's Field and dump them.'

'You'll take *what* over to Thompson's Field, Dickie? What's happening here, Kitty?' It was my da. I hadn't heard him coming in, with all the noise and excitement in the living room. And he wasn't drunk. Not much anyway. Not blind staggering drunk like he is sometimes. Maybe now we'd get something done. Maybe my da *would* take charge. Liam must have thought that, too, because, from behind the big chair, you could hear him moaning again, even louder than before. 'What's he doin' in there?' my da shouted. 'In under God, Kitty, what's up? What's happened to our Liam?'

By this time, my da had pulled back the chair and lifted Liam up, holding him tight, and saying to him, 'You'll be all right now, son. You'll be okay now, wee son. Don't be afraid. Your da's here.'

And that's when it hit me. The feelings of guilt. The feelings of sorrow. The feelings of regret. And a terrible fear. A fear that maybe we'd gone too far. Liam and me. That we'd soon regret carrying out the plan, good and all as it seemed at the time. And that we'd be sorry for days and weeks and maybe months, or even years, for putting my da and ma and the twins through this torment over Liam.

What if my ma or my da had a heart attack over it, and became crippled? *God bless the mark*, I was thinking, because Kevin Doherty always said that if he saw a cripple. Aye, the guilt of it could last a lifetime.

But nothing like this seemed to register in Liam's mind. He was enjoying himself. Lapping it all up. Acting the part of the martyr. And doing his very best for the plan we'd hatched. I couldn't blame him at this minute and I was half-hoping that he'd now begin to wind it down a bit, to calm things, seeing that it was already starting to do the trick. But no, not Liam. He just got worse. Or was it better? As my da hugged him and soothed him, you could see the tears and the snotters starting all over again.

'He saw the guns in the attic, Barney,' said my ma. 'I don't know why he went up there.'

I knew it. My da did know stuff.

Then she turned to me, tears in her eyes, and fear, and some rage, too.

'Was it you that took him up, Dickie? Was it you, ye brat?'

That's when the guilt feeling left me. And the sorrow feeling. And the regret feeling. And any fears about my ma getting a heart attack. She was nearly giving me a heart attack the way she was going on. She was accusing me, in front of everybody, of causing Liam the distress that he was supposed to be in. She was blaming me for everything again, when really it was nearly all her own fault, for making us do what we were doing. She should know better. She was our ma. Well, I wasn't having it any more, not from her, not from anybody, because it wasn't my fault, and it wasn't Liam's fault. All this stupid dangerous stuff, with guns and everything, and Uncle Jimmy, was not our fault. Liam was right when he'd sounded as if he was getting worse and worse. He was right to keep it going when I would have given up. Liam knew that we were at the point of no return. Now it was up to me to turn the screw.

'Naw, Ma,' I lied. 'It wasn't me that brought Liam up to the attic. He just went up, off his own bat, because he thought Uncle Jimmy was there. He ran up before I could stop him. He wanted to ask him about what he saw last night out in the back lane. It's hard to believe it, Ma.'

This was it. This was the big one. This was the one that would now set the cat among the pigeons. My ma stared at me, wanting me to stop. But I didn't.

'It's like this, Ma,' I went on, and I wasn't lying now. 'When Liam told me a wee while ago that he'd seen Uncle Jimmy in disguise goin' into Constable Johnston's house last night, in through the back door, I was shocked. Liam was, too. So I'm not surprised that he wanted to ask him about it.'

My ma put her hand up to her mouth as if she was speechless at the news. As if *she* was shocked. But I knew she wasn't. She was lying. I could see it in her eyes. She definitely knew everything about Uncle Jimmy. Except maybe about the suitcase full of money. But then again, she could know about that, too. And about him being a traitor as well. So what did that make her? Aye, we were getting answers now, all right. And the shock she was showing on her face wasn't because I'd told her what I told her. It was the shock of me and Liam knowing about it at all. And it was the shock of knowing that Kate and Laura now knew about it, because as I was speaking, I looked at their faces, too. All I could see was amazement.

'Ma, what's Dickie talkin' about?' said Kate, turning to her ma. 'About Uncle Jimmy goin' into a cop's house?'

'Kate,' stammered my ma. 'Kate, it's a . . . it's . . . it's—'

'Look, girls,' my da butted in quickly. 'This isn't the time nor place to be talkin' about these things.'

And when he said this, he was pointing with one forefinger at Liam and me and the other forefinger up to his lips. But the girls didn't agree, and even though Liam was still sobbing and moaning into my da's big neck, they were standing their ground. They wanted answers, too.

'There's no better time or place,' shouted Kate angrily over Liam's sobs. 'We want to know, and we want to know now. Where *is* Uncle Jimmy anyway? If you don't give us answers, we'll go and talk to *him*.'

'Look, look . . . it's not what youse think, girls,' said my ma, and she wasn't stammering now. 'I know it seems bad, and what Dickie's sayin' sounds bad, but all I can tell youse now is this. Your Uncle Jimmy saw no cop. What do youse think he is, an informer? Is that what youse were thinking? Shame on youse. Bloody shame on youse.'

As soon as my ma said that, about Uncle Jimmy not seeing Constable Johnston, and not being an informer, I looked over at Liam. I could see his eyes widening and then going half up into his skull and his mouth opening in surprise. For all I knew, I looked the same to Liam. Because this was another turn-up for the books. 'Your Uncle Jimmy saw no cop'. Her words were still ringing in my ears, and rattling round my brain. 'Your Uncle Jimmy saw no cop'. Had Liam got it wrong? Was it somebody else who'd gone into Johnstons'? My mind went into another whirl at this turn of events.

'What are we supposed to think,' shouted Laura, 'when we heard Dickie sayin' what Liam had told him? Are they makin' it up, Ma?'

'Naw, Laura, they're not makin' it up. But what Liam saw is not what happened.'

'You're talkin' in riddles now, Ma. He either went into the cop's house or he didn't. Which is it, Ma?'

Now *my* head was spinning. Did Uncle Jimmy go into the cop's house or did Uncle Jimmy not go into the cop's house?

'Aye, girls, he went into the cop's house,' said my ma, breathing hard now, 'but he didn't go there to see the cop.'

'What are ye sayin', Ma?'

She hesitated for a few seconds, then took a few big deep breaths. She looked worried, and worn out by everything. And she closed her lips tight as if she wasn't going to say anymore. At the same time, she shrugged her shoulders and looked straight at my da, wanting him to say something. And he did.

'Okay, girls,' he said as he got up from the armchair and sat Liam down in his place. 'About Uncle Jimmy. It's very, very hard to explain this, but it's better that youse know now, because by the sound of things in here the day, youse are gettin' the wrong end of the stick, and only half the story. And the end of the stick youse are gettin' is very dangerous talk that could cause a whole lot of bother when there's no need to cause bother.'

There was complete silence in the room when my da was speaking. Even Liam had stopped pretending to snivel. Everybody was staring, first at my ma, then at my da, not sure if he was going to say any more or if she was going to continue where he'd left off.

'You see,' my da went on, 'Jimmy is a strange sort of man in a whole lot of ways. He might be a big-time captain in the Movement, but he's . . . he's . . .' He looked at my ma before going on, but her lips were still tightly closed, and her face looked green. 'He's only a small-time man when it comes to women. Aye. Aye, small-time.'

My da was slurring his words now and again and you could see spittles coming out of his mouth as he began to stammer a bit. He didn't look one bit comfortable as his eyes flitted between the girls and my ma. And he wasn't making any sense. Not to me anyway, and not to Liam, because I could see that his wee face was just as puzzled looking as mine. Laura must have felt the same, because she suddenly burst out in an angry voice, 'What are ye bletherin' on about, Da? What is it you're tryin' to tell us?'

'Aye, when it comes to women,' he went on, 'he never, he never, ah . . . had much sense. And then he joined the Movement way back, and that's when he met this wan. He was all over the place then, in more ways than wan. Aye, all over the place.'

I still didn't know what my da was on about, and neither did the twins, but my ma's eyes were rising, and she was shaking her head slowly from side to side in a frustrated kind of way. And annoyed with my da, too, by the look of things.

And that's when she jumped in, shouting again, 'Will ye, for God's sake, Barney, tell them, and stop your ramblin'. It's time they all knew, anyway. Even Dickie, and wee Liam, sure they

139

know nearly as much now as you and me, and them only wains. Go on, Barney, out with it all now.'

But my da said nothing. It was as if he had given up. He wiped the spittles away from his mouth and sat down on the chair, taking Liam on his knee. He leaned back and rolled his eyes. Liam snuggled into him again, still wide-eyed like myself and wondering what was going to happen next. My da was the one that looked annoyed now. Probably because my ma had shouted at him, and swore at him, and mocked him about rambling, and then the way she'd ordered him to tell us everything. That wasn't very nice, the way she did that. It was like an insult. That's what I thought. Sure wasn't Uncle Jimmy *her* brother, not my da's? And she was the one who was allowing him to stay here, not my da. My da didn't want him here at all. So it should be her that was doing all the telling and not him. She must have read some of my thoughts, because she started again, but this time she wasn't shouting so loud.

'Sure isn't that why he came back to Derry, the eejit, when he heard she was here in Rosemount Terrace?' she said. 'Back with his stupid disguise, and him thinkin' that he'd kill two birds with wan stone. With a few guns and stuff from across the border. Sure the fool still thinks he's in with a shout. Well, he's bitten off more than he can chew with that trollop.'

Now it was my ma who was rambling a bit. But nobody spoke, because we knew there was more to come. And I was hearing something that I was beginning to understand, even if it was hard to understand.

'And if her husband finds out,' she went on, 'if that cop finds out, there'll be hell to pay. In more ways than wan.'

She began to breathe fast, looking around at everybody as she spoke. You could see fear in her eyes and there was great anger in her, too, and her voice got louder. I looked at my da. His eyes were shut fast, but he wasn't sleeping. Nobody could sleep through this. Liam's eyes were wide open, and he'd gone quiet.

'Just because he went after her, all those years ago, to Belfast, before the cop married her,' she shouted angrily, 'he thinks he has the right to start up with her again where he left off. Well, he's makin' wan big mistake there. And I told him that, but he wouldn't listen. And I'm sick of it. I'm sick of the whole thing. I've had enough, and youse can tell him that, if youse see him before I do.'

She was almost hysterical now, waving her arms about and roaring out of her, and crying and wailing at the same time. My heart sank. Had we gone too far? Me and Liam.

My da rose slowly from the chair, gently lifting Liam away from him. He walked slowly towards my ma, his arms outstretched, wanting to hug her, but she pushed him away, shouting, 'As for you, Barney McCauley, you're worse than useless. You're nothin' but a waste of space. Just get out of my sight.'

There was a deathly silence in the room when we all heard my ma talking to my da like that. She'd never been like this before, slagging him the way she was doing now. In front of everybody.

'And another thing,' she went on, turning away from him but still shouting, 'if he thinks he's stayin' in this house any longer, he's far mistaken, because I've had enough. Republican or no Republican, I'm not standin' for this carry-on anymore. And youse girls should feel the same. Don't get mixed up now with that man. Even if he is your uncle. And forget about goin' to Donegal with him in August. I'm tellin' youse. It's my wains from now on. Nothin' else matters now but the wains.'

And that was it. All out in the open. Questions asked and questions answered. I looked at the twins. Their mouths mightn't have been hanging open like mine but their eyes were staring in amazement at my ma.

'Ma,' said Kate, her voice husky, 'we didn't know. How could we? Ye should have told us sooner. About the cop's wife and Uncle Jimmy. This is desperate. I can't believe it.'

As Kate was speaking, she walked over to my ma and held her hand, but before she could say anything else, Laura butted in, shouting, 'This is bloody ridiculous. It can't be true. There must

141

be some mistake, Ma, Uncle Jimmy couldn't be that stupid. I've never heard anything so crazy in all my life.'

But as she was speaking, I knew by the way she'd said it that she did believe it. It was just that she didn't want to believe it. Because now she was probably feeling foolish herself. About her plans, I mean, plans about her and Kate joining the IRA. You could see the tears of disappointment in her eyes as she rushed out of the living room and thundered up the stairs. Kate was going to follow her, but my ma stopped her.

'Let her be, Kate. She's in shock. And she'll just have to bloody well get over it, like the rest of us.'

I looked at my da again as all this was going on. He was breathing heavy, but his eyes were open, his teeth were clenched tight and he was shaking his head from side to side in disgust. He then quietly rose from the chair and let Liam sit there again. 'I'll make a cup of tea for us all,' he said as he walked out to the kitchen. 'Maybe it'll settle this madhouse down.'

Nobody seemed to take him on. I decided it was time for me to leave as well, but before walking out of the living room I looked back to check if Liam was following me. He wasn't. He just sat where he was, in my da's big armchair, his head in his hands and his knees up to his chin, watching my ma and Kate hugging each other. He wasn't snivelling anymore, or even whimpering. He didn't need to. The plan was working. He knew not to milk it.

I walked slowly up the stairs to the bedroom, to do a bit of thinking or maybe lie down for a wee while. I was knackered. It had been a long day so far, and it wasn't even two o'clock yet.

CHAPTER 17

Ye Can't Have Two Das

'Dickie, wake up. Wake up, Dickie.' It was Liam, shaking my shoulder excitedly. I could hardly open my eyes. And I felt cold and numb.

'What, what is it? What's happenin'?' I shook my head a bit and squeezed my eyes shut and then tried to open them wide to keep them from closing altogether. It felt as if they didn't want to open.

Liam kept prattling on. He was annoying me. I wanted to sleep.

'Dickie, it's me. Liam.'

'Go away, Liam, I'm tired.'

'Dickie, I heard more stuff. I've more news for ye.'

I didn't want to hear anything at this minute. My mind was a fog. But Liam kept on.

'It's about Uncle Jimmy, Dickie, and Eva. I heard my ma whispering to Kate about it downstairs.'

'What are ye talkin' about, Liam?'

I didn't really want to hear anything else about Uncle Jimmy. I'd had enough. My brain couldn't take any more. Not now anyway. But there was no stopping Liam.

'I stayed on in the armchair, Dickie, and listened to them whispering. My ma and Kate. They didn't even notice I was there. My da was out makin' the tea.'

As Liam was speaking, I began to come round a bit. One half

of my brain didn't want to know, but the other half began to get curious. About what Liam was saying. And about what was making him so excited. Now I was a bit more awake. But there was something I had to say to him first. I sat up and looked at him. Straight into his eyes.

'Liam, before ye tell me what it is, about Uncle Jimmy and Eva, I mean, can I say somethin' to you?'

'Aye, what, Dickie?'

'I want to tell ye that you were great downstairs a while ago, the way ye did the actin', I mean. Ye were brilliant, Liam.'

He laughed when I was talking.

'I learned it all from you, Dickie. Sure aren't we gettin' the guns and all out, and didn't we get most of the information we wanted, too? About secrets?'

'We did, Liam, thanks to you.'

'And you, too, Dickie. It was your plan.'

'Aye, well, I suppose it was. But you carried most of it out.'

'We're a good team, Dickie.'

I laughed when he said that, hardly believing that he was only nearly eight.

'So what is it ye were sayin' about Uncle Jimmy and Eva?'

'Oh, aye. They didn't know I was listenin', Dickie, my ma and Kate. After youse left the room, my da and you, they kept on and on with more stuff, Dickie, about Uncle Jimmy and then about Eva.'

'What more stuff, Liam? I thought we'd heard it all. And what's that about Eva?'

'Well, first, Dickie, I think ye know the bit about Uncle Jimmy bein' Mrs Johnston's boyfriend, but that was before she married the cop. My ma said she lost interest in Uncle Jimmy, but he was still wile to marry her. There was a big row between them about it all and she left Derry to live in Belfast. And wait till ye hear, Dickie. Uncle Jimmy followed her up to Belfast and tried to get her to come back to him, but she wouldn't. He stayed there for weeks, pleadin' with her, but she wouldn't budge. Soon after that, she met Mr Johnston. He was just startin' off to be a policeman then. But she married the cop after goin' out with him for just a month or so. But that was years ago, Dickie. Then they all came back to live here in Derry last September.'

'Wow,' I said for Liam's sake, 'imagine that.'

That's all I could say, because I was really bored and sick of listening to stuff now about Uncle Jimmy. And I felt like lying back on the bed again and going to sleep. I couldn't understand why Liam was so excited about all this, because he was really only repeating much of what I'd already heard myself. And I couldn't understand, either, why stupid Uncle Jimmy was still wanting to visit Mrs Johnston after all these years when she was now married to somebody else. And in disguise, too. It didn't make much sense. All I wanted at this minute was to get Uncle Jimmy out of my mind, and his guns and stuff out of my way, out of our coalhouse, so that our family could live a normal life.

Liam could see I was getting fed up as I closed my eyes and shook my head from side to side.

'But, Dickie,' he whispered, still excited, 'there's the stuff about Eva. That's what I really wanted to tell ye.'

'What stuff, Liam? What are ye talkin' about?'

'My ma told Kate that Uncle Jimmy might be Eva's da.'

'That's stupid, Liam,' I said. 'Sure Constable Johnston is Eva's da. Uncle Jimmy couldn't be her da as well. Ye can't have two das. That's silly, Liam. Ye must have picked that up wrong. Ye must have got mixed up. Maybe ye didn't hear things right because of the way they were whisperin'.'

'But I did, Dickie, I did hear her right. That's what my ma said to Kate. And she even said that wee Eva looked a bit like Uncle Jimmy. That's what she said, Dickie. Honest.'

'Sure that couldn't be, Liam. Ye have to be married to have wains. Ye can't be a da or even a ma if you're not married. That's the rules, Liam. Naw, ye got that wan wrong. Uncle Jimmy couldn't be her da.'

But I knew as I was speaking that I was wrong, because there's a boy in my class who has no da. And his ma isn't married. But she's going out with somebody and if she marries him, he could be his da then. Nearly everybody in the school knows that. So that's nearly the same thing as this carry-on with Uncle Jimmy. That's what I was thinking now.

'Are ye still goin' to have that meetin' the night in the air-raid shelter, Dickie?'

'Oh, aye, Liam, the meeting . . . Aye, seven o'clock. As a matter of fact, you can go and tell the gang, instead of me, about the pictures and the chips, and I'll give them the rest of the details when they get to the meetin'.'

'Right, Dickie. I'll do that in a wee while,' Liam said as he was leaving, 'I'll let them all know.'

But before he went, he turned back to me, grinning. He took the ten-shilling note out of his pocket that I'd given him from the suitcase and handed it to me. 'Here, Dickie,' he said, 'here's the ten bob I took from under the mattress. Just you let them all think that it's you that's payin' for everything. But don't forget to give me the four bob change. And another thing,' he laughed, 'have this as well.' It was another ten-shilling note. I couldn't believe it. He must have taken it out of the suitcase when my back was turned in the attic. 'This is for you. To get your bike fixed for goin' to the College.' I was speechless. And I was shocked, too. But he was away before I could even think of saying anything.

I followed him out of the bedroom and looked over the banisters from the landing as he went down the stairs. I was hoping that he wouldn't go out the front door. Not yet anyhow. But he did. And I knew immediately that he was carrying out my order to tell the gang about the pictures and chips on Friday night. I was disappointed, because it could have waited. But that was Liam for you. I really wanted him to go first into the living room where my ma and da and Kate were. And to still show signs of being shocked and frightened. I'd wanted him to keep up the act. If he didn't, they might suspect something.

Luckily, that's what Liam did when he came back into the

house a couple of minutes later. I watched him as he walked slowly towards the living room, his head lowered; sad, like. I heard voices greeting him when he went into the room. Sympathetic and concerned voices. From my ma and da and Kate. He'd done it. Liam was milking it this time. He was doing it for me because he knew that I might need him again when I went downstairs later for my dinner. It wasn't over yet, because, from what Liam had told me about Uncle Jimmy and Eva, there were more questions to be answered.

I went back into the bedroom. I was still knackered. I lay down again and closed my eyes. If I got more sleep, I was thinking, I'd be able to handle things better. Aye, if I got a sleep now, my brain would be able to cope when things exploded again in the living room later this evening. Especially if Uncle Jimmy came for his dinner. And I couldn't get it out of my mind, either, about the wee fart stealing the ten-bob note from the suitcase when my back was turned.

CHAPTER **18**

Stop Asking Stupid Questions

The first thing that struck me when I opened my eyes was that I must have been having a dream, because my hands were up high in front of me, moving about. How else could I account for the strange images that had been flashing before me? Images of faces. Eva's ma's face. Eva's da's face. Then Eva's face again and Uncle Jimmy's face. Together. Dancing in front of me, circling around me. Uncle Jimmy's face looked at times like Eva's and Eva's ma's face looked a bit like Eva's, but Eva's da's face didn't look like Eva's at all. I felt confused. And away behind all these faces, there was another one trying to get in amongst them. It was Uncle Jimmy's disguised face. And it didn't fit in with the rest. Hands were appearing from everywhere, trying to push it away. I was sweating; as if I'd been running, chasing somebody. I felt confused. I tried to sit up but I couldn't. I closed my eyes to concentrate and think of what might be happening to me.

It was the shout from my da that brought me to my senses.

'Dickie, your dinner's ready. Come on down now.'

His loud voice calling me had released me from the spell I was under. I jumped up, looking around for signs of faces. There were none. But the images that I'd dreamed were as clear in my mind as if they were still in the room.

I stumbled out to the bathroom and threw some water on my face. To waken me better. I felt stiff. I then went downstairs slowly, still rubbing my eyes. My ma and Kate were in the kitchen, rattling about, but not saying anything. It was the same in the living room. My da still in the armchair and Liam at the table. Silence. There was tension in the air. You could cut it with a knife. But that wasn't a surprise after all that had happened earlier. And Liam's head was still down a bit. Still acting. There was no sign of Laura. As I sat down beside Liam, he looked at me and winked. I gave him a knowing smile. Luckily, my da didn't notice. I glanced at the clock. It was just after six o'clock. Dinner was earlier than usual.

Kate came into the room and put down some knives and forks. Her face looked very serious. At first, I didn't know if I should say anything because of the whole atmosphere in the house. Then I thought, why not.

'Where's Laura?' I said to Kate as she leaned over the table. I thought that would break the ice. Just a simple question. 'Is she still upstairs?'

'Naw, Dickie,' came the sharp reply, 'she's away out in a huff, not that it's any of your business where she is.'

There it was again, the same old attitude, the annoyance at me for even trying to be normal, the hateful look as if I hadn't the right to speak, or even be there at all. As if I shouldn't exist.

'I only asked,' I said. 'Can ye not ask a civil question in the house anymore without gettin' your head bit off?'

I'd heard the twins saying this sort of stuff a whole lot of times, but this was the first time I'd said it. It made me feel good. It made me feel more grown-up.

'Shut up,' hissed Kate through her almost closed mouth and gritted teeth. 'Just shut up, Dickie, will ye? There's nothin' to be gained by askin' stupid questions.'

'That'll do,' said my da. 'Do youse not think we've had enough rows in this house for wan day? Can youse not give it a rest for a while?'

'How can we give it a rest, Da,' shouted Kate, turning to him, 'when we're hearing things now that we should have been told

149

about before this? You and my ma should have told us, and ye know what I'm talkin' about.'

I knew what she was talking about, too, but she didn't know that, and my da didn't know that, either. And it was thanks to Liam that I did, even if I didn't fully understand it yet. But I was determined to understand it before long, and what better time than now when it had been raised in another secret kind of way by Kate.

'What things are ye talkin' about, Kate?' I asked innocently.

But she didn't answer. She just gave me one of her 'shut up' looks.

'That's enough, Dickie,' said my da before I could say anything more about it. 'Nothin' that ye have to worry about, son. So leave it at that. And you, Kate, stop going on about these things in front of the wains.'

'Will youse close up, the three of youse?' It was my ma speaking as she brought in three plates of dinner from the kitchen. Sausages and spuds and peas and gravy. It looked nice and I was starving. 'And I can't keep this dinner warm all day for that Laura, wherever she is. Did she say where she was goin'?'

'Naw, Ma, she said nothin',' Kate answered civilly as she went out to the kitchen to bring in the other plates of food. But she shouted back in, 'She went up the stairs after the row, and five minutes later she went out and slammed the glass door behind her.'

I heard my ma taking three big breaths as she set the dinners down in front of me and Liam. And then a big sigh.

'I put Laura's dinner in the oven, Ma,' said Kate, when she came back in, 'but I noticed ye have another dinner in there, too. Who's that for?'

My ma didn't answer for a few seconds. 'That's for your Uncle Jimmy, in case he comes,' she said quickly. 'Right, Barney, your dinner's out,' she added as if she didn't want to talk about Uncle Jimmy any further.

But Kate did. 'You're not serious, Ma,' she said. 'I thought ye told us a while ago that that was it. No more Uncle Jimmy in this house.'

My ma didn't answer her. But she spoke quietly. 'Now, sit youse all down, and tuck in. Right, Barney? Right, wains?' It was as if she hadn't heard Kate.

As we ate the meal, Kate said nothing but her face said everything. She was raging. Another row was brewing. And the rest of us knew it. We weren't halfway through eating when we heard the glass door opening. It was Uncle Jimmy and Laura. And from what I could make out, Laura had a face on her to match Kate's as she poked her head in the living-room door and shouted, 'Look what I bumped into in the street, comin' back from gettin' my head showered.' Behind her, I could see Uncle Jimmy's face, too. It looked like thunder. Liam nudged me and I nudged him back. And we knew what each other was thinking. That the stage was now set for the big showdown.

After Laura's outburst, nobody spoke for a wee minute except my ma. 'Sit down there, Jimmy,' she said quietly, 'for a wee bite to eat. And, Laura, when you're comin' in, bring in them two meals in the oven.'

Uncle Jimmy took the nearest empty chair.

'I will not,' Laura shouted. 'He can bring in his own food if he wants it. I'm not his skivvy, and I'll never be his skivvy.'

She went to the kitchen and within seconds was back in the living room, carrying her own plate to the table.

'How dare ye!' shouted my ma, taking the food away from her and putting it in Uncle Jimmy's place. 'How dare ye, Laura McCauley, for bein' so disrespectful to your uncle!'

My ma's eyes were blazing, and she was about to say something else when Uncle Jimmy broke in. 'What's this all about?' he said. 'What's happenin' here?'

'Now,' said my ma, trying to ignore Uncle Jimmy's questions, 'you go out, Laura, and get your meal from the oven and we'll all sit down in peace and quiet and enjoy it. It's not often that we're all here at the same time, is it? Like a family? Together?'

151

But by the looks of it, Uncle Jimmy wasn't going to be ignored, because he came back, quick as a flash with another question. 'Would somebody please tell me what's goin' on here? What's all the dramatics for?'

And his eyes were blazing as he was speaking.

Now it was Kate's turn. She'd been dying to butt in for ages.

'Should we not be settin' another place at the table, Ma? Or even maybe two places, Ma? Wan for an adult and wan for a child? Like the big family get together you're talkin' about. Except that it would be two families, wouldn't it, Uncle Jimmy? And it wouldn't be happy families. Not by a long chalk.'

Everybody stopped eating after Kate's outburst. Some of us looked at Uncle Jimmy, because we knew this was it. And he knew, too, that there must have been some talk about him. Probably about him and Mrs Johnston. You'd have been stupid not to have known if you were in his shoes. He pushed back his chair and half-rose. His face was even angrier than before.

'Sit down, Jimmy,' shouted my ma. 'Remember the children. Sit down and eat your meal. And Kate,' she roared as she turned to her, 'if ye can't keep a civil tongue in your head, ye'd be better to leave the table this minute and let the rest of us eat in peace.'

'This isn't over yet, Ma,' said Kate breathlessly. 'Far from it.' But she went back to eating her food.

Even Laura had gone out to the kitchen again and brought the other plate in. They were both doing as my ma had bid them, but they were far from happy. And because the tension in the room was still high, I thought it would be better to let things settle a bit before I put my spoke in. But it had to be soon or the opportunity could be lost and we'd be back to square one. With Uncle Jimmy the winner. And after everything that had been said and done, I couldn't let that happen. No way. That would be the biggest mistake of my life. Letting Uncle Jimmy off the hook, and us still in big danger. I would wait my chance. I would say something when the time was right. It was just that I was very, very puzzled at what my ma had said earlier about having nothing more to do with Uncle Jimmy, and telling the girls the same, and now, just a minute ago, telling us all to sit down in peace and quiet and enjoy a family meal together. It didn't add up. And then, into the bargain, just a wee while ago, her shouting at Laura about being disrespectful to her Uncle Jimmy when she herself was roaring and shouting and squealing against him herself a few hours ago. Naw, this wasn't on. It didn't add up at all.

Before I spoke, I took a very quiet, deep breath. It was now or never. 'Uncle Jimmy,' I said with an innocent kind of voice and a mouthful of spud and sausage, 'our Liam saw ye goin' into the cop's house last night. In from the back lane. He told me about it this morning.' I said it deliberately like that – 'the cop's house'. I felt there was no point in saying 'into Johnstons' house' or 'the policeman's house' or even 'Eva Johnston's house' – 'the cop's house' sounded better.

Everybody stopped chewing. Waiting to see if I was going to say anything else. But I wasn't. Not at this moment anyway. Liam kicked me gently. Egging me on. I decided to wait.

Uncle Jimmy turned to me with a shocked look on his face. He then looked at everybody else, checking if they'd heard me. He knew immediately that they had. And that his game was up. I glanced at my da's face. He looked as if he was about to choke, or maybe burst out laughing. My ma was shocked, her angry eyes darting between me and Liam and Uncle Jimmy, but mostly directed at me. But why was she so shocked? That's what I was thinking right now. Sure she already knew what Liam had seen. And she knew that Uncle Jimmy was visiting Eva's ma. So what was the point of being shocked? No point. It was all show. Uncle Jimmy would just have to face up to this. And give us his answers. That's what I was thinking. So why was my ma pointing her angry eyes at me?

Aye, blame me, Ma. Blame me for him going into a cop's house. Blame me for him seeing Eva's ma in secret. Blame me for his stupid disguise. Blame me for Liam seeing him in the lane in the first place.

And when you do all that, blame me as well for the guns and am-
munition that are buried under a quarter-ton of coal in the back
yard. I can take it. I can take it right now, especially because I know
that everything's coming to a head. That we're all going to be safe
again, maybe before this night's out.

I was about to say something else to Uncle Jimmy that would
really have set the cat among the pigeons again, but my da got
in first, and with a sneering voice, too.

'So that's what the disguise is all about, Jimmy, isn't it? It's
so that the neighbours won't recognise ye. And there was me
thinkin' when I saw ye first that it was the cops ye were hidin'
from.'

That's all he said. He just sat back then with a satisfied smirk
on his face. But as my da was speaking, I could see Uncle Jimmy's hands clenching the edge of the table. His knuckles had
turned white and his face was red. And he looked annoyed as
well as shocked. But I didn't care. Everything was going the way
I'd planned. My ma was squirming in her seat, not knowing
what to say. She was as pale as a ghost. And looking very scared.

Now it was Laura's turn to jump in again. And she went to
town, shouting at him. It was like sticking the boot in. 'Aye,
it's all comin' out now, Uncle Jimmy. Some IRA man you are,
datin' a cop's wife when he's out on night duty. A secret rendez-
vous with an old flame, eh, Uncle Jimmy? Gettin' acquainted
again with the woman that wouldn't have ye all them years ago?
Maybe even checkin' up on how the wee girl's gettin' on, too?
Her that looks like ye. Is that why you're in Derry, Uncle Jimmy?
Some IRA business that. And something else, too—'

Before she got that something else out, Uncle Jimmy had
pushed back his chair as if he was going to rise, but he didn't.
There was still an angry look on his face but he was calmer than
I thought he would be. That worried me a bit.

'Well, well, well,' he said, 'so youse all know everything, do
youse? Well, let me tell ye that youse know very little. And what
youse do know is of no consequence to anybody. And that's all

I'm sayin' for now, because I'm not goin' to waste my time or my breath on youse. I've more to be gettin' on with than that. And as for you, Kate, and you, Laura, I can tell youse now that youse won't be doin' any trainin' in August, for the both of ye are too stupid, and too excitable, and too impetuous to be in the Movement. Youse are too big a risk. That's what youse are.'

I could hear Liam beginning to whimper a wee bit, and then sniffle. He must have felt it was time to start the act again. But now Kate was on her feet, shouting even louder than Laura. 'Is that right, Uncle Jimmy? Well, let me tell you that if we're stupid, then the Movement must have been in a bad way when they hired you. Big-time captain is it? Sure you wouldn't even be fit to captain the Rosemount football team. And another thing, does the Movement know that even after all the shenanigans in this house last year when wee Liam got hurt, did your bosses know that you're still stupid enough to bring in guns? Stupid enough to think that this would be a safe house?'

The spittles were flying from Kate's mouth as she shouted. My ma tried to stop her a couple of times, but she just went on and on. And I knew she wasn't finished yet. But this time, my ma interrupted her, at least for a second.

'Dear God Almighty, Kate,' she called out, 'can we not all sit down and talk this through, civilly? Sure isn't—'

But Kate didn't give her a chance to finish what she was going to say.

'Naw, Ma. We can't, Ma. But you can tell that precious brother of yours there, in as civil a way as ye want, what ye told us this very day. Go on, Ma,' continued Kate, 'tell him what ye told me about that trollop Johnston, and the wee girl. Go on, Ma, tell him now to his face. And tell him when you're at it what ye said about wee Eva lookin' the spittin' image of him.'

'Shut up, Kate,' my ma shouted angrily. 'Shut up. You've gone too far this time. And I didn't say that Eva was the spittin' image of him. I said she looked a bit like him. There's a big difference.'

With that, she turned quickly to Uncle Jimmy, apologising to

155

him. 'I'm sorry, Jimmy. Sorry. I shouldn't have said that about the wee girl bein' like ye. It was just an off-the-cuff remark I made because I was that annoyed at ye after ye told me that ye were goin' to visit that woman again. I just put two and two together and got five. I'm very sorry, Jimmy. It just came out and then everybody got the wrong impression. It's my fault. Sure I know that the wee wan's not yours. I'm sorry, Jimmy.'

I didn't like the way my ma kept apologising to Uncle Jimmy, but when she'd said that about Eva not being Uncle Jimmy's wain, I looked around at everybody. At Kate first. She had shut up, all right; taken aback she was. Then I looked at Laura and my da. They didn't need to be told to shut up. You could see that they had nothing much else to shout about. And that was definitely down to what my ma had just said. It had taken the wind out of their sails. Their trump card had been the notion, now a wrong notion, that Uncle Jimmy was Eva's da. So all they had left was maybe to shout some more about getting rid of the guns and ammunition and force him out of the house as well.

That suited me.

But the wind hadn't been taken out of Liam's sails, for his whimpering and sniffing had already begun again and were getting louder by the second. He must have sensed, the same as me, that Uncle Jimmy was getting ready to pounce. I think my da might have felt the same, because his arm went round Liam's shoulder, as if he was protecting him. My ma was to blame for this, because she was the one who was apologising all the time to Uncle Jimmy. She was the one who'd started the rumour about Eva. But I was glad of one thing. I was glad it was just a rumour, because I didn't want Eva to be my cousin. I liked her too much. But I wasn't glad when my ma then went into another fit of crying. I didn't like to see her like this even if nearly everything was her fault.

'Oh, dear God Almighty,' she squealed out as she turned to the distressed-looking Liam and then back to Jimmy. 'How have I let things get this far? It's not right, Jimmy. All this carry-on's not right. Not in our house. Not anymore. It's just not right, Jimmy.'

You could see the disappointed look on Uncle Jimmy's face as she was making her loud protests to him. You could see the anger rising in him as she went on.

'It's a mistake, Jimmy, ye must see that yourself. Nothin' else matters now but the wains. I want you and all your stuff out before this day's over. Do you hear me, Jimmy?'

You could see the agony all over her as she breathed heavily after her outburst. You could sense the tension in the room. You could feel the fear. But as the seconds ticked by, you could also see the relief on my ma's face. She had done it. She'd told Uncle Jimmy what she really thought now. That she wasn't backing him anymore, even if he was her brother. Everybody else felt the relief, too. Except Uncle Jimmy. As well as all that, Liam's whimpering and sniffling had turned into low moans. I liked that, especially as Uncle Jimmy had suddenly pushed his chair further back from the table and stood up, his eyes blazing and his teeth clenched. He was badly rattled.

He slowly took a revolver from his pocket and held it up before he spoke. You could have heard a pin drop in the room except for the odd moan from Liam. And you could see that everybody felt a bit afraid.

'So this is it?' he shouted, looking around at everybody. 'Betrayed, am I? By my own family. And after all the sacrifices I've made over the years, it's come to this. Well, it's a good job Ireland isn't dependin' on the likes of youse. Let me tell youse all right now that this,' and he held the gun up higher, 'and the likes of this, will be what gets rid of the foreigners out of this country. And all I'd asked youse to do was to store a few guns for a couple of days—'

'But, Jimmy,' my ma interrupted, 'it's not fair on the wains, it's not right—'

'Not fair? Not right?' he roared. 'Is it fair that this country is divided the way it is? Is it fair the way the North of Ireland is run? Naw, not wan bit fair. Sure all you've got to do is look at the way this very town is organised, by that Corporation down there. A crowd of bigots, they are, with a minority of Unionists lordin' it over us Nationalists. What could be fair about that, or right about that? And there's no better time than now to be doin' somethin' about it when they're up against it themselves with Hitler. Naw, no better time to put the boot in when we can. I'm ashamed of ye, Kitty, and the rest of youse. Youse aren't fit to call yourselves Irish.'

We could hardly breathe with the tension. And we couldn't take our eyes off Uncle Jimmy. None of us. I even felt a wee bit afraid because he was shouting. Especially when he was waving the gun about. I think the others felt the same, but it didn't stop my ma from doing her bit of shouting too, for she suddenly got up off her chair, turned on Uncle Jimmy in a wild rage, and told him to get out. To get out of her house and never come back. Now we couldn't take our eyes off our ma. She was brilliant.

But Uncle Jimmy was a very stubborn man. I'd heard people saying that often. And I knew as my ma was shouting at him that he'd be hard to shift. And I knew as well that he wouldn't want to be seen being ordered about by his sister Kitty. I was right. He didn't turn to go the way most people in the room thought he should. Instead, just then, by the way he was standing, I knew that he had more to say, more to shout about. Everybody was a bit fearful about what would happen next. Except Liam, because you could see from the look on his face that he had something important to say as well.

'Uncle Jimmy,' he said, his voice shaking with false nervousness, 'I forgot to tell Dickie this morning about Cecil Colhoun seein' ye in the back lane last night as well. Seein' ye goin' into Johnstons' house. I'm just rememberin' now, so I thought I'd better tell ye before ye go. In case it's important.'

'What's this?' snapped Uncle Jimmy. 'What are ye on about?'

'Let the wain speak. He's only tryin' to be civil to ye. Can ye not see that?' shouted my da in anger. 'Or maybe ye don't want to hear any more home truths.'

But Liam was determined to finish. 'Aye, Uncle Jimmy. Cecil Colhoun saw ye, the same as I saw ye, goin' in through the cop's back gate.'

There was a heavy silence in the sitting room as Liam was speaking. Everybody, including me, was waiting on the next part. It was Uncle Jimmy who spoke. Before he did, he took two big deep breaths. He was afraid. And this time, he put his face up very close to Liam's.

'Did you tell him who I was?' he snapped.

Liam put on a special scared look, then moaned out loud as if he was frightened. But he wasn't frightened. I knew that, but nobody else did.

'Jimmy,' shouted my ma, 'leave the wain alone. Ye have him nearly out of his wits the way you're goin' on. Just go now and leave us all in peace.'

That's when Kate and Laura joined in the shouting again, telling Uncle Jimmy to get out, to get out of the house and stay out. My da said nothing but he hugged Liam closer to him.

'Naw, I didn't tell him, Uncle Jimmy, honest,' wailed Liam loudly. 'Sure I don't talk to Cecil Colhoun anymore. And he doesn't really speak to us since the IRA killed his da. His ma doesn't allow him. He's not in our gang anymore, either, and he doesn't play with us in the street.'

'So there ye are, Liam, he didn't recognise me, did he? And if you didn't tell him, then there's nothin' to worry about, is there?'

'But, Uncle Jimmy,' sobbed Liam, 'he knew ye as soon as he saw ye, because before he went into his own back yard again he shouted to me about your disguise. That it wasn't very good. "That's your Uncle Jimmy with a beard and a moustache," he told me. I said nothin' to him.'

Uncle Jimmy left the room without speaking. And in a big hurry, too. He then thumped his way up the stairs like a madman. Nobody spoke. Liam cuddled closer to my da. Two minutes later, we heard him thundering down again. We all listened in silence, holding our breath. Then we jumped with fright as the living-room door suddenly banged open. He shouted in, his eyes wild looking, 'All that stuff'll be gone before the night's out. Somebody'll call to collect it.'

With that, he was away, out into the hall and then slamming the glass door behind him. Everybody in the room breathed a sigh of relief. Except Liam. He just winked over at me. The wee fart had done it. He'd lied like a trooper and got away with it. The plan was working. But the guns and bullets were still in the coalhouse. At least for another wee while. And the suitcase of money was probably still in the attic.

Just then, out of the blue, my ma turned on my da, shouting at him that he should have stood up more to Uncle Jimmy.

'You're a wastrel,' she roared at him, 'nothin' but a bloody wastrel, and ye shouldn't have let him badger wee Liam like that.'

I could see that my da was badly shocked at my ma's outburst. But he said nothing. He just looked at her with sad eyes. Then he got up from his chair and left the room quietly. I heard him climbing the stairs, probably to lie down for a while. But my ma kept shouting more insults after him. Stuff like him being a coward and a drunkard. And, worst of all, that she didn't want to see him anymore. Kate and Laura went to comfort her as she slumped into the chair and began to sob violently. Her whole body was shuddering. But I was feeling more sorry for my da. And I didn't blame him one bit when I heard him coming down the stairs about ten minutes later and then leaving the house. He was probably heading downtown again. To give his secret knock on some pub door.

I looked at the clock on the mantelpiece. It was half six. I had plenty of time before the meeting in the air-raid shelter. Without saying anything, I left the room and slipped upstairs. To pass the time, I read some of the comics that Cecil Colhoun had given me. I was beginning to feel good.

***

160

'Dickie . . .'

It was Liam. I hadn't heard him coming into the room.

'Hello, Liam,' I said.

'I'll go down now, Dickie, and get the air-raid shelter ready for the meeting.'

'Great, Liam,' I replied. 'And, Liam . . .'

'What, Dickie?'

'Ye were great downstairs again, the way ye handled Uncle Jimmy.'

'No bother, Dickie.'

'Ye had him fairly scared, too, with the lie about Cecil recognisin' him in the lane.'

'It wasn't a lie, Dickie. I forgot to tell ye. Cecil Colhoun knew who it was right away. Honest, Dickie, he said that Uncle Jimmy's disguise wasn't very good. But he didn't ask me why he was disguised.'

'My God, Liam,' I said, 'how could ye forget that? About tellin' me, I mean?'

'Does it matter now, Dickie? Sure it did the trick, didn't it?'

I was very, very shocked. Too shocked, in fact, to reply to Liam for a few seconds, because my mind was racing with very dangerous questions. What if Cecil Colhoun told his ma about seeing Uncle Jimmy? What if Mrs Colhoun then quizzed Mrs Johnston about it? What if she even told the cop himself? Or maybe intended to and didn't get round to it yet. These would have been the thoughts going through Uncle Jimmy's mind as he rushed out the door earlier. And they were probably the thoughts, too, of my ma and Kate and Laura. But not me. Because I was the only one who believed that Liam was telling lies at the time.

'Aye, it did the trick, Liam,' I said as calmly as I could. 'Ye were great. Just you go on to the air-raid shelter now. I'll be down in a wee while.'

Liam left without any more questions. But I felt afraid. Uncle Jimmy had promised that all the stuff would be out of the house before the end of the night, but I was thinking now that the sooner someone came to take everything away the better, because we could be raided at any minute. As I closed the glass door behind me and headed for the meeting with the gang, I suddenly felt a terrible burden on me. As if I was to blame for this whole mess. And just because my plan had worked, with Liam's help, it didn't seem to have made things any better for the McCauley family. But then again, it wasn't because the plan worked that things might now be worse. It was still all down to Uncle Jimmy and my ma, and Kate and Laura, that things were bad. Aye, it was their fault, especially Uncle Jimmy's, that we were all still in danger. It had really nothing to do with the plan working. But the danger was definitely greater now since Cecil Colhoun had seen Uncle Jimmy in the lane. Liam telling us about it all had only made us all realise that. That's when I said a quick prayer that Cecil hadn't told anybody about Uncle Jimmy going into the cop's house.

CHAPTER 19

Ye Don't Lie To A Friend, Dickie

Liam had the candles lit in the air-raid shelter when I got there just before seven o'clock. Nobody else had arrived yet. I expected the Deeney twins to be here first. They were nearly always on time for everything. But I wasn't sure if Danny or Kevin or Eva would come. All I could do now was wait and hope that the pictures-and-chips bribe for next Friday night would do the trick, at least with Danny.

But as my mind began to dwell again on my problem with Eva, I knew that I still wouldn't be able to tell her the truth about Danny and Kevin doing the spying job for me on the disguised Uncle Jimmy. If only her da wasn't a cop, everything could have been different. But that was stupid thinking, because her da was a cop and there was nothing I could do about that. If she did come to the meeting, that would be a start. Maybe I would then be able to think up something that would turn things around. At this moment, I couldn't think of anything. But I would have to, soon, because I liked her too much. And she could be gone from Derry before I even knew it. It didn't bear thinking about.

'Dickie . . .'

'Aye, Liam?'

'Is that the end of the guns and everything in our house from now on? And Uncle Jimmy, too?'

'Aye, Liam, it is. After the night, that's it. That's what he said;

the guns and stuff are all goin' the night. And he's not comin' back, Liam.'

'That's great, Dickie. I'm glad it's all over.'

I could see his wee face in the candlelight. He looked a bit pale, tired-looking. Not surprising after everything that had happened. You'd have thought now after all he'd been through that he wouldn't want to talk about anything. But he still had questions.

'Is Uncle Jimmy really a soldier, Dickie?'

'Well, it's like this, Liam,' I replied. 'He is and he isn't.'

'Does he have a uniform, Dickie? Like the soldiers you see trainin' sometimes down in the back field?'

'I don't know, Liam. I never saw him wearin' a uniform. He probably has. You have to have a uniform if you're a soldier.'

'Where does he keep his uniform, Dickie?'

'I dunno, Liam.'

'Will Uncle Jimmy fight Hitler if he attacks Derry, Dickie? I heard on the wireless that the Germans might be coming.'

I was getting tired of Liam's questions so I just told him to ask my da tomorrow.

'Okay, Dickie,' he said. 'Will I go now and look for the gang? It must be after seven. I already told them that the meetin' was at seven, and about the pictures and chips and all.'

'Aye, okay, Liam, good idea. If ye see them, tell them to hurry. I haven't got all night.'

A minute later, I heard footsteps outside. That must be them. But it wasn't. It was Eva. On her own.

'Am I the first here?' she said. 'I saw Liam runnin' up the street. What's up?'

'Nothin's up,' I told her. 'Liam's away to get the others.'

It felt good being with her in the air-raid shelter, with nobody else about. I was almost hoping that the rest wouldn't come, because I had never really got talking much to Eva on her own. But the problem was now that she was here, I didn't know what to say to her. For some reason, I couldn't come out with it: that she looked nice, that her hair was lovely or that I liked the way her eyes seemed to dance and shine in the candlelight. And as I was thinking these things, I could see her looking at me in a strange, smiley sort of way that gave me the impression that she could read my mind. I didn't want to say to her about her going away.

And I didn't want to say to her, either, that I was sorry about last night. About the lies I'd told her. I just couldn't, because I'd have to tell her why, and I couldn't do that, either. So I said nothing, probably hoping that she'd forgotten all about it. But she hadn't forgotten.

'About last night,' said Eva, her smiley face now gone, 'the things ye said, and the lies ye told me. That hurt me, Dickie.' Then she blurted out the rest. It looked as if she wanted to get it off her chest. 'And ye don't lie to a friend, Dickie. Ye don't hurt your friends.'

My heart sank. If it had been any other members of the gang that were saying things like this to me, I'd have told them where to get off, in no uncertain fashion, and I'd have given them a back-of-the-throat job right up their ugly faces. But I had no answers like that now. You couldn't say rough things like that to a girl, and you could forget about the spit job. It just wouldn't be right. Not to Eva anyhow. I didn't want to apologise to her, because that would have been another lie, because Dickie Mc-Cauley doesn't apologise to anybody. And she knew that.

'And another thing, Dickie McCauley,' she said, and she didn't seem to be annoyed as she was a minute ago, 'I'm a girl, and I'm in the gang, and if there's things to be done, gang things, missions and things, I want to be included. Do you hear what I'm sayin', Dickie? And you can get it out of your head as well about me going to Dublin. Because I'm not. No matter what my da says.'

She wasn't angry now as she spoke, but I was getting a wee bit annoyed with her. I wasn't used to being told what I should do or shouldn't do when it came to gang rules. Because it was my gang, and I made the rules. Before I knew it, I had spoken.

Spoken even before my brain got time to think properly. That was the trouble with me sometimes. Mouth before brain.

'Okay, Eva,' I said. 'From now on, everybody in the gang's the same. Whether it's a girl or boy. And if there's a mission organised, then whoever I pick to go will go. Okay?'

That was the best I could do with the words that came out, but I knew immediately that I'd made a mistake. Because a girl is a girl and a boy is a boy, and there were definitely missions and things that a girl couldn't carry out.

'That's all right with me, Dickie,' she said.

And I knew by the look on her face, even in the dim candle-light, that things would be okay with us from now on. It wasn't the full smile like the ones she usually had for me, but it was a good enough one. And it made me feel better. Because I reckoned when it came to it anyway, when I gave the order about electrocutions and skinny-dipping with the gang, Eva wouldn't be up for it. Because she was a girl.

Now it was my turn to smile, because when one of the Deeney twins suddenly came into the air-raid shelter and I said, 'Hello, Joey,' I could see the puzzled look on Eva's face, because she was wondering how I knew it was him and not Hughie. She hadn't noticed that their hair was combed in opposite ways. But I'd explain it to her later. A few seconds later Hughie came in as well.

'Dickie,' said Hughie excitedly, 'Danny and Kevin want ye in the street. They said it's wile important.' I told Eva and the twins I'd be back in a minute. Eva just shrugged her shoulders, puzzled like, as I turned to leave.

'What's up?' I asked when I got outside.

Both of them were sweating and red-faced. Kevin was breathing very heavily. His right hand was in his pocket. I knew why. But I didn't know yet why they were so flustered.

Danny pulled me lightly by the sleeve and down the street a wee bit, looking around him at the same time to make sure nobody was within earshot. He was a bit hoarse when he spoke.

'Dickie,' he said, 'me and Kevin followed your Uncle Joe when he came out of your house a while ago. We carried out the mission, Dickie, and he didn't spot us. We know where he went.'

'You do?' I asked in disbelief.

You could have knocked me down with a feather. Here was Danny, even after the big row we'd had last night, here he was, all proud of himself, reporting to me, dying to tell me what had happened, when away at the back of my mind I was still trying to work out how I'd get him back into my good books again. By the sound of things, he *was* back, without me having to do anything. And I knew I had Kevin to thank for that.

Before I could say another word, they had the rest out. I didn't have time to ask them anything. Kevin just stood there, obviously pleased with himself, and waiting his turn to speak.

'Aye, Dickie,' whispered Danny, 'we let him go down the hill a bit before we tailed him. We were a good bit back, on the other side of the road, so he didn't see us. And he was goin' very fast, too.'

Now it was Kevin's turn. His glasses were steamed up, but it didn't stop him. He was bursting to get his spoke in.

'It was a great mission, Dickie. A great success. And we ran the whole way back up to tell you. That's why we're late for the meetin', Dickie—'

'Shut up, Kevin,' said Danny, interrupting him. 'He went to Kellys', Dickie, into Bap's house, in the Bogside, but he only stayed about five minutes. We hid behind a gable wall and wait-ed. When he came out, he went on down the Bogside and to-wards the town. We didn't follow him anymore, Dickie. We just ran back up to tell ye.'

All I could do now was praise them, because they really had done what I'd asked them to do, even if it was a day later, and even though it didn't matter to me where Uncle Jimmy went. Not now. He was out of our house. That's all I cared about.

'Great job, boys,' I said. 'Youse have done great.'

And I meant it. Mainly because they hadn't burst into the

air-raid shelter and blurted everything out in front of Eva. If they had, it could have been another disaster. And it was still better to keep stuff about Uncle Jimmy secret. From everybody. Especially from Eva. But just as I was thinking that I should warn them again, about the secret thing, Kevin came out with something very important.

'Dickie,' he said quietly as he looked around him again, 'we didn't talk to anybody about this, not even to the Deeney twins. We didn't blab to a soul.'

'I know youse didn't, Kevin. Youse were great. And, Kevin . . .'

'What, Dickie?'

'Thanks,' I said, smiling at him.

Before heading back into the shelter, I heaped more praise on both of them. They were beaming from ear to ear. And so was I, because a lot of things seemed to be going my way for the first time in a good while. And that gives you a great feeling.

Even though Liam hadn't come back yet, I started the meeting with what they all wanted to hear.

'Right,' I said. 'Liam has already told youse about the pictures and the chips on Friday night. But that's only part of the programme. After we get the chips, we'll capture two of the North Street Bunch. Me and Liam and Joey and Hughie will do the capturin'. We'll drag them to Cnoc na Ros, where Danny and Kevin and Eva will be waitin'. As soon as we arrive, you, Danny, and you, Kevin, will hold the prisoners. Then Eva will electrocute them, wan at a time.'

They all nodded excitedly, even Eva. That surprised me. About Eva being excited, I mean. About the electrocutions. She really was a tomboy, all right.

'Then on Saturday,' I went on, 'we'll raid their dam and wreck it. After that, we'll all go for a dip in the reservoir. Okay, everybody?'

They all cheered. Including Eva. For the next ten minutes, the gang chatted excitedly about the plans. It had been a long time since we'd all done stuff together. And it felt fantastic being back in charge again without anybody arguing with me.

But before the excitement had fully died down, Liam came running into the air-raid shelter. He was in a bit of a state, wild-eyed.

'Dickie, Dickie,' he hissed through his teeth. 'Bap Kelly and his da and two men are up in our house. C'mon quick.'

I knew why they were there. But I didn't want the rest of the gang to know, so I shushed Liam quiet by putting a finger to my lips. And without anybody else seeing me. I didn't want him to blab anything by accident. Especially about guns.

'It's okay, Liam,' I then said quickly. 'They're up to see about some work,' I lied. 'Some decoratin' that my ma wants done. They're goin' to do our bedroom, too, Liam. I'll be up in a wee minute.'

Liam cottoned on immediately that he'd nearly blabbed after he heard me talking rubbish about the men coming to paint the place. At first, he looked a wee bit embarrassed at being so stupid, but then he perked up when he saw me winking and smiling at him on the quiet.

'Right, Dickie,' he replied with a knowing grin. 'I'll tell my ma that you're comin'. Ye might want to help pick what colour of distemper we're gettin'. So hurry up, Dickie, before the men leave.'

Liam turned away, a cheeky look on his face, and left without saying hello or cheerio to anybody, but I don't think they noticed. They were still too caught up talking about the plans I'd made for them. But I was thinking that I'd have to have a wee talk with Liam again about letting his brain do the thinking before he opened his mouth. Because by the sound of things, we weren't fully out of danger yet.

But as regards the meeting, I decided to stay on for at least another five minutes or so before I followed Liam home. It wouldn't look good, the gang leader leaving when everything was still being discussed. But when the five minutes were up, I would make my excuses and tell them that I'd be back in a wee

169

while, and that they could tie everything up themselves about times and things. And they could then let me know later what had been decided. And that's just what happened. Eva was the only one to notice me leaving. She gave me a wave and a smile. The others didn't notice. There was still great excitement in the air-raid shelter.

Chapter 20

A Suitcase Full Of Money Doesn't Go Missing

I was more than angry when I saw Bap Kelly sitting in our living room, eating a piece and drinking milk. My ma must have given it to him. More fool her. I was fit to be tied. He smiled up at me, but I glared back at him with a real dirty look that said I didn't like him and I didn't want him there. He was always sticking his nose into other people's business. But I was really surprised that he was here at all. Under the circumstances, you would have thought that his da would have left him at home. Naw, Bossy-Boots Kelly had to be in the middle of everything, even dangerous stuff. To my mind, that made his da a very stupid man, the same as my ma was a very stupid woman.

'Did ye like the bike, Dickie?' he asked as if that was an important question to be asking at this very minute. And as if it didn't matter to me that him sitting there was annoying me, to say the least. Especially when he knew he was annoying me. Or as if it was a normal thing that his da had just done, taking two IRA men into our house to collect stuff. And normal that they were upstairs in our attic, probably with my ma and Kate and Laura. It was on the tip of my tongue to tell him to get out, that he had no right to be sitting at our table, taking our food. But I knew in my heart I couldn't, because what was now happening upstairs was really down to me. And to Liam. And the plan was working. And if Bap had to be here for some stupid reason that I couldn't understand, then well and good. That was up to his da, so I'd just have to put up with him for another wee while until Mr Kelly and the other two men had taken everything with them. But it was still hard to stick, watching him sitting in our house as if he was a normal visitor. And he was far from it. As were the rest of them. So I held my tongue for the sake of what was going to happen and I let him ramble on.

'Aye, about the bike, Dickie, I know it needs a wee bit of repair done to it, but ye should be able to sort all that out before the end of August. It should be handy for the College, eh, Dickie?'

I still didn't answer him. Instead I took my usual two big deep breaths and left him sitting there in the living room. I had more important things to do. I went upstairs to the landing. Liam was in the bedroom, looking at a comic. He spotted me and whispered out loud to me to come into the room. I was torn between going into him or slipping quietly up the attic stairs to find out what was happening. I decided to see Liam first. He might know something.

'Dickie,' he said, 'they're all up there. Mr Kelly and the two men. With my ma and Kate and Laura. I heard them shoutin' a minute ago. The men, I mean. Dickie, they sounded angry.'

'It's okay, Liam,' I replied in a whisper. 'I'll slip up and let ye know in a wee while what's happenin'.'

'Right,' he whispered back.

He looked a bit afraid. I could see it in his eyes. I hugged him before I left the room and told him not to worry. That our plan was working. The way we said it would.

'Great, Dickie,' he whispered a bit nervously as he sat back on the bed. But I noticed before I left him that the comic he was holding was upside down.

As I walked quietly up the attic stairs, I could hear voices arguing. Then I heard Bap Kelly's da.

'There must be some reasonable explanation for this, Kitty, it can't just have disappeared. This is very, very important now, Kitty. A lot of people are dependin' on it. People have to be paid and stuff has to be bought. Do ye understand what I'm sayin' to ye?'

'Jimmy must have taken it with him,' said my ma. 'He probably forgot.' Her voice was loud. Protesting.

I didn't know what they were talking about but I sensed by the tense atmosphere in the room that something was badly wrong. Something very serious was happening. And the twins were definitely scared.

Mr Kelly was staring straight at my ma. You could see that he was worried, too, whatever it was about. I tried to appear calm as I went further into the room and stood in front of her – as if I was protecting her. The other two men, one black-haired and the other fair, had grim faces on them. They had obviously been searching the place for whatever they were looking for. Their cheeks were red and their faces sweaty. I didn't like the look of them.

'This is stupid,' shouted Kate at the three men. 'Sure youse have got the guns and ammunition out of the coalhouse and youse can see there's nothin' else here. Uncle Jimmy must have taken the suitcase with him when he left this evening. Nobody else would have touched it.'

'We're not leavin' till we find it,' said the black-haired man. 'Jimmy told us it was here in the attic bedroom. He said he hadn't taken it with him. You don't forget something as important as this.'

So that was it. The suitcase of money. The two thousand pounds minus two ten-bob notes. My heart began to thump. I thought everybody would hear it. Pounding away in my chest. This was big trouble. A suitcase full of money just doesn't go missing. But somehow it had. Unless, I was thinking, Uncle Jimmy really did forget that he took it with him. But I couldn't believe that. Naw, not for a second. Uncle Jimmy was too cute. The IRA man was right. Uncle Jimmy couldn't make a mistake like that. There must be some other explanation. But what?

I reached back and held my ma's hand. She was trembling.

Her nerves were wrecked. I'd have to try and do something before she collapsed. I couldn't think of anything. Just stay calm, I thought, and maybe say something when I got the chance. And I did, because the men began frantically searching the room again.

'Hello, Ma, hello, Mr Kelly.' I said. 'What's up? Is somethin' wrong? What are these people doin' in our house?' I continued as innocently as I could. 'Where's Uncle Jimmy?'

As I spoke, I put on a wee bit of a crying voice and then tried to look scared. It didn't work.

'Get that wain outta here,' shouted the fair-haired man, his eyes blazin'. 'As a matter of fact, the whole lot of youse go back downstairs. And stay in the living room till we come down. We have a whole house to search here, startin' now.'

The black-haired man began to usher me and my ma and Kate and Laura out of the room, very roughly. We didn't need to be told twice.

'Hold on there, boys,' said Mr Kelly. 'Calm down. There's bound to be a simple explanation for this. Youse don't have to be wreckin' the whole bloody house. We'll all go back down the town and see Jimmy. He'll have the answer for youse. The case'll turn up. You'll see.'

As Mr Kelly was pleading with the two men, I tugged at my ma's hand, pulling her after me as we left the attic room. The twins followed. We went straight down to the living room, nobody speaking. But on the landing, I glanced into our bedroom. Liam was still there, pale as a ghost. I'd go up to him later.

As soon as I saw Bap Kelly again, sitting at our table and smiling, when we went in, I exploded.

'C'mere,' I shouted to him. 'Out to the hall!'

My ma and the twins hardly noticed. Or didn't care. I pinned him up against the hall wall, deliberately letting my spittles land on his face as I spoke. He knew I meant business.

'Get outta here, Kelly, outta this house and never come back. You're not welcome here. You're nothin' but trouble, you and your da and the likes of youse, and youse can keep Uncle Jimmy for all we care. Now, out!'

I didn't kick him up the backside as he was leaving, but I felt like it. And I swore under my breath at him as I slammed the glass door behind him. But I knew in my heart I shouldn't be blaming Bap. It wasn't his fault that these people were in our house, maybe about to wreck it. It really had nothing to do with him. It was his da that was involved in some way. With Uncle Jimmy. And with the Movement. And with the two boyos up in the attic. Bap Kelly was just nosey, always wanting to know what was happening. Now I was annoyed with myself. And feeling a bit guilty, because I knew that Mr Kelly wasn't a bad man. He'd helped us last year to get the house back in shape after a police raid. And it had been Bap who'd told him we needed the help. Aye, I'd just taken it out on Bap when he didn't deserve it. It was the frustration of everything that had made me do it. And I felt even more rotten when I thought that the whole house might be wrecked again inside the next half-hour. This time by the IRA. I'd have to get Liam out before that. Before the whole carry-on sent him gaga.

But first, I ran back into the living room. My ma and the twins were just sitting there, still shocked by everything, and saying nothing.

'Where's my da?' I asked. 'He should be here sortin' all this out. When's he comin' back?'

'I don't know, son. He didn't say.'

But I felt she was lying. She knew something but she wasn't going to tell me.

Her voice was tired. She was a beaten woman. And by the look of the twins, they were the same. Clamming up, too. More secrets.

'I'm takin' Liam out of the house, Ma, down to the air-raid shelter, away from all this.'

'Aye, okay, Dickie. Good boy. Look after wee Liam.' That's all she said. The twins didn't speak.

As I was running up the stairs to get him, I was thinking that it should have been my ma or the twins' job to keep Liam safe. It was their responsibility, not mine. Even now, they couldn't see the danger they were allowing him to be in. Just like the last time, when he nearly went mental altogether. But I knew what was bothering them now. It was this money business. The suitcase of money. And it was bothering me, too. Because it was a mystery. And we were all wondering the same thing. Where was it? Who had it? More bother, I was thinking, just when I'd thought that everything was going to be okay. But for now, I put it to the back of my mind. Before going into the bedroom, I listened from the landing. They were still arguing up in the attic. And Mr Kelly was still trying to settle things down.

I went in and whispered to Liam that we were going back down to the meeting in the air-raid shelter. I stayed calm, because I didn't want to frighten him anymore than he was, or say anything about what might happen next in the house. He followed me right away. Down the stairs and out the front door. On the way to the shelter, I noticed that Bap Kelly was sitting in his da's van, just staring in front of him. And it crossed my mind that the rifles and ammunition were probably in there with him. Liam waved to him, but I didn't bother. What would be the point? The damage was done. Between me and Bap, I mean. Maybe someday we could make it up again, even though we had never been on very friendly terms at the best of times. I felt now that it was better to stay out of his way.

'What's happenin', Dickie?' asked Liam before we reached the air-raid shelter.

My first reaction was to lie to him. To tell him that Mr Kelly and the two men had settled all their differences with my ma and the twins. That everything would be sorted by the time we got back. That our plan was still working well. That there'd be no more trouble in the house. That everything was working out fine. But I couldn't lie to him. Definitely not. Because if we went home in another half an hour or so and the place was wrecked

176

from top to bottom, he would be raging. And he'd never trust me again. So I decided to tell him everything I knew, since he knew most of what I knew anyway. But he didn't know about the missing suitcase of money. So I told him. Otherwise, if I hadn't, he would be wondering what all the fuss was about back there when everything should have been straightforward.

'Where is it, Dickie? The money?'

'I dunno, Liam.'

'Maybe Uncle Jimmy hid it behind the water tank, Dickie. I hide stuff there sometimes.'

'Naw, Liam, they must have searched there. Sure they searched the whole attic.'

'Maybe Uncle Jimmy took it with him and forgot to tell the men that, Dickie.'

'I don't think so, Liam. Uncle Jimmy doesn't forget stuff like that. It's a mystery.'

'Is that what all the shoutin' was about, Dickie? The money?'

'Aye, Liam. But hopefully, Mr Kelly's sortin' things out now.'

'And where's the guns and ammunition?'

'In the van, Liam.'

'Is Bap mindin' them?'

I laughed when he said that.

'Aye, he is, Liam. Bap's mindin' the stuff.'

'He's brave, Dickie. Bap's a brave man.'

Before going into the air-raid shelter, I whispered to Liam to nip out near the end of the meeting to check if Mr Kelly's van had gone. And warn me if it hadn't. I didn't want the gang to be bumping into a whole crowd, maybe an angry crowd, coming out of our house, arguing with each other and then jumping into a van as we were walking home. That would set tongues wagging, and I had enough on my plate without the likes of Danny and Kevin and Eva asking questions. I knew the twin Deeneys would say nothing. They weren't gossiping types. I suppose Eva wasn't, either, but I wouldn't want her to see or hear anything. For different reasons.

When we went back into the air-raid shelter, they were all standing around, laughing and talking. I liked that. This was my gang. And I had control over it.

'Hello, Dickie. Hello, Liam,' shouted the twin Deeneys together as soon as they spotted us coming in. 'Did youse get the decoratin' thing sorted?'

They'd said it together. Weird. Maybe it was something to do with them being identical twins. I stared at them, puzzled for a second, because I didn't realise immediately what they were talking about. But Liam saved the day.

'Aye, Mr Kelly and his workers are goin' to distemper our bedroom. Me and Dickie want it done blue. Isn't that right, Dickie?'

I just nodded, thankful to Liam and hoping that I'd be able to carry on with the meeting for another while. And hopeful, too, by the time we all went back out to the street, that Kelly's van would be gone, and the IRA men in it.

Then Eva piped up. 'Sounds great, Dickie. Maybe I'll ask my ma if they'd allow me to get my bedroom done. I'd like pink distemper. Do you think your painters would do it?'

I just gave her a stupid smile in reply, thinking at the same time how crazy that would be. I could just imagine it: Mr Kelly and two IRA men painting a cop's house. Aye, that was one for the books, all right.

'Dickie,' shouted Danny over the noise, 'everything's arranged as ye asked. Friday at half three for the pictures, then a plate of chips each in Harley's afterwards. And an hour after that, we capture two of the North Street Bunch and electrocute them. Okay?'

'And then,' roared Kevin, his big jamjar glasses glinting in the candlelight, 'on Saturday afternoon, we're goin' to wreck their stupid dam.'

'And don't forget as well,' shouted Joey, not to be outdone by the rest, 'we're all goin' for a skinny-dip at the reservoir after that.'

178

'Aye, at five o'clock,' shouted Eva, 'and we'll meet outside the girls' school at five to.'

When I heard that, about the time we were meeting outside the school, I was very surprised, because it takes well over an hour to get to the Killea reservoir, where we always go. But it struck me right away that they intended for us to go to the wee reservoir behind the school.

'Great,' I shouted over all the noise, 'youse seem to have everything well organised.'

Even though I didn't think they had. But I didn't argue. I had too many other things on my mind. And I was conscious, too, that Liam had already nipped out of the shelter, and was back again in seconds. Nobody but me knew what he was up to. And when he gave me the nod that the van was gone from the street, I winked at him with a grin. I just hoped that the IRA men were gone too.

On the way up the street, I deliberately praised Danny and Kevin for holding the fort and keeping the meeting going while I was away. They were more than pleased. They were beaming with pride.

'Just wan more thing,' I whispered to them casually, without anybody else hearing. 'Did my Uncle Jim . . . Uncle Joe . . .' – I nearly made a big mistake again – 'did my Uncle Joe have a wee brown suitcase with him when he left our house?'

'Naw, he didn't,' said Danny.

'Definitely not,' whispered Kevin, 'because he was swingin' his two arms fast as he walked down the hill. We'd have noticed, Dickie. He had no case on him.'

So that was it, beyond doubt. And if Uncle Jimmy didn't take the money, who did? I'd have to find out, and why. There was nothing else for it. That mystery had to be solved. Because that could be a matter of life and death, too.

As Danny and Kevin ran on up the Terrace after the twin Deeneys and Liam slipped into the house, probably to see what had happened, I was conscious of Eva's footsteps behind me. She called out, 'Dickie, I've blown out the candles and done a quick tidy-up.'

I'd forgotten about her still being in the shelter when we left, probably because of everything that was going on in my mind. She always liked clearing up any mess after the meetings. Nobody ever said thanks to her. Not even me. You sort of expected her to do it. Took it for granted. But not anymore. From now on I would thank her, but it crossed my mind, too, that everybody else, except me, should take their turn to tidy up. I'd organise that at the next meeting. That's what I was thinking anyway when she spoke again.

'It was a great meetin', Dickie. Everything's well organised now.'

'Aye, Eva. Sorry I had to leave early, but it was better to get things sorted out in case the painters would order the wrong colour.'

'I know, Dickie, I know what ye mean.'

She was making me feel bad again. Well, not *her* making me feel bad. But myself. Making me feel bad. About lying to her again. About a stupid painting job that wasn't going to happen. But what could I do? I couldn't tell her the truth.

She was very close to me now as we walked up the street together. I told her that I'd see her up to her door.

'That'll be nice, Dickie.'

She smiled as she spoke and her hand touched mine again. Accidentally, this time. I think. But I still liked it. Touching her hand, I mean. So much so, in fact, that I decided there and then to let my fingers wrap around hers for a wee minute. Then I let go in case people would see us. They might laugh, and I wouldn't like that.

But good and all as I felt as we walked the rest of the way up the Terrace, there was still something I had to find out from Eva. And when I did, I knew it would make me feel bad again because I would be tricking her once more. But I just had to know something, out of curiosity, mind you. I had to know if her da

180

was out of their house last night when Uncle Jimmy called. I knew he must have been, but I had to be sure, because a lot of lies were being told.

'Eva,' I said quietly, 'do ye remember last night, after I left you and Liam?'

'Aye. I was annoyed with you, Dickie, for leavin' me with wee Liam when I could have been doin' something more important.'

'And were ye still annoyed when ye went home, Eva?'

'A wee bit, Dickie.'

'And did your ma or da ask ye why ye were annoyed, Eva?'

'Naw, Dickie, my da was out and she didn't notice, probably because she seemed to be upset herself about something. She looked sad and I think she'd been cryin'. It made me sorta sad, too, lookin' at her like that.'

When Eva was telling me this, I felt like a traitor. A sneak. A creep. There she was, saying stuff about her ma feeling sad, and her feeling sad, and me knowing now why her ma was sad, and her not knowing. I felt worse than a creep but I could do nothing about that right now. I just said cheerio and told her I'd see her tomorrow.

Now I had something else to do before I went home. And that was to slip round to Deeneys' and explain to Joey and Hughie that the important mission I had planned for them was off because I had been able to sort the problem out by myself. But I did say that I would definitely use them again when dangerous stuff came up, and that they were still the deputy leaders of the gang.

They looked a bit disappointed about the mission being cancelled but very pleased about the deputy-leaders thing. In fact, they were all smiles as they waved goodbye to me from their doorstep. But as I was talking to them, it did strike me that this plan with the Deeneys had been a good one, and that the guns and ammunition *would* have been better under the clay in Sergeant McBride's marrow bed instead of in some other boy's attic bedroom. I waved goodbye to them as I headed home.

When I was passing Colhouns' on the way back down the Terrace, I heard Cecil calling me. He was standing in his porch.

'Dickie,' he whispered, 'I saw youse all goin' into the air-raid shelter earlier. Were youse havin' a meetin'?'

'Aye, Cecil, we had a great one. We're goin' to electrocute two of the North Street Bunch on Friday. That's after the pictures, and the chips in Harley's. Then we're goin' to wreck their dam on Saturday, and after that, we're all headin' for a dip at the wee reservoir, the wan behind the girls' school.'

It was all out before I'd time to take another breath. I think it was the excitement of speaking to Cecil like this. It was like old times in the gang. But he didn't say anything at first. And he looked a bit upset. He swallowed a few times before he spoke.

'Dickie, I wish I was back in the gang. I miss youse all.'

He began to sniffle a bit so I broke in.

'Why don't ye ask your ma, Cecil, if she'll let you play with us again? You're badly missed. It hasn't been the same since you and Billy left. The twin Deeneys and Eva are great, but it's not as good as it used to be.'

Cecil seemed to ignore my question, shaking his head slowly from side to side before saying something else.

'And I see wee Liam's in the gang, Dickie. That's great.'

His sniffles got worse. I thought he might cry.

'Aye,' I said. 'He's a bit young, Cecil, but he's brilliant.'

'I know he is,' whispered Cecil. 'He's smart, like you.'

When Cecil said that, I felt a lump coming to my throat. Next to Billy Burnside, Cecil Colhoun had been my best friend – before the IRA shot his da.

'And thanks again for the comics, Cecil. They're great, and Liam loves them.'

When I was speaking, a terrific thought struck me. And it was Liam who had put the idea into my mind in the first place. But as well as that, this could be the opportunity of getting Cecil and Billy back in the gang. Even if it was only for a wee while. And in secret, because if their mas or Billy's da found out, there'd be hell to pay. So before I said cheerio, I put the idea to him, about maybe him and Billy going to the pictures with us. And about going to the dam and the skinny-dipping. I told him everything. The whole plan.

You could see the beam coming over his face. Like the sun coming out from behind a cloud.

'That would be brilliant, Dickie, just brilliant. I'll tell Billy about it all.'

Before I moved off, I told him I'd work something out about meeting up with him and Billy after school tomorrow.

'I'll call up in a wee while when I've worked out the details about where we could meet.'

'That sounds great, Dickie, just great,' he whispered through the porch window. 'I'll be here, waitin'. And, Dickie . . .'

'What, Cecil?'

'I hope I haven't blabbed somethin'.'

'What do ye mean, Cecil? About blabbin' somethin'?'

'It's just that after I saw your Uncle Jimmy goin' into Johnstons' last night, I happened to mention it to my ma. I hope I wasn't blabbin', Dickie. I knew it was him, even with the beard and all.'

My worst fears were realised.

All I could do was stare at him, feeling disbelief but not wanting to show it in case he would stop speaking to me for nearly another year.

My mouth was now telling him, with a false laugh, not to worry, that it wasn't blabbing, that Uncle Jimmy was just visiting an old friend. But my brain was in a whirl. About his ma knowing. And the possible consequences of that.

'Oh, that's okay, then, Dickie,' he said as he turned and went back into the house.

My heart had sunk right down to my stomach, because this was blabbing at its worst. Especially if Cecil's ma happened to mention anything about it. To a cop, for example.

As I walked down the street, all I could do was hope that

she hadn't. And pray that she hadn't. And then put it out of my mind, because there was nothing I could do about it now anyway.

There was a terrible silence in our living room when I got home. My ma and Kate were sitting there in a sort of daze. It wasn't as if they had suddenly stopped talking when I walked through the door the way they did sometimes when they didn't want you to hear what they were saying. Even the wireless was turned off.

'Where's my da?' I asked, more to start a conversation than anything else, because I already guessed that he was still in some 'closed' pub down the town, drinking loads of Guinness.

Nobody answered me. I tried again.

'Did youse get everything sorted, Ma, about the suitcase of money?' I just had to know.

Suddenly, Kate screamed at me, making me nearly jump out of my skin. Everybody else was shocked, too. You could see that from their expressions.

'Shut up. Shut up. Shut up, you stupid, stupid boy. Just shut your mouth and git up them stairs. You should be in your bed anyway at this time of night. And shut up from now on as well about guns and money and everything else that's none of your business. Ye shouldn't be listenin' to grown-ups talkin' anyway. About stuff ye don't understand. Stuff that's got nothin' to do with ye. Just go on up now. Take Liam with ye, too, and get him washed. Look at the state of youse. Youse are a disgrace.'

I knew we were getting no supper made for us this night, because my ma and Laura said absolutely nothing when Kate was screaming at me. They just sat there, staring at the floor as if they'd heard nothing. They were like zombies.

Liam threw down his comic and walked out to the hall to go upstairs. I followed him for a bit, thinking I might get some information from him since he'd been in the house for about ten minutes before me.

'You go up to the bathroom, Liam, and get washed,' I said

quietly. 'I'll be there in a few minutes. I've somethin' to do first.'

He didn't reply, just looked at me sadly and walked slowly up the stairs. He looked knackered.

I went out to the kitchen and made two pieces of bread and jam. That would have to do for our supper. It was better than nothing. By the time I got up to the room, Liam was fast asleep. I didn't waken him. And he still looked a mess. He hadn't even bothered to clean himself. He could do it in the morning, the same as me. I was too knackered as well. It had been another very long day. I ate the two pieces before climbing into bed. I'd been very hungry. Liam must have been starving.

Before I went to sleep, the only things I could think about were Eva Johnston's smile and me touching her fingers on the way up the Terrace this evening. For now, everything else that had been bothering me seemed to go out of my mind.

CHAPTER 21

Can I Join Your Gang, Dickie?

Bap Kelly was watching me closely when I walked into the classroom. Mr Philson was at the board, writing something about the rules of English grammar. It was his pet subject. He always did grammar stuff first thing on Monday mornings. Nearly everybody hated it.

I sat down at my desk, at the same time taking a quick glance to my left, where Bap sat. I gave him a half-smile, nodding friendly, like, just enough to let him know that we were still on speaking terms. Of sorts. I knew by the look on his face that something was up, and I intended to find out what at lunch time. It was probably to do with what happened in our house last night. But it would have to keep for now.

As Philson rambled on, with his back to us, about singular and plural nouns, my thoughts began to drift to more important things. Like what happened before me and Liam went to bed.

And then there was this morning. The twins out in the kitchen, with shocked faces, washing up last night's dinner dishes, and my ma still in a daze, saying nothing. She seemed so caught up in her thoughts that she didn't even answer me when I asked her why the girls hadn't gone to work and if my da was okay. She just handed me and Liam a cup of tea and a slice of dry toast each without even looking at us.

But all this hadn't distracted me from checking up on a couple of things before we went to school. The first thing I did was to slip up to the attic. I expected the place to be wrecked, but it wasn't. On the way down, I'd juked into my ma and da's room. Da wasn't there, so I assumed that he'd gone to work at the docks. And I remember feeling relieved that the guns and ammunition were gone, even if the mystery of the missing suitcase of money hadn't been solved yet. But the fact that the house hadn't been wrecked looking for it was a good thing. Mr Kelly must have persuaded the two IRA men that Uncle Jimmy had made a mistake, that he'd already taken the money with him and forgot to mention it. But then again, if that was the case, why were my ma and the twins in such a state of shock? Naw, something else must have happened. Maybe my ma and the twins were threatened.

That's when I remembered what Danny and Kevin had told me. That Uncle Jimmy had no suitcase with him when they followed him. Could that be it? Were my ma and the twins being accused of taking the money and hiding it somewhere? Naw, they couldn't be that stupid. But still, why were they in such a state of shock? It didn't make sense. But something did begin to make a bit of sense when me and Liam were going into school this morning. It was when we were running up the corridor that Liam tugged me by the sleeve and whispered a question to me.

'Dickie, why did my da not come home last night?'

I couldn't answer, but he'd left me standing there dazed, because a mad notion had begun to rush through my mind. And the notion was that my da had the suitcase of money. And my ma and the twins knew that. And they didn't blab. But the IRA men and Mr Kelly must have asked where my da was. And when they couldn't tell them exactly where he was – in some pub downtown, they might have said – that's maybe when they made their threats. That's what I was thinking right now. And I was very far from happy. The more I thought about it, the more shocked I felt. No wonder my ma and the twins were in the state they were in. It all made sense now. But then again, when I really did think about it some more, and knowing my da, I mean, it didn't make any sense at all. Not to me anyhow. Because I knew my da better than that, and there was no way he could do such a thing. Surely not. Maybe at lunch time Bap Kelly would tell me something that would clue me in.

In the playground, me and Liam played marbles. I didn't want to tell him yet about my worries, in case I'd upset him. If need be, I'd tell him everything later, when I found out more. My ma hadn't given us any food to bring with us this morning. We were starving. Within a couple of minutes, Kevin and Danny sauntered over to us. They didn't say anything about us not having a lunch or that they had spare food, but they knew we hadn't eaten anything. They just talked about the great meeting last night and that they were looking forward to the pictures on Friday. After a while, when they had eaten what they wanted from their own lunches, they asked us if we'd like a piece of bread. Danny also offered us a bit of extra cake that he didn't want. We tried not to look too eager. If you look too eager at times like this, you can let yourself down. And Liam knew not to gobble the food as well. We didn't want to appear like gulpens. We even ate Danny's ma's cake. It was rotten, but beggars can't be choosers.

I noticed all the time we'd been eating that Bap Kelly was standing just a few feet away from us. He didn't come over, but I knew by his face that he wanted to talk to me. And because I wanted to talk to him, I made the excuse that I had to go to the toilet. I walked slowly to the far side of the playground, Bap following. None of the others appeared to notice.

'Right, Bap, what's the story?' I asked him when I reached the playground wall.

'What story, Dickie?'

I knew he was being crafty, and cagey. He didn't want to give anything away that he didn't have to. He wanted me to ask the right questions. I knew that but I didn't like it.

'Okay, Bap,' I said, 'if that's the way you want to play it. But you remember this: if you don't tell me what I have to know, then don't ever come to me or the gang if you need help. And remember, you won't be blabbin' if you tell *me* things. You know that, Bap.'

I could see his good eye glinting as I spoke. He was thinking about what I'd said. And thinking very hard. I knew by looking at him that he knew things.

'Right, Dickie,' he said. 'You just ask the questions, and if I know the answers, I'll tell ye.'

'Okay,' I said. 'First of all, did the two IRA men threaten my ma or the twins in any way?'

'I think they might have, Dickie, because when they came out to the van, wan of them said, "That letter from Barney Mc-Cauley could be a fake."'

'What letter was that, Bap?' I asked quickly. 'What's that about a letter?'

'I dunno, Dickie. It must have been somethin' about a letter they found in your house.'

'What else did he say, Bap?'

'He said, "She's a crafty wan, that oul' doll. She could have written that letter herself and left it there for us to find. To put us off the scent."'

I deliberately didn't look worried when he was telling me all this. But I was.

'Is that it, Bap? Is that everything?'

'That's all he said, Dickie. But I don't know what was in the letter. Oh, and the other boyo said something about your ma knowin' the score now, so she'd better watch out if lies were bein' told. That sounded like a threat to me, Dickie.'

It sounded like a threat to me, too, a serious one, because I'd often heard about people like this settling scores. I was badly shocked at what I was hearing, even though it just confirmed what I'd already guessed. That my ma knew a lot more than she was letting on. And I would love to know what was in the letter that my da was supposed to have left. It had me worried.

'Did they say anything else, Bap?'

I tried to keep a calm face on me as he began to speak again.

'All I know, Dickie, is that when they came out of your house, they were in a very bad temper. My da tried to calm them down, but they were very, very annoyed. When they did settle, they told him to drive to some safe house where they thought your Uncle Jimmy might be. They left me home first and then drove off, but I don't know where they went after that. And I don't know where the safe house is. That's all I can tell ye, Dickie. Honest.'

'Right, Bap,' I said quickly. 'There's just wan more question. Did anything else come up in your house about my da, about maybe where he might be? I'm askin' because he didn't come home last night. And we're very worried about him.'

'Naw, Dickie. His name wasn't mentioned again, not while I was there anyway. But if I hear anything about him, I'll let ye know right away.'

I didn't say thanks to him for the information. He owed it to me for things I'd done for him in the past, and maybe for things I might do for him in the future. And he knew it, because he wasn't long in asking me for a favour before I went back over to the boys.

'Dickie . . .'

'Aye, what is it, Bap?'

'Can I join your gang? I'd love to be in your gang, Dickie.'

Well, this was a turn-up for the books. And not what I had expected.

'I'll see, Bap,' I said as casually as I could. 'I'll think about it.'

With that, I walked away from him and across the playground.

I couldn't settle when we went back in after lunch time. How could you when you were sick with worry about your da, and when you knew that the rest of the family were still in grave danger? And especially after I'd thought that we were in the clear. With Uncle Jimmy out of the house, I mean. And with the rifles and ammunition away, too. Everything was supposed to be straightforward from here on in. But by the looks of things, we were as far back as ever. Maybe even further than I thought. This whole missing-money business, and Cecil blabbing to his ma, had really set the cat among the pigeons, and no matter how much I thought about it all, I knew in my heart that there was nothing I could now do to sort things out. I was at a complete loss. This was way out of my league. And I was getting a very bad headache even thinking about it. If only I had . . .

'So, McCauley, is this really true, or have I just woken up from the worst nightmare imaginable? Fill us in, McCauley. A nightmare or a joke? Or both?'

I could hear some laughter from around the class as Mr Philson spoke. But not too much. Probably just from people who didn't like me, or who wanted to see me in trouble, or who were sucking up to Philson. But because I hadn't been listening to what he'd been saying, I hadn't a clue now what he was on about. But he kept on and on in that droning, sarcastic voice that he always uses when he thinks he has me cornered.

'Is it true or not, McCauley?' he went on. 'Put us out of our misery. Go on, please. Please, *Mister* McCauley.' He always called me Mister when he was being nasty. Like the priest at the College did.

I looked up at his sneering face. I still hadn't a clue what he'd been talking about but I didn't put on a puzzled look. I didn't want to give him the satisfaction of knowing that I hadn't been listening. I wracked my brains for some clue, maybe a word or two that I'd overheard and hadn't taken in. Naw, nothing was coming. He had me over a barrel. Now he'd try to be even more sarcastic.

But that's when I noticed he had something in his hand. A black book. It didn't look familiar. And he was waving it about as he was speaking. At first, I couldn't make out what book it was or what was written on the front cover. If only he'd stop moving it, I might see the title.

Some people were still laughing as Philson kept goading me to answer. I knew I had to do something or say something. And

191

soon. I couldn't sit here like a gawk for the rest of my life. I looked again at his face. At his sneer. Watch him, I thought. That's what my da had always advised me about Philson, 'Watch that boy, Dickie.' So I watched him.

'Sir,' I called out, for an idea had hit me. And it worked. He stopped moving at my shout. That should give me enough time, I was thinking, to read the gold lettering on the front cover of the book. I peered at it, squinting my eyes to focus on it properly. He didn't notice. He was still too intent on goading me further.

'Well, McCauley,' he sneered, 'I'm waiting on an answer. The whole class is waiting on an answer. The whole of Derry wants to know your answer. Maybe even the whole world, McCauley.'

More laughter. He was milking it and he was enjoying his moment. So I needed to do some milking myself. If only to shut him up. This was only a small-time predicament that I was in, and one that was easily solved. I wished for a second that the problems at home could be sorted out with as little difficulty.

I looked again at the title on the book. *Mass Responses For Altar Servers*, it said in gold lettering. Now I knew what he was at. I stood up. I was ready.

'Yes, Sir,' I said as if I was the calmest person in the room. 'Yes, Sir, it's true. I would like to be an altar boy. I think it would be a great privilege, Sir, and an honour. Were you an altar boy when you were wee, Sir?'

Philson's sarcastic look suddenly changed to annoyance. I could see it in his eyes. But I was now determined to make him a lot more annoyed before I was finished with him. Nobody was laughing now. They were waiting. Sensing a contest. Philson versus McCauley. It had happened before. Many times. And Philson hadn't won yet.

'I asked you a question, McCauley. Is this a nightmare or a joke? That's what I'm asking you. You . . . you . . . you . . . you . . . McCauley, an altar server?' he stammered. 'Don't make me laugh! No. No, McCauley, don't make me cry. Please.'

Philson's face was getting redder by the second and his eyes were beginning to bulge. That's the way I liked him. Flustered. I knew I had him.

'You . . . you, McCauley,' he repeated, 'having the nerve, the audacity to think that you would be a suitable person to don an altar server's soutane . . . and assist the priest at Holy Mass.'

Now the class was totally hushed. They knew that the battle had commenced. And I liked it, because it was taking my mind off the more serious problems that I had. Philson droned on.

'In the Cathedral, McCauley, in front of hundreds of people?'

Spittles were dribbling from either side of Philson's mouth.

'I couldn't bear it, McCauley, not even for a second could I bear it, looking up at you on that altar . . . and knowing you the way I do . . . you rude, insolent boy. How dare you put yourself forward for such an honourable position. Shame on you, you brat, for attempting to degrade such a worthy vocation. You're nothing but a—'

'But, Sir,' I interrupted with all the innocence I could put into my voice and my face. 'Sir, I didn't put myself forward to be an altar boy. Honest, Sir, I didn't . . .'

Philson began to breathe very heavily as he stared down at me in disbelief, his eyes searching mine for some sort of an answer. But I was giving nothing away. Not just yet. And I still had no intention of letting him off lightly, even though it had crossed my mind seconds ago to let this all drop. Because of our Liam. I mean, Liam would be in his class next year, and the year after that, and I didn't like the idea of Philson badgering him week after week the way he had done with me. But naw, I wouldn't let it drop. Because our Liam would have no problem dealing with Philson. Liam was smart. He'd be able to deal with him when the time came.

'What do you mean, McCauley, you didn't put yourself forward, when I have it here in black and white in this letter from Father Mooney that you have? Along with Timothy and John and Francis, with your name as the fourth candidate. How can you sit there and tell me that you didn't approach the priest and put your name down the same as the other three boys? You're nothing but a liar, McCauley, an impertinent brat and an utter disgrace. That's what you are, McCauley.'

'But, Sir,' I replied with a false look of hurt and innocence, 'I didn't put my name down. It was the priest that put my name down without me asking. It happened at the Parochial House. I was there on Saturday morning, Sir. Father Mooney was arranging for me to get a lift in his car to the College. To the meetin', Sir. The meetin' about timetables, and subjects, and uniforms and seein' round the place, Sir. For parents and children, Sir.'

Philson went dead quiet and his eyes were bulging even more. He couldn't believe what he was hearing. And he couldn't even speak. You could have heard a pin drop in the room. It was sickening him. That's when I decided to prolong his agony.

'But it wasn't Father Mooney who gave me the lift to the College, Sir. It was Father Donohue, the new priest. He's very nice, Sir. And he took me up there in Father Mooney's car. To the meetin', Sir. And he put my bike in his boot. I mean, the bike that Bap Kelly . . . Charlie Kelly gave me. The one that needs fixed. And I'm goin' to get it seen to before September. And then I can use it to go to the College. And save on bus fares.'

I looked around the classroom as I was speaking. Most of the boys were grinning from ear to ear.

Philson exploded.

'Shut up, McCauley. Shut up, you brat. You impudent brat. I know your game.'

'What game, Sir? There's no game, Sir. And I was goin' to tell you about the bishop, Sir, but I got carried away talkin' about the kindness of Father Mooney and Father Donohue.'

I'd just at this minute decided to throw in a lie about the bishop in the whole saga, because I knew it would flummox Philson altogether. And it appeared to be working, for he suddenly blurted out hoarsely, 'What's this about the bishop? What are you talking about now, McCauley?'

'Oh, yes, Sir. It was when Father Mooney was arrangin' with Father Donohue to give me the lift. That's when the bishop came out the door of the Parochial House, Sir.'

Philson didn't speak. But I continued. I was enjoying myself now.

'Father Mooney introduced me to the bishop and told him that I'd got the scholarship to the College. The bishop congratulated me, Sir, and said that I'd make a fine altar boy. And that's when Father Mooney asked me again to become an altar boy. The bishop smiled, Sir, when he heard him asking me.'

Philson was breathing fast, his eyeballs staring at me.

'What do you mean by *again*, McCauley?'

'Oh, aye, Sir. Did I not tell ye, Mr Philson?'

'Tell me what?'

'Father Mooney had already asked me to be an altar boy the day after I got word about the scholarship. And he gave me sixpence for passing, Sir. But it was on Saturday morning last that he told me that he'd be lettin' you know on Monday, Mr Philson, that I'd be a candidate as well. And I'm really looking forward to you teaching me the Latin responses.'

Philson left the room without saying anything. He couldn't speak. That's because he was coughing and spluttering so much. The class were enjoying this. So was I, but I knew there'd be hell to pay later.

Chapter 22

A Sudden Chill Down My Spine

When me and Liam got home from school, the twins were in the house, listening to the wireless. My ma was in the kitchen. Something was definitely up. I'd say nothing and ask no questions. That way, they wouldn't shout at me, and I'd probably learn things as the rest of the day went on. There was still no sign of my da. My ma gave us a piece and a cup of tea each. She said nothing, either. After we'd eaten, we went upstairs to the bedroom and talked for five minutes about what we should do. Then Liam started his homework. I sat reading a comic while he worked away at his books for about half an hour. When we were both finished, we went downstairs again, hoping that we might hear something important about our da. Things didn't look good. There was a terrible atmosphere in the house. My ma and the twins must know something. The three of them looked as if they had been whispering stuff together, but when we appeared, they just clammed up. Aye, something was definitely up. So we put the wee plan we had hatched into action. And it was a good one.

Liam would sit at the table with a bunch of comics and stay there all evening if need be. After a while, they mightn't even notice he was in the room and begin to talk among themselves again. Liam would take a mental note of what was being said and repeat it all to me later. In the meantime, I would make myself scarce and carry out a mission of my own, which I would tell Liam about later. And he'd be delighted. As would the other members of the gang when they heard.

I ran on down the Terrace into Warke's Lane and through the wee gate into Brooke Park. I felt really excited, because for the first time in nearly a year, I'd hopefully be meeting up with Billy Burnside and Cecil Colhoun together. I'd been able to arrange it last night with Cecil. The plan was that the three of us would meet at the statue of the Black Man at the bottom of the park after school at four o'clock. I quickened my pace in the last hundred yards or so because I heard the Guildhall clock striking the hour. But when I arrived, there was no sign of anybody.

I sat down on the grass beneath the statue and waited. When I heard the clock in the distance striking a quarter past, I rose slowly and began to head back to Rosemount.

Now I felt really sad, because I'd been looking forward to meeting my two old friends again. Cecil mustn't have been able to arrange it. Maybe his ma had found out about our plan, or maybe Billy wasn't interested anymore.

I wasn't twenty feet away from the Black Man when I heard the shout.

'Dickie, Dickie.'

My heart leapt for joy at the sound of the familiar voice. It was Billy roaring at me. Both of them came running up the path towards me, their schoolbags flying all over the place. When they reached me they were out of breath.

'What kept youse?' I said as if I was annoyed.

They both stared at me and then burst out laughing. I did the same.

'Nothin' changes, Dickie McCauley,' said Billy, grinning as he threw his schoolbag to the ground. 'Still as bossy as ever, I see.'

'Didn't I tell ye that,' screeched Cecil, delight in his voice, 'sure hasn't he half of Rosemount scared out of their wits?'

'And it used to be the whole of Rosemount,' laughed Billy.

Within fifteen minutes, it was as if the ten months since the break-up had passed in a flash. Here we were now in Brooke

Park on a warm summer's day, talking together like we used to. It was as if Billy Burnside was still the same Billy Burnside and still lived in the Terrace beside us. As if his da, the cop, hadn't been the bad man that he was. It was as if Cecil Colhoun hadn't been forced to hide away from the rest of the gang, in his own house, in our own street. It was as if *his* da, the B-Special, hadn't been shot dead by people that I knew. And as we stood there and talked and laughed together, it was as if we'd never been apart. For there was no mention of the things that had separated us.

'So what's happenin', Dickie?' asked Billy when the excitement had died down. 'Cecil was fillin' me in about your new gang members, especially about somebody called Eva Johnston.' And he laughed when he said that.

'Aye,' said Cecil with the eagerness in his voice that you always heard when we used to plan missions together, 'and about the plans ye have, Dickie. I told Billy what ye told me about the pictures and all, about the electrocutions and the attack on the dam, then the swim in the reservoir. It sounds brilliant, Dickie.'

It was great listening to them. Hearing their voices again and watching their faces light up. But I wasn't stupid. I knew that things could never be the same as they were. There was no way that Cecil's ma would allow him out to play with us again. And there was no way that Billy Burnside would trek a mile or more to Rosemount on a regular basis when we had something coming up. Naw, there was no turning back the clock. But at least we could make a good weekend of it.

'Right, Cecil,' I said when their excitement had died down a bit more, 'it looks as if you have filled Billy in on everything. And if both of youse are game, then we're back in business.'

'I'm game,' shouted Billy. 'I wouldn't miss out on this for anything.'

'And so am I,' said Cecil, laughing, 'if I can arrange for Danny's ma to keep my ma talkin' long enough to keep her eye off me. All coddin' aside, Dickie, I'm in, too . . . I'll work it, some way.'

'So okay then,' I said to both of them before we broke up. 'For a start, if youse are free on Friday after school, it's everybody to the pictures, then chips afterwards in Harley's. My treat if youse want to come. We're meetin' at the top of William Street, at the billboards, at half three. I'll give you the details then of what's going to be happenin' on Saturday.'

Their eyes were standing out in their heads. I didn't tell them that it was Liam's idea to ask them in the first place.

'Great,' said Billy. 'If I can make it, I'll be there.'

'Same here,' said Cecil excitedly.

'Right, Dickie, right Cecil, I'm away. See youse all on Friday. Except you, Cecil, I'll see you at school in the mornin'.'

And Billy laughed as he left, running down the path towards the park gate into Infirmary Road. He waved as he looked back before disappearing round the corner at Christ Church. It lifted my heart when I saw him waving like that, because it wasn't a 'goodbye forever' kind of wave. It was a 'see you soon' kind of wave.

'Let's go,' I said to Cecil. We turned and made our way up the park towards Rosemount. As we walked we couldn't stop chattering. We had a lot to make up, but when we reached the top gate, at Warke's Lane, Cecil asked me if he could go on ahead. I knew why right away. He didn't want his ma to see him with me. He didn't have to say it. And I understood. Getting friendly with Cecil again was a lot easier than getting friendly with his ma.

But before he went through the gateway, he said something to me that sent a sudden chill down my spine and a knife through my heart. His words struck me dumb. Rooted me to the spot. And as he spoke, I had to pretend somehow that I was aware of what he was on about. For if I appeared shocked, even a bit surprised, Cecil would know immediately that something wasn't just right. And there was no way I would let myself do that. It would be like giving myself away. Or blabbing.

'Billy was tellin' me,' he remarked casually, 'about your da, Dickie. I hadn't heard it myself until he told me the day. My ma mustn't have heard, either, or she would have said somethin'. Is it work he's away for?'

I nodded automatically, dreading what he was going to say next.

'Aye, it's a pity he had to go, Dickie, but maybe he'll get a good job over there.'

I still couldn't say anything, for there was now a terrible fear on me. But I kept trying my best not to let it show. I felt myself going numb. And there was worse to come.

'Billy was sayin', Dickie, that his da saw your da yesterday evenin' gettin' on the cattle boat at the docks. The Liverpool boat. And him with just a canvas bag on his back and carryin' a wee brown suitcase. I hope he gets over safely, Dickie, what with Hitler and the war and all. See you on Friday, Dickie, if not before that.'

I was glad that Cecil walked away just then, because I felt like screaming, and I could hardly hold it in. My head was spinning and I felt sick. My body began to shake and I wasn't able to control it. Cecil's words kept repeating themselves inside my head. Over and over again. About my da stepping onto the Liverpool cattle boat with a canvas bag over his back and carrying a wee brown suitcase. In those few seconds, I felt as if my world was falling apart, that any control I had over it was gone. That there was no way back from this one.

I suddenly took flight. Across the park I ran, howling like an animal. I had no idea where I was going, where I was running to. It just happened. As if it was the right thing to do, to get away from what I'd just heard. That my da had run away and left us. Left me and Liam, and my ma, and the twins. Away to another country. Suddenly, it felt as if he was dead, like Cecil's da, and Danny's da, and like some of the das of the boys in my class who died of TB. And that I'd never see him again.

That's when the screaming stopped and the retching and the vomiting started. And the anguish and the pain of it all overcame me. And when that had passed, I threw myself down on the grass and sobbed until I was sick again. And I didn't care if anybody saw me, or heard me. I was past caring.

I don't know how long I lay there, but when the sobbing got less and the words of Cecil came to the front of my mind again and again, I tried to think it all through. And as the impact of what Cecil had told me began to sink in properly, when it was dawning on me what had happened, and what could now happen, I just wondered in another blind panic how we were all going to cope. When this came out. About my da. And about the suitcase of money. This wasn't something that could be kept secret.

Now I was angry. And disgusted, and I hated my da. And I hated my ma, too, because she must have known something about it. And the twins as well. So that's what all the big faces were about in our house before I left. Then I thought of wee Liam, back there now in the living room, pretending to read comics, but really, on orders from me, to pick up any scraps of information he might hear from my ma and Kate and Laura.

I got up from the grass, brushed myself down a bit, and wiped my mouth with my sleeve. I could feel a cold sweat on my forehead which I hadn't realised was there. Slowly, I began to walk home. I had a lot of thinking to do. Especially about how the McCauleys were going to get out of this one. And how we would all cope now. Because this was worse than my da dying and leaving us all behind to fend for ourselves. This was my da who'd skedaddled with a suitcase full of dosh. This was my da who had now left us all in the lurch to face the consequences of what he'd done. My stomach wasn't churning anymore, but my anger was rising very quickly as I went through the park gate, up Warke's Lane, and into Rosemount Terrace. I tried to calm myself but I couldn't. I wanted to walk into the house as usual, quietly, and see the twins sitting there, talking, and laughing. I wanted to see my ma out in the kitchen, baking a scone, with Liam helping her, and flour all over his face. And I wanted them all to tell me when I asked them that Cecil Colhoun was talking rubbish about my da going away on the Liverpool boat and that he'd soon be home from the pub.

But I didn't go into the house quietly. I burst in, shouting and roaring, and banged the glass door shut behind me. I rushed towards the living room, smashing the door open with my foot. I was breathing faster now and my heart was racing as I went in, screeching. But I was screeching to an empty room. And I was screeching to an empty house. And it frightened me. For I immediately felt a terrible loneliness. And I cried out to God to help us. To help all the McCauleys.

***

The six o'clock Angelus bells were ringing when I turned at the Cathedral gate. I must have run the whole way down the hill from Rosemount. Not must. I had. It was weird. I was still sobbing and whimpering and I couldn't stop, even though I tried. I was inside the chapel, walking very fast up the middle aisle. I stopped at the altar rail and put my hot, sweaty forehead down on the cold marble. It made me feel a bit better. But not much.

'Please God,' I said out loud as I lifted my head, 'please God, help me. Help my da and my ma, and Kate and Laura, and Liam, and even Uncle Jimmy. Keep us all safe, God, please.'

'Richard, is that you, Richard?'

I heard the voice behind me but I didn't turn round, even though I knew it was Father Mooney. I just closed my eyes and kept praying into myself.

'Richard, are you all right?'

I then turned slowly and stared up at the face of the priest. I knew I must have looked a sight, but I didn't care. And I didn't want to answer him.

'What happened, son? Is your mammy all right? Is your daddy all right?'

Without saying anything, I got up from my knees and ran down the aisle. I couldn't talk. I had no words for the torment flying around inside my skull. If I'd answered the priest's questions,

I would have blurted everything out. And I didn't want to. Because I would have been telling him stuff that I might regret later.

When I got outside the chapel grounds, I walked on up Creggan Street, wiping my face with my coat sleeve. But I knew it would be harder to wipe away the memory of how I had reacted in the park after Cecil told me about my da, or in the house afterwards, but especially in the Cathedral. No coat sleeve could do that. Luckily, no-one had seen me or heard me in the park, or in the house, but I was thinking now, just because I was feeling calmer, that I'd definitely let myself down in the Cathedral. And in front of Father Mooney, too. But if I was going to let myself down in front of anybody, Father Mooney would have been the one, and the least of my worries, because he understands things like that better than anybody else.

CHAPTER 23

All I Could Do Was Own Up

I was in a much better state of mind, but still annoyed, when I reached the house. They were all back. My ma in the kitchen as usual and the twins in the living room. Liam was probably upstairs.

'Where were youse all a while ago?' I shouted. 'Nobody was in when I got home.'

Kate glared at me as if I had two heads but said nothing. She looked worn out, and worried. And scared looking.

'We were out searchin' for Uncle Jimmy,' said Laura. 'We have to find him. And we're goin' out again later.'

'I know where my da is,' I shouted, angry at them for being more concerned about where Uncle Jimmy might be. 'He's on a boat to Liverpool, and he went last night.'

They didn't act surprised; they knew. Now I was angry again. And my face showed it.

'Shut up, Dickie,' shouted Kate, 'and listen. We were looking for Jimmy because of the way he left the house, with the IRA men lookin' for him and all. We're very worried, Dickie. We have to find him.'

I wasn't listening. I didn't care about Uncle Jimmy. He could look after himself.

'Did youse not hear me?' I shouted again, getting angrier by the second, because I knew now that they'd known already where my da was, and they hadn't told me. More secrets. They sickened me. But I knew everything now, and I was going to let them know the rest as well. Aye, they'd be the ones who'd be badly shocked after this.

'And he took the brown suitcase with him,' I roared, 'and the money, and we'll never see him again.'

I began to cry and wail again. I couldn't hold it in because the words of Cecil Colhoun were still running around in my skull.

'Oh, dear Jesus, oh my God.'

It was my ma who was now crying as she walked in from the kitchen. I turned to her as she came towards me, her arms out to hug me. But I wasn't listening, and I didn't want her hugs. I pushed her away, shouting out that my da was more important than stupid Uncle Jimmy.

'Why didn't youse stop my da goin'? I would have stopped him.'

'Oh, Dickie, we should have told ye at the time, but we just couldn't. I was waitin' for the right minute. There was nothin' we could do about it, son. He was set on leavin'. You're right about him gettin' on the cattle boat to Liverpool. And, please God, the Germans don't get him. There was no stoppin' him, Dickie. He said that things were gettin' him badly down here and he had to get away. Maybe it was me, son, that pushed him too far, with the things I've been sayin' to him and all. Oh, God, Dickie, I'm sorry.'

'But he stole the money, Ma. The IRA money, in the brown suitcase. How could he do that, Ma?' I cried out as I turned away. I didn't want to look at her. 'Big Burnside saw him gettin' on the boat with the suitcase. Cecil Colhoun told me.'

'Oh, dear, dear God,' sighed my ma, taking a big deep breath. 'I'm glad your da's not here to listen to ye, Dickie. He might be a lot of things, your da, son, but he's not a thief. No way did he take that money. Sure it was your uncle that took it with him before he left. And he must've had good reason for takin' it. There'll be some explanation. You'll see. He probably just emptied the suitcase and stuffed the notes into his pockets. For

205

handiness. Your da just borrowed the empty case, son, that's all. I didn't know about any of this until I saw the letter he left. The IRA men saw the letter before me. I should have told you, Dickie. I'm sorry, son.'

For a minute I was speechless. I glared at Kate and Laura. They knew about this, too. If only somebody had told me earlier, it would have saved me a lot of grief. And anger.

Before I knew it, my ma was hugging me. But she had a terrible fear in her eyes. Okay, so Uncle Jimmy had scarpered with the money. For whatever reason. Well, good luck to him, for all I cared. But I still felt very sad, and afraid, at the thought of my da going away on an old cattle boat to Liverpool.

***

When the dinner was over and the dishes were cleared, I sat in my da's big armchair, listening to the music on the wireless, even though I was still feeling guilty about even thinking that my da could have taken the suitcase of money. I kept saying sorry to him over and over again under my breath. I was looking down at the floor and closing my eyes tight now to try and shut out bad memories. But it was hard, because everything that had been happening kept flooding back.

I heard a cough. I looked up and couldn't believe it, because there was Father Mooney standing in front of me, my ma beside him. I hadn't heard them coming into the room and it gave me a bit of a start. I jumped off the chair and stood up, stammering, 'Hello, Father . . . Hello, Father . . . I didn't see you there for a minute.'

'Lost in thought, eh, Richard?' he said with a big smile. 'And how are things with you?'

'I'll get you a wee cup of tea, Father,' said my ma as she left to go out to the kitchen. The twins must have been out there, because you could hear dishes rattling. And Liam must be upstairs.

'And, Dickie,' my ma continued before she closed the door behind her, 'turn that wireless off, will ye, son?'

'I'm okay now, Father,' I told him as I flicked off the electric switch. 'I'm sorry about runnin' out of the chapel the way I did. I was very upset at the time, Father. I was very annoyed about somethin'. I'm sorry, Father. I shouldn't have run off like that without speakin' to ye.'

I knew by the way the priest was looking at me that he wanted me to tell him why I'd been so upset in the Cathedral. Probably that's why he was here now, to check on me. You could see the concern on his face. Father Mooney was very good like that. Always thinking of other people. So I just went on to explain. 'I was very, very annoyed, Father, because I'd just heard that my da had gone away in the cattle boat to Liverpool, and I didn't know he was goin'. Nobody told me. He's away to try and get work, Father, because there's not much here for him.'

I didn't tell the priest that I'd been shouting and sobbing, and cursing my da up and down.

'Everybody gets upset when a loved one leaves home, Richard, but, please God, the war will be over soon and he'll get more work here in Derry then.'

'Yes, Father,' I said, hoping that he wouldn't talk about it anymore, because I was beginning to feel rotten again.

'There's just something else has come up, Richard, that I wanted to ask you about as well.'

I looked at him, my heart sinking, because I knew that what he had to say wouldn't be good. I put on an innocent kind of face, just in case.

'It concerns you and Mr Philson . . .'

Now my heart sank completely, to the bottom of my stomach.

'About what you said to him today, in school. Something about the bishop saying that you'd be a fine altar boy.'

As my heart hit the bottom of my stomach with a dirty big thump, all I could think of was Philson running down to the Cathedral after school to blab to Father Mooney, with spittles flying out of him.

'This was not true, as you know, Richard, and you may have had your own reasons for saying such a preposterous thing, but it is after all, tantamount to a lie. And for obvious reasons, Mr Philson was most upset by the whole episode. Wondering why the bishop would be involved, in any way, in your selection as a candidate for the altar. I have to tell you now, Richard, that he was even more upset with you when I informed him that the bishop was not involved at all.'

There was no way of escaping this. I couldn't talk my way out of it, and I couldn't very well say to Father Mooney that Mr Philson was nothing but a big nose-picker, and that he was forever taking delight in annoying most of the people in our class – mostly me. All I could do was own up. To admit that it had been a poor joke and that I was sorry. Except the part about being sorry. If I told the priest I was sorry, I'd be telling a lie. And you don't lie to priests.

'It was just a wee joke, Father,' I said, 'to get Mr Philson goin' the way he gets us goin' sometimes in the class. He says stuff about some boys that make other people laugh, even when it's not funny, and the boys he makes fun of don't laugh, Father, because they don't think it's funny. Do you know what I mean, Father? They don't think it's fair what he says!'

In other words, Father Mooney, Philson is nothin' but a sarcastic nose-pickin' bully, and a hypocrite.

And as I was thinking this, I was hoping that he couldn't read my mind.

'I think I know what you mean, Richard,' said the priest. And as he spoke again, I could see a twinkle in his eye. 'We'll leave it at that now, son. But I expect you'll sort all this out with Mr Philson first thing when you go to school tomorrow. One way or the other.'

'Yes, Father, I will,' I said, breathing a sigh of relief that this subject, at least for now, was over.

'And, Richard . . .'

'Yes, Father?'

'Maybe I'll get a wee run up to the school in the morning as well. Just to make sure that everything will be okay between you and Mr Philson.'

Oh God, I thought, I'm really in big trouble now.

But all I could say was, 'Thanks, Father . . . And, Father,' I blurted out, just wanting to get away from the subject quickly, 'thanks again for gettin' the President of the College to change things around for me last Saturday. Only for you, Father, I would have missed the meetin'.'

'I was glad to help, Richard, even if the whole episode was most unorthodox. And I hope that your years at the College will prove that everybody's unusual efforts on your behalf were not in vain.'

I wasn't totally sure what he was on about, but I nodded to him with a big smile on my face.

That's when my ma came in with a cup of tea and a biscuit for Father Mooney. I noticed there was nothing for me.

'Thank you, thank you so much, Mrs McCauley,' he said. 'I was just having a wee chat with Richard, here. He seemed a bit upset about his father leaving for England. I'm sure it's not easy for you, either, Mrs McCauley, and for the rest of your family, for that matter, but, please God, Mr McCauley will arrive safely and find work.'

My ma looked at me for a split second. I could see by her face that she was a bit worried that I might have blabbed stuff to the priest. About the suitcase and the money and about Uncle Jimmy disappearing.

'Aye, Father,' she said quickly, looking away from me, 'poor Barney wasn't havin' much luck with the work in Derry. He's a hard goer, Father, and he gets frustrated with havin' so little to do.'

After that comment of my ma's, I had to get out of the room as fast as I could before I exploded. Even Father Mooney began to choke on his biscuit and cough to keep himself from laughing, because he knew my da well, and what he got up to in the Guinness department.

I muttered a quick goodbye to the priest and said to my ma that I was going upstairs to Liam. Although that was an excuse to get away quick, I really did have to see Liam, because there were a couple of questions I had to ask him.

When I got to the bedroom, Liam looked up from his comic as I walked in.

'You look a mess, Dickie. Are ye all right?'

'Aye, Liam, I had a bit of bother earlier but I'm okay now.'

'Who with, Dickie?'

'It doesn't matter, Liam, it's all sorted. But have ye anything to report to me?'

'What about, Dickie?'

I stared at him, annoyed at first, then amazed. You would have thought that he'd be dying to tell me all the news about what he'd overheard from my ma and Kate and Laura earlier in the living room. That's what I'd asked him to do. A simple request.

'What about? What about?' I mimicked, frustrated with him.

'You should see your face, Dickie. You look a sight,' he laughed. 'Of course I have news for ye, I'm just kiddin' ye,' he went on, laughing.

All I could do was laugh with him.

'Okay, Dickie,' he said when we'd settled down. 'The first thing is, after you left, nobody said anything for a good while, but when my ma began to sob and cry about Uncle Jimmy, Kate and Laura said to her that the best thing to do would be to go out and search for him. And that's what happened, Dickie. They all went out and took me with them. I was knackered after a wee while, because they must have knocked on half the doors in Derry. But nobody knew where he was. My ma's wile worried, Dickie.'

'Aye, I know she is, Liam,' I said, 'but was there anything else that I should know about?'

'Naw, Dickie, nothin', except when we were out, we got a bag of chips each. Kate said that would do us instead of dinner the night. I think your bag's in the oven.'

'Right, thanks, Liam,' I whispered as I slipped out to the landing and listened. I heard muffled voices from the living room. It sounded as if Father Mooney was still down there with my ma and the twins. I felt very tired, even though it was still a bit early, not even nine o'clock, but I didn't want to go to bed yet, because I needed to see my ma again. I was really worried about her.

I sat on the landing floor and watched Liam through the half-open door of the bedroom. He didn't see me. I was proud of him and I didn't feel annoyed when he threw the comic he was reading onto the floor and began reading another one. Or when the next two comics went the same way. He was a loveable brat.

I must have sat there for the guts of an hour with my back to the banister rails, listening to the voices downstairs. Eventually, when I heard my ma and Kate and Laura saying cheerio to Father Mooney and closing the glass door after him, I slipped down to the living room. All three of them looked exhausted. I felt I had to say something.

'So youse didn't find Uncle Jimmy, Ma? Maybe he'll turn up soon!'

'We searched everywhere, Dickie. We must have knocked on twenty or more doors. Nobody saw him, son. It's as if he's disappeared off the face of the earth.'

As soon as she said that, she broke down. The tears were flying from her and she began to moan out loud that it was all her fault. That she had driven him away. 'Just like Barney,' she wailed, 'I've driven the two of them away.' Now she went into hysterics. Kate and Laura rushed to her, shouting to me at the same time to go to bed. Once again, I was the baddie. I left, but before going to bed I went out to the kitchen to get my chips. They were cold. Rotten. Nobody had switched on the oven. I wasn't even hungry anyway.

Liam was asleep when I went up. I was feeling bad but I had to smile when I saw the place. The room was a mess with about a million comics all over the floor. I looked at him. The wee fart was snoring, and by the look of him he hadn't a care in the world. And I wondered if anything had been going on in his head before he went over. If he had been trying to work things out. Things that might be bothering him.

After I tidied the room, I knelt down and said my prayers. And I asked God to do two things for me. The first one was to look out for my da and keep him safe. And the second one was to look out for Uncle Jimmy and keep him safe, too.

And before I went to sleep, there was another thing that kept running round and round in my head. A special promise thing. And the promise was that I'd try to do everything I could to find Uncle Jimmy for my ma. And I got the feeling that I would. And soon.

CHAPTER 24

Final Showdown With Philson

I knocked at the classroom door, hoping that Philson would be in there by himself. He was.

'Come in,' I heard him shout.

I hated having to do this but I had no choice. I knew that when I woke earlier than usual this morning that I just had to do it. For Father Mooney. I'd deliberately left the house at a quarter past eight after eating a quick piece and gulping down a cup of cold tea left over from Kate and Laura's breakfast. My ma didn't hear me going out because she was still upstairs in her bedroom. I'd heard her moving about when I quietly slipped across the landing. She probably had a sleepless night, worrying about my da and Uncle Jimmy. She'd see to Liam in a wee while. I took a short cut to school through Thompson's Field. I did that some-times instead of going down Creggan Hill and up Helen Street. I noticed that the workmen had the walls of the new B-men's hut almost built. Some of them were singing. They sounded happy.

I walked into the classroom and closed the door behind me, trying to look like somebody who was sorry for something he'd done wrong, even though I didn't feel sorry. Not for a single second had I felt sorry for lying to Philson yesterday, and even if I had, there was no way I was going to say sorry. But I still had to put a face on that might give the right impression. And now I had to say something very important to Philson that I didn't really want to say. Something that would make me feel very sad.

And I'd say it for Father Mooney's sake. Definitely not for Philson's sake.

'Ah, McCauley, is it?' he asked sarcastically as I moved towards him.

'Yes, Sir,' I replied, 'I came in early to see you.'

'And I wonder now what *Mister* McCauley would want to see me about. Oh, I just wonder. This should be interesting.'

'I won't be goin' on as an altar server, Sir. I've changed my mind.'

Mr Philson stared at me with that look of contempt that he always had for me. He also had a look of relief, probably because I wouldn't be on the altar after all. But I didn't give him the impression that I noticed, because I wanted to get this all over with before anybody else came into the classroom. So I just rambled on with what I had to say.

'I shouldn't have said that to you, Sir, about the bishop congratulating me or smilin' at me, or anything. The bishop wasn't there at all, I just made that part up, as a joke, Sir.'

So far, I hadn't mentioned anything about telling lies. Unless I was forced into a corner, I would never admit to that. Getting caught telling lies was one of the worst things that could happen to you. Especially with the likes of Philson.

'Let me get this straight, McCauley,' he whined. 'Yesterday, in front of the whole class, you said that the bishop had congratulated you about getting the College examination and had said, too, that you'd make a fine altar server and that you hadn't put your name forward. Lies, McCauley, and then more lies. And then you had the cheek and audacity to waffle on in front of everybody that you went to the College meeting in Father Mooney's car, and about Father Donohue driving you there. Just one lie after the other. All you tell me is lies, McCauley, lies and more lies.'

'Not so, Mr Philson, not so, my dear man. What you're saying about Richard is not totally true.'

It was Father Mooney's voice coming from behind us. We

hadn't seen him coming in, but he must have overheard what the teacher was saying to me. Or at least some of it. And he would have heard the sarcastic voice nagging away at me, and seen the look of contempt in Philson's face. His timing couldn't have been better.

Philson stood up quickly and pushed his chair back. I could see that he was shocked. I liked that.

'Ah, good morning, Father,' he said as he stretched out to shake the priest's hand. 'Good morning,' he said again, 'I wasn't expecting you in today.'

He then turned back to me and told me to sit down, that he'd deal with me later.

'Mr Philson, as I was saying just now, about Richard here, I think perhaps you've got the wrong end of the stick about him. Indeed, as I explained to you yesterday after school when you called to see me, he may indeed have told a few wee white lies about the bishop, but I think that would be more in the nature of a joke, a childish prank, a young boy's foolishness, Mr Philson. He is, after all, as you well know yourself, a mischievous-natured boy, full of life, an adventurous boy, Mr Philson, and very prone to act sometimes before he thinks things through. And I can assure you that, most times, he does mean well.'

Mr Philson didn't say a word as Father Mooney was speaking, but his jaw had dropped open. I kept the innocent look on my face in case Philson would suddenly turn round and hope to catch me grinning from ear to ear. But I wasn't stupid.

'But besides all of that, Mr Philson,' continued Father Mooney, 'I can vouch for the fact that Richard was telling you the truth regarding the other aspects you were referring to when I came into the room just now. Indeed, it was very remiss of me, if anything, not to have informed you in the first place that I did indeed ask him to become an altar server. Twice. And that he *didn't* put his name forward like the other boys. So he's correct there, too, Mr Philson.'

At this stage of the proceedings, Philson had taken his hanky out and was wiping away the spittles that were dribbling down the sides of his mouth.

By now, about thirty of the boys had come in, slipping quietly into their seats when they saw Father Mooney talking to Philson. They all knew something was up.

'I don't know what to think now, Father,' said Philson hoarsely. 'I mean, this boy, McCauley, has given me so much grief over the past two years. In fact, his overactive imagination is very difficult at times to fathom, and it's not always easy to distinguish between truth and lies with him.'

He didn't realise that about half the class were now listening to every word he said. I loved that.

'Well, I can assure you, Mr Philson, that on this occasion, Richard is telling you the truth. And bizarre and all as it may seem, Father Donohue did indeed give the boy a lift to the College meeting on Saturday morning. As a matter of fact, and he may have mentioned this to you as well, he had an old bicycle with him, probably with every intention of cycling to the meeting, but because it was in grave need of repair, I asked Father Donohue to put it into the boot of the car.'

I could see the amazed look on Philson's face. So could everybody else who was watching and listening. They knew that he was getting a telling-off from the priest. And they liked it. Nearly as much as I did. But what they probably didn't hear then was the last frantic effort of Philson going out of his way to bad-mouth the McCauley family, saying terrible things about us. And I didn't like that one bit, even though I only heard some of what he said. I then cocked my ears to listen more intently. He was now telling Father Mooney what I had told him just five minutes ago, that I had changed my mind about being an altar server after all. And as he whispered that to the priest, with a stupid look of triumph on his face, he reached round to his desk and picked up one of the four altar servers' books and proceeded to hand it to the priest. That's when Father Mooney looked across at me with a questioning glance. But I didn't indicate one way or the other that I knew what was happening, or what was being said. And when Father Mooney held up his hand and refused to take the book, I guessed right away that I was back in as a candidate. They whispered some more stuff that I couldn't make out, but Philson was nodding his head up and down and wasn't looking one bit pleased. After the priest left, and for the rest of the morning, there was no mention of anything from a very grim Mr Philson, except the ordinary stuff about sums and reading. I deliberately kept my face looking innocent.

At lunch time in the playground, after me and Liam got the usual share of lunch from Danny and Kevin and a gobstopper each from the twin Deeneys, Bap Kelly came over to me and whispered, 'I've some information for ye, Dickie, but we can't talk here. Somebody might be listenin'.'

Half of the gang and a few others were standing about chatting and laughing, so I pulled Bap to one side and told him to meet me at the school steps next to Helen Street. You couldn't get much further away from the playground than that.

'Okay,' I said two minutes later when we got there, 'spit it out, Bap. What have ye got?'

'It's about your Uncle Jimmy, Dickie. The IRA are lookin' for him. He's vanished! Vamoosed. Just like that.'

That's the way he said it. Blunt. And snapping his fingers at the same time.

'He's definitely on the run, Dickie. And there's something about him headin' off with a wile load of money that doesn't belong to him. That he stole. They even went down to Donegal to search for him in your Aunt Minnie's house. That's all I know. Honest.'

Bap kept turning round as he was speaking, to make sure nobody was listening. I couldn't believe what he was telling me. Or maybe I didn't want to believe it. Especially not after my ma had said about there being some good reason why Uncle Jimmy had taken the money with him.

My heart was racing, because when Bap was telling me all

this, I had a bad feeling that everything he was saying sounded true. It must have been just wishful thinking on my ma's part that Uncle Jimmy didn't steal the money, because it looked now, from what I was hearing, that he did. And it was looking likely, too, that I'd never be able to keep the promise I'd made, that I'd find him for her. If the IRA couldn't find him, how did I think I could? It was a stupid promise.

The bell rang as I was still taking everything in. I didn't even get time to thank Bap for the information. I probably wouldn't have thanked him anyway. You don't thank people who give you bad news. But because I was grateful for the information he'd given me, I told him he could join my gang. He looked very pleased.

We ran back to the classroom. Philson was sitting at his desk. He called me over before people had settled. He handed me the Mass responses book and told me to write my name inside the front cover, and to stay behind for an extra half-hour, starting today, to begin learning the Latin. He didn't turn to me as he spoke, but I could still see that his face looked ashamed. And embarrassed, probably because of what Father Mooney had said to him. It was as good as Philson apologising to me, but not quite. Philson's a bit like myself. He doesn't apologise to anybody.

After school, after the four of us had been put through the first part of the Latin pronunciations by Philson, I ran the whole way home. I was bursting to tell my ma what Bap Kelly had told me about Uncle Jimmy. She was sitting in my da's armchair, listening to the wireless. Liam was at the table, doing a jigsaw puzzle. He didn't seem to notice me coming in. My ma was very pale and I could see when she looked at me that her eyes were afraid. And I knew why: Uncle Jimmy. And she knew right away that I knew something, because she put her finger to her lips as a warning to me not to say anything in front of Liam.

'I'll put the kettle on, Ma,' I said as I went out to the kitchen, nodding for her to follow me. Before I had half the water in, she was beside me.

'Ye know, Dickie,' she whispered, 'don't ye, about your Uncle Jimmy?'

I nodded aye.

'How did ye find out, son?'

'Bap Kelly, Ma. Bap told me. He knows nearly everything, that boy. He heard his ma and da talking about it. About Uncle Jimmy being on the run from the IRA. Is it really true, Ma?'

'Aye, son, it's true. Mr Kelly came up this morning to let me know, and I told Kate and Laura at lunch time. Now we're worried sick about him. It looks as if he stole the money, Dickie, out of the suitcase, before he left on Sunday night. I really thought that there would be a good explanation, but I'm not so sure now. I still can't believe Jimmy would do that.'

'Right, Ma, but Liam doesn't know, does he?'

'I don't think so, son. If he does, he didn't mention it. Maybe you could find out. And if he does, tell him not to be sayin' anything about it.'

She began to cry quietly into herself.

'Leave Liam to me, Ma,' I whispered. 'I'll check if he knows anything. But don't worry, he won't blab.'

'Dickie, son,' she said, sobbing harder now, 'what are we goin' to do with your da away and all?'

I put my head down for a second. I didn't know how to answer that one. Then I said, 'Why *did* Uncle Jimmy steal the money, Ma? Sure it wasn't his to take.'

She didn't reply. Her eyes were red with crying and there were tears running down her cheeks. She just gave a big sigh.

'What's for the dinner, Ma?' It was Liam, standing behind us.

'I don't know yet, son,' she whimpered. 'Maybe a stew. I got a wee bit of mince the day.'

She could hardly get the words out. I knew she needed a bit of peace to be by herself for a while. So I spoke up. 'We'll go upstairs and do our homework, Liam. That'll give my ma a chance to start the dinner. Okay, Liam? Right, Ma?' I said as I pulled Liam away.

'Great, Dickie. I'll call youse down for a piece in a wee while. Okay, boys?' she shouted feebly after us. I could hear the tremor in her voice. So did Liam. He wasn't stupid.

'What's wrong with my ma, Dickie?' he asked when we reached the landing. 'Is it still all this carry-on about Uncle Jimmy?'

'That's what it is, Liam, you've hit the nail on the head.'

'I thought it might have something to do with the big row in the street the day, Dickie. We saw it all happenin', me and my ma, when you were still at the school.'

'What big row, Liam?'

'With the cop, and Eva's ma, and Eva and her wee brother. It was a whole screamin' match, Dickie. Half the neighbours were out watchin'.'

'What are ye talkin' about, Liam?'

'Some woman came in a car, Dickie, and the cop put wee John into it. And he was tryin' to get Eva to go, too, tryin' to drag her out of the house, but her ma held onto her and wouldn't let her go. And Eva was screechin' that she didn't want to leave.'

'And what happened then, Liam?' I asked him, my voice shaking.

'Well, Dickie, her da gave up and the woman drove off with just wee John. It was a whole bargin' match, Dickie, and there was a wile bit of shoutin' and roarin' and cryin'. Eva and her ma were in a terrible way and the cop was mad with them. And my ma was wile upset, too, Dickie, watchin' it all.'

What I was hearing from Liam was making me feel very bad in one way. But very good at the same time. Bad for what Eva had to go through but good for me that she hadn't left Derry. And I was glad as well that Liam didn't say anything else. He just got on with starting his homework as soon as we went into the bedroom. But I was pleased that he had told me about Eva, about what happened in the street, and I knew that I'd have to fill him in shortly about Uncle Jimmy being on the run from the IRA. He deserved to know, because he was smart and he knew nearly everything else that was going on. So why not this, too? For as far as I knew, he had never really blabbed about any of our family business to anybody. And later this evening when Kate and Laura came home from work, I was thinking that it might be a good idea if I told everybody that I was going to be an altar boy. That would make them all sit up. But for a different reason.

***

When we finished our homework, I asked Liam if he wanted to go outside for a while. He said he'd go later. That he was starving with hunger.

'Okay,' I said, 'I'll race ye down. Last there has to eat the other's crusts.'

I sometimes said that to him because I knew he hated crusts. But I always let him win the race because *I* loved the crusts. And I think he knew that. We took the stairs two at a time laughing the whole way down.

My ma wasn't in the kitchen, or the living room, or the sitting room, or even in the yard. Liam ran back upstairs to check. She wasn't there, either. She must have gone out for a message. Maybe there was no bread. I looked. There was. Nearly a full loaf. I cut two thick slices and spread jam all over them. That would do us in the meantime. I then told Liam I was going out to see Danny and Kevin and asked him if he wanted to come with me, but he said he'd rather wait in the house for my ma to come back. I headed for the street. Eva Johnston was the only one out there. She was kicking a ball up against the air-raid shelter. She asked me if I wanted to play tippity-kick. I said okay, so she lifted the ball and threw it to me. That soon made me forget about Danny and Kevin.

'Your ma's up in our house,' she said after a while. 'She called about twenty minutes ago. My ma asked her in and offered her a cup of tea. That's the first time she was ever in our house.'

'What did they talk about, Eva?'

'I don't know, Dickie. My ma told me to go out to play before

221

they really said much, but I guessed that something was up, because the two of them looked that serious, and your ma seemed to be cryin' about somethin'.'

'Is your da there, too, Eva?'

She didn't answer at first and hesitated a bit more as if she didn't want to talk about him. 'Naw, my da's away out.'

I didn't like the sound of all this. I mean, about my ma going into the cop's house. It really worried me. But Eva kept on talking.

'Dickie, I'm stayin' in Derry. Wee John's away to Dublin with my aunt, but I'm stayin' put. Nobody's shiftin' me.'

I swallowed hard as she was telling me this. I knew I had to say something.

'I'm glad you're stayin', Eva.'

'I know ye are,' she laughed. 'And, Dickie . . .'

'What, Eva?'

'Maybe now I'll be able to visit you in your house.'

She laughed again as she said this. Then she grabbed the ball off me and dribbled it all the way up the Terrace like an expert. And I was thinking, too, as I looked after her, how pleased I felt about her visiting our house. And that the cop wouldn't be one bit happy if he hears about it.

But it was the thought of Mrs Johnston and my ma up in Eva's house right now that was mostly in my mind. Because it seemed really strange. My ma being there, I mean, in a cop's house, talking to a cop's wife, when only a couple of days ago Uncle Jimmy was in there, too, talking to the same cop's wife. Aye, it was all very strange. And I prayed there wasn't going to be a big row between the two of them. About Uncle Jimmy.

I ran up the street after Eva, shouting to her that I wanted to play a game of tippity-kick. But this time, it was really just an excuse for me to hang about waiting for my ma to come out of Johnstons'. I'd know then by the mood she was in if she'd had some sort of bust-up with Eva's ma. But that didn't mean I wouldn't enjoy the football game.

About ten minutes later, Eva said she had to go in to do her homework. I left her to the door, hoping that when she opened it I might hear my ma and Mrs Johnston talking. I heard nothing. That was a good sign, I thought. Seconds later, as I was walking back down to the house, Eva came running after me.

'Dickie,' she whispered, 'your ma must have gone home. Out the back way. That's why we didn't see her.' She laughed a little as she spoke because she knew I was anxious about this meeting of the two mas. Even though she didn't know why. But the laughter soon turned to a look of concern as she told me that her ma seemed a bit upset, and that she'd been crying. I didn't say anything, because I didn't really know what to say. Eva turned and ran back to her house. I just hoped that they hadn't come to blows.

But I had something else to do before I went home. A very important wee plan that I'd been working on. Without anybody else knowing. It would only take about fifteen minutes, and I'd have to be careful in case any of the gang spotted me. Because they would be really puzzled about what I might be up to. It was something special I had to see about by myself. This was Dickie McCauley's lone, secret mission. To negotiate a deal. With the North Street Bunch. I'd tell the gang later if I succeeded. I headed up the Terrace and turned right towards North Street.

***

Later, when I got home, I could smell the stew cooking. My ma must have been here a good while. Liam was in the kitchen with her, the two of them laughing together. This was a good sign, but it was also very hard to understand, because an hour ago she was sobbing her eyes out. I'd even got Liam out of her way then to give her peace and quiet, but here she was now, in great form, as if she hadn't a care in the world. It was a complete turnaround. And a mystery. But I knew I'd soon have answers. In the meantime, I thought I'd let them hear *my* good news.

'Ma, Liam,' I said, putting on my biggest smile, 'I forgot to tell youse earlier. I'm going to be an altar boy. Father Mooney picked me, Ma, and Mr Philson is teaching us the Latin responses. But I know most of them already. The Latin words, Ma.'

'Well, well, well, do ye hear that, Liam? Imagine that, your big brother being an altar boy. Just wait till the girls hear this, and wait till your da . . .'

She stopped for a second when she mentioned my da, then took a big deep breath before she went on excitedly, 'Come over here, son.'

When I went to her, she gave me the biggest hug ever. Liam was excited, too, and shouted out that he was going to be an altar boy when he grew up. And would I teach him the Latin words. I said I would.

'This is lovely, Dickie, just lovely. Imagine, my boy on the altar! Dickie McCauley an altar boy, eh! Who would ever have thought it?'

She was beaming from ear to ear. It was the happiest I'd ever seen her. The hassle I'd had with Philson was well worth this. That's what I was thinking now as she danced around the kitchen floor, swinging me and Liam with her.

***

'How did ye wangle that wan, Dickie?' laughed Kate when my ma told the twins about me.

'Aye, but does the bishop know yet?' smirked Laura with a big cheeky grin all over her face.

I just laughed with them, because I could sense from the way they were talking that they felt proud. But maybe not just as proud as my ma was. Or me, for that matter.

'Now, eat up, everybody,' my ma said, 'youse must be starvin'.'

Nobody argued with her.

I got the impression during the meal that the twins were a bit puzzled about the big change for the better in my ma's humour. And they knew as well as I did that it wasn't just because of me getting on the altar. But they didn't say anything. Like me, they guessed they'd find out soon what had happened. But I knew, too, that she'd want to tell Kate and Laura first, whatever it was she'd talked to Mrs Johnston about. And she wouldn't want me and Liam there when she was telling them. So when the dinner was over, I nudged Liam to follow me upstairs.

'What's up, Dickie?' he asked me as soon as we got into the bedroom.

'It's about Uncle Jimmy, Liam, I wanted to tell ye about Uncle Jimmy.'

'What about him?'

'The IRA are lookin' for him, Liam. And if they get him,' I said, 'they'll throttle him.'

'Hell rub it up him,' said Liam as he walked out of the room and down the stairs, 'he deserves all he gets.'

All I could think of as I followed him was that if Mr Philson thought he'd had a hard time with me over the past couple of years, he wouldn't know what hit him when he got Liam in his class.

***

When we got back down to the living room, you could see right away that my ma had told the twins some good news. Whatever it was, it was Kate who spoke first. 'Dickie, Liam,' she said, 'there's somethin' we have to tell youse, because we know youse were worried, too. It's about Uncle Jimmy. Well, he's safe . . . in Dublin . . . he's away back to Dublin, boys. Mrs Johnston told me ma a while ago—'

'I'm away to bed,' interrupted Liam suddenly, slamming the door behind him as he left the room.

It was obvious that he didn't want to hear any more about Uncle Jimmy. Or Mrs Johnston. But I did. And as I listened to Kate, I felt a relief coming over me. Relief for my ma, too. And for Liam. And for Kate and Laura as well.

It turned out from the rest of what I was hearing this minute that Uncle Jimmy, since he arrived back in Derry, had been calling regularly at the Johnston house when the cop was out, trying his best to get into Mrs Johnston's good books. But she wasn't having it. Even if she was very fond of him. And before that, he'd been sending her letters, too, wanting her to go away to Dublin with him. But she definitely wouldn't leave the cop. And that's why Jimmy left. For good.

Maybe now, I began to think, things would settle down a bit in our house again. With the danger gone. And the twins back to their normal, hateful selves.

I slipped out of the living room as my ma and the twins kept talking excitedly to each other. I don't think they noticed me going, but I wouldn't have cared anyway. All this carry-on about Uncle Jimmy had really upset the applecart. In every way. And him being here in Derry had nearly driven us all mental. I was glad he was away. Liam was dead right. Hell rub it up him!

The wee fart was sound when I went into the bedroom. I was knackered, too. It really had been a very long day. But there were a few things that were annoying me a lot about all this, and I think they must have been nearly the last things on my mind before I went to sleep myself. First, I thought it was very strange that the twins hadn't mentioned anything about Uncle Jimmy skedaddling with nearly two thousand quid that didn't belong to him. Or about him being on the run from the IRA. As if it wasn't really worth talking about. And another thing annoying me was that they didn't mention anything about my da being away. All they were concerned about was that Uncle Jimmy was safe in Dublin when they should have been worried that my da could be lying at the bottom of the ocean with a load of dead cows. It didn't seem right. But there were two other things that made me really happy this very night. One was that Uncle Jimmy couldn't get Mrs Johnston to go with him. And the other was that the cop wasn't able to shift Eva.

CHAPTER 25

The Skinny-dip In The Reservoir

During the next couple of days in our house, not a single word was spoken about the terrible events that had been happening.

Not a peep about my da, or Uncle Jimmy, or Mrs Johnston or the cop Johnston, or guns, or bullets or suitcases, or money. Nothing. Not a sausage. And when my ma or Kate and Laura spoke to me or Liam, it was just ordinary stuff like 'sit down' or 'keep quiet' or 'go on upstairs, now' or 'here's your piece'. Ordinary stuff that didn't really matter much. There were no raised voices, or tears, or even whispers. It was as if life in the McCauley household was back to normal. When it was still far from normal. And very strange.

And besides all that, in the school playground Bap Kelly didn't come near me. You would have thought that at least he would have asked me if I'd heard anything else about Uncle Jimmy. Not that I would have told him. But no; Bap Kelly was playing marbles with the twin Deeneys as if nothing important had been going on. Aye, all very strange indeed. Maybe it was because everybody was worn out.

Even Liam didn't talk much when we were going to school or coming from school. And when we took the short-cut through Thompson's Field on the Wednesday and Thursday, Liam put little pass on it when I nudged him and mentioned that the B-men's hut was nearly built. In fact, he didn't even look up, just grunted something when I said that they'd probably have the roof on it in another week.

Today was my last day at St Eugene's Boys' School. And if Liam was going to go to the College, like me, he'd have to stay here for another two years, from September, probably in Mr Philson's class. Maybe that's why he was being so quiet. Maybe that's why he had been waiting behind after school, while I was in with Philson and the other three boys. Aye, that could be it. He probably didn't want me to leave the place.

And as usual, this past few days Philson was up to his old tricks with me, but I didn't care. He couldn't help it. During these times, after school, when he was teaching us the Latin, not once did he look in my direction. And at the end of the lesson when I was preparing to leave the classroom, he didn't say a word to me, but he deliberately kept chatting and laughing with the three others. Strange as it may seem, me being ignored by Philson gave me a very good feeling.

But on each of those lunch times in the playground, I was being sickened by Danny and Kevin. They'd kept on and on about the pictures in St Columb's Hall and about getting chips afterwards. And about the plans for the electrocution of two of the North Street Bunch and the attack on their dam. And about the skinny-dipping in the wee reservoir. It was no wonder that I hadn't mentioned to them yet that Billy Burnside and Cecil Colhoun would be joining us for all that stuff. Because that would have sent them totally crazy with excitement. So I decided that I wouldn't fill them in until later.

But during those quiet days when nothing much was happening, I'd been thinking a lot about some of the stupid plans I'd made. For there were a couple of things that didn't sit right with me. In fact, they were annoying me badly. So I quickly decided that I'd have to do something about them. And I did. Without anybody else finding out. On Wednesday, I went to the man in charge of the Cnoc na Ros snooker hall and warned him about the dangerous bare electric wire. And on Thursday, I sent Danny and Kevin – on a fake mission – to check if the dangerous wire was still there. It wasn't. That made me feel good. The electrocutions were cancelled. Two of the North Street Bunch were off the hook.

Another thing that had been niggling away at me as well was the dam, so after the twin Deeneys had reported back to me that it was now complete and ready for swimming in, I went to inspect it for myself. It was brilliant. My gang could never have done as good a job. And there was no way that I could ever order an attack on it. That's why I'd gone secretly the other evening to the leader of the North Street Bunch and negotiated a simple deal. That we wouldn't destroy their dam as long as they allowed us to use it, too. He agreed. And I'd let the others know as soon as possible about the change in the plans. And I did, the following morning, before we went to school. Nobody objected. So that was that. I even slipped a written message through Cecil's window, telling him about the new arrangements, and to let Billy know as well.

***

Me and Liam ran home from school after the final Latin lesson. I now knew all the responses. The next stage, we were told, was that the four candidates would be called to the Cathedral within the month for a week's training, when Father Donohue would teach us the movements on the altar. I was looking forward to that. And I was glad to be finished with Philson.

As she'd promised, my ma had a piece and a cup of tea ready for us when we got into the house before we went to the pictures. I told her that we wouldn't need any meal this evening because we were getting chips in Harley's afterwards. But what I didn't tell her was that Liam was paying for everybody out of the ten-bob note that I'd taken from Uncle Jimmy's suitcase. After we'd eaten, we said cheerio to my ma and set off down the hill. Eva came with us. She'd been waiting for us at her door. Her ma knew she was going, but her da didn't. That's what she told me.

The arrangement with the gang was that we'd all meet under the billboards at the top of William Street, across the road from Strain's shop. We were first to arrive, but only seconds before the Deeney twins.

Five minutes later, when we were getting a bit worried about Danny and Kevin, we spotted them in the distance, running as fast as they could down Creggan Street, past the Cathedral. When they reached us, they were sweating and Kevin's glasses were steamed up as usual. And just as they'd got their breath back, Bap Kelly arrived, sauntering over the Little Diamond with his hands in his pockets. You could see the sun reflecting off his glass eye. I'd already told the rest of them that he was coming with us. And that he was now in the gang. They were pleased. And Liam hadn't minded when I told him earlier on the q.t. that he'd be out an extra eightpence. For Bap. I knew by the look of Bap as well that he felt proud to be with us. But they were all even more pleased when Billy Burnside and Cecil Colhoun appeared. They hadn't expected that. And really, if the truth were told, neither did I. Because I wasn't sure if they'd turn up at all. Liam was pleased the most because it was his idea in the first place. You could see it in his face. There were cheers all round, and the cheers got louder when I announced that Billy and Cecil were coming to the flicks with us, and to the chip shop, and then to the reservoir after that. Within seconds, you'd have thought that Billy and Cecil had known Eva and the Deeney twins all their lives by the way they were chatting and laughing. I felt good. I'd done it. I'd done what I'd promised myself. That someday I'd get the whole gang together again. I felt great about it, even if it was only going to be a one-off.

***

Being at the pictures in St Columb's Hall was great. Danny and Kevin had never seen anything like it before. And it was Liam's first time too. The three of them couldn't take their eyes off the screen most of the time. They thought the people up there were real. Like on a stage. But I liked the wee picture the best. Charlie

Chaplin was in it. We all screamed laughing at him. I didn't fancy the big picture much. It was called *Footsteps in the Dark*. A man called Errol Flynn was the main actor. It was supposed to be a fast-moving mystery comedy. But not one of us laughed. I thought it was boring.

Afterwards, we ran the whole way to Harley's. We were starving. We sat in two stalls and ordered ten plates of chips. The man said we were the best-mannered boys he'd ever seen. He gave us a free sausage each. We'd never tasted anything as good. The only thing I was scared of now was that Danny and Kevin would start farting. That would have spoiled everything. But I think they knew better. This wasn't the time or the place.

It was around half six when we reached the top of Creggan Road, near the barracks. Everybody now knew the new arrangements that I'd made.

We were to meet outside the girls' school at seven o'clock, and when it was safe, we'd slip through the hole in the wire fence to get into the lower reservoir. I would have preferred going to the Killea reservoir, about three miles away. That's where we always went before, but Eva had picked this one, so that was now okay by me. And it would be too late anyway going to Killea at this hour. Eva was right when she organised the change of plan. A smart move. And Cecil had arranged that Billy would stay in his house until nearly seven o'clock while the rest of us showed our faces for a while at home.

Everybody was excited and looking forward to the skinny-dip. They kept chattering on and on about it until they split up.

As we walked down Rosemount Terrace, Eva gave me a big smile. Luckily for me, nobody else noticed. In the same way that nobody had noticed when we'd held hands at the pictures.

My ma was sitting on my da's armchair when me and Liam went into the living room. Nobody else was there. She seemed to be listening to the music on the wireless, but I noticed right away that she'd been crying. Again. Liam spotted that, too. Her eyes were red and her face was a bit puffy.

231

'What's up, Ma?' I said as we went over to her.

'Oh, Dickie, Liam, it's youse. Did youse enjoy the pictures?'

'Aye, Ma, the flicks were brilliant,' said Liam excitedly.

I knew by the way he was talking that he wanted to cheer her up, but it wasn't working. She wasn't even listening. She seemed to be looking past us, as if we weren't there.

'Are ye all right, Ma?' asked Liam. You knew by the sound of his voice that he was really concerned. 'Were ye cryin', Ma? Your eyes are wile red.'

She took a couple of big deep breaths, then blew out a long blast of air between her tight lips. Before she answered, she took a hankie from her apron pocket and blew her nose.

'Aw dear, boys, it's just that I'm sittin' here in the house by myself. The girls have gone out somewhere and I was just thinking of Barney . . . your da, I mean. Sure I can't get him out of my mind. I'm worried sick about him, boys, ever since he got on that cattle boat for Liverpool.'

'He'll be all right, Ma,' I said quickly, because her tears were coming thick and fast again, 'he'll be okay, he'll be over there now, Ma, probably workin' at the docks.'

'Aye, Ma,' Liam broke in, 'my da's a great docker. He'll get a wile lot of work over there, and send ye money back.'

I couldn't believe what Liam was saying. He sounded great.

'Aw, boys, it's nothin' to do with the money. That's not what I'm worried about. Sure we don't even know at this minute whether he's alive or dead.'

I was about to cut in and say something. Probably something stupid, but she just kept on, and the tears were still flying,

'It's this bloody war, and even there on the news a wee while ago, before youse came in, the man was sayin' that German U-boats were attackin' ships all over the place. Even merchant ships and cattle boats. It's nearly a week since he left and there's no way of knowin' whether he reached Liverpool or not.'

Her crying turned into a high-pitched wail when she spoke those last words. Liam and me just looked at her, not knowing what to say next. But it was Liam who made the first move. He walked closer to her and put his arms out as if he was going to hug her. And she squealed out even more as she hugged him to her. She then reached one arm out towards me, wanting me to come to her as well. Before I knew it, the three of us were sniffling and blubbering away about my da. And it did seriously cross my mind at that second that he really was dead. The thought of it made me feel numb.

I don't know how long we stayed like that – hugging, I mean – but it was only when the sobbing stopped and we had wiped the tears and snotters off our faces that Liam nudged me and nodded to the clock. It was five to seven. If we didn't leave now, we'd be late. All the gang would be there waiting on us. It would look bad if we didn't turn up on time, but the way things were at this minute, we couldn't leave my ma. The gang would have to wait, but they'd need to know that there was to be a delay for the skinny-dip. And if they didn't like it, they could lump it. Liam guessed what I was thinking as I looked at the clock again.

'I'm away to the toilet,' he lied, 'I'll be back in a minute, Ma.' I knew where he was really going.

'That's okay, son,' she said as he flew out through the living-room door like a rocket.

'*He's* in a hurry,' she laughed, nodding after him and sniffling at the same time. She said nothing more and within seconds gave another big sigh and closed her eyes as she leaned back on the chair. I sat down quietly and waited.

About five minutes later, you could hear Liam deliberately thumping down the stairs. Bluffing he was. He was red-faced and sweating when he came back into the living room. He put his thumb up to let me know he'd seen the gang, and whispered half seven to me. I had to smile. And he made me feel proud of him.

My ma opened her eyes and mumbled something, then closed them again. We stayed with her, keeping as quiet as we could.

***

A wee while later, I peeked up at the clock. Twenty-five past seven. We'd have to go. Now. I nudged Liam and whispered about the time. My ma wakened. That's when I told her that we were going out to play. She smiled and waved. As we went out of the room, I looked back. Her eyes were closed again.

'Just go slow, Liam,' I said as we walked casually up the Terrace. 'Don't give them the impression that anything was up. And no excuses, either. They don't need to know why we were delayed or anything. It's none of their business. Just say nothing. That's the best way, Liam.'

He nodded without replying. He didn't need to. He understood.

'Right,' I said when we reached the girls' school, 'are we all set?'

I looked around as I spoke. Everybody was there. Nobody mentioned anything about us being late. I think they knew better. You could see that they were still excited about the skinny-dipping. We hadn't been to a reservoir since last September when we got caught by the man in charge. But there was nobody in charge of this place, nobody that I ever saw anyway.

'We're all ready, Dickie,' said Danny, 'and look what Eva brought with her: a pink towel.'

He wasn't acting the smart alec when he said it, he was praising her.

'You'd think that was the normal thing when you're goin' for a dip,' laughed Eva.

Everybody laughed with her. Even Danny. But I was more concerned just now that we'd be spotted if we made too much noise, so I told them all to shush up.

We walked on slowly down the hill towards the reservoir fence. Within a minute, we were through the gap in the wire, scrambling up the steep banking. Kevin had to be helped by the twin Deeneys and I saw fat Danny being half-dragged by Billy and Cecil. Everybody was out of breath when we reached the top, but we didn't rest. In case we would be seen. That was the order. I'd told them that we would head on up the gravel path, to the halfway mark of the reservoir. That way, if anybody spotted us, we could clear off in the opposite direction. Me and Eva were leading the way, but she suddenly ran ahead like a greyhound. She was probably the best runner in the gang. That's when I took a quick look behind me. At Liam. He was walking with Bap Kelly. You could see the excitement on his face. Bap winked at me. It was a wink that said that he was glad to be with us. But it crossed my mind as he closed his good eye that he must have been totally blind for a split second.

Eva was sitting on the grass banking at the halfway spot when the rest of us arrived. Here, there was a gentle slope that led down to the water. It was a good place for the dip. Without saying anything, we all sat on the grass and began to take off our stuff. Shoes and socks first. But before we even had our shirts off, Eva went flying past us, into the water, in the pelt, whooping and shouting and laughing and splashing the water with her feet. Nobody had noticed her getting stripped. She was fast all right, and while the rest of us were still struggling to get undressed, she was already in up to her knees. And when she turned and began splashing water towards us with her hands, and shouting 'cowards' at us, there was a sudden silence from everybody. My mouth dropped open. Probably the others were the same. Then there were gasps. We couldn't speak. It was as if we were dumbstruck. And astounded. Paralysed to the spot and not able to react. For at least ten seconds. Kevin was the first to squeal out. He had his rosary beads in his hand, held up high as he fell to his knees.

'Almighty God in Heaven,' he wailed out, 'save us this day. Mother of God, protect us. Dear Jesus . . .'

As Kevin prayed, all hell let loose. There were cries, screams. And then general panic. But when I got my wits about me a wee bit, I lifted Eva's towel from the grass and ran towards her. She must have thought we'd all gone mad, and I could see concern in her eyes as I got closer. I quickly wrapped the towel around her and began to guide her out of the water, without saying anything.

She didn't know what was happening. But we did. All of the rest of us. For behind her, floating in the water, face down, was the body of a dead man. And as we waded to the shore, Eva and me, I took another terrified glance over my shoulder. The corpse was floating in behind Eva, just inches away. The screaming on the shore got louder, with screeching prayers still coming from Kevin. I could see Bap and Liam and Danny scrambling away with their socks and shoes in their hands. And still screaming their heads off. Billy and Cecil stayed for just another few seconds before heading off in blind panic.

'Don't look behind you,' I suddenly shouted to Eva when we reached the banking. But she did. I couldn't stop her. And when she saw the body, she stood there, frozen to the spot. She was shocked into silence at first, and then an almighty scream left her lips as the blood drained from her face. But before the scream had died down, she was falling in a faint on the grass. I felt helpless. Useless. I could do nothing. She was as white as a ghost. And I felt sick.

But I still had enough wit about me to shout to the Deeneys to run for help. And to take Kevin with them. They dragged him away as they ran down the path towards Rosemount. He was still screaming out prayers like I'd never heard him before.

I looked back down at Eva. Her eyes were closed but her lids were flickering. As if she was trying to wake up. And when she didn't, I rushed back to the edge of the reservoir to cup some water into the palms of my hands to throw on her face. And I made sure that I was as far away from the dead man as possible. But before I ran back to Eva, I couldn't help taking another glimpse at the body. Because it had turned over, face up. And that's when *my* head began to spin as the blood seemed to drain away from me, too. I didn't have to look twice at the bashed-in face of the dead man. Because I knew it was Uncle Jimmy. And that's when I blacked out.

***

Eva had been the first to come round from the fainting. And when I wakened, she was bending over me, shouting, 'Dickie, Dickie, are ye all right?'

I nodded aye, but I still couldn't speak. I was too weak. Eva helped me to put on my socks and shoes, but when I stood up, I still felt a bit dizzy. She held on to me. She was great. But as we stood there together, we kept our backs to the water. Minutes later, when the police came, they took us aside and asked us some questions about what we saw. And before a policeman led us back towards the fence, he wrote our names and addresses into a wee book. He then told us to go straight home. When we were going out through the hole in the wire, into Creggan Road, you could hear the ambulance bell clanging in the distance. By that time, too, a large crowd had gathered. Some rushed forward and began asking us what had happened, but we said nothing. We went straight home. And we didn't even speak a word to each other, either, as we walked up hill and into Rosemount Terrace. It must have been the shock.

***

The most amazing thing about the weeks after Uncle Jimmy's death was that nobody in our house said a word about us being at the reservoir. Maybe nothing was mentioned because we hadn't been swimming in it.

But I could hardly get it out of my mind, night or day, about us finding Uncle Jimmy the way we did. About his head being bashed in the way it was. About him being murdered. That's what I'd read in the paper. That he'd been murdered and thrown into the reservoir. But nobody in our house mentioned murder. They probably didn't want to talk about it.

But the worst of the whole lot was the way it had left my ma. There she was, day after day, sitting in my da's big armchair, not really talking to us, or anybody else, but crying most of the time. And every night, too, we could hear her moaning in

237

her bedroom, sometimes calling out stuff like 'Barney, Barney, where are ye?' and 'we need ye home, Barney'.

Kate and Laura told me and Liam that my ma was in a state of shock. Because of how Uncle Jimmy had died. And that she had a terrible guilt on her because of the way she'd treated him. About how she drove him away. But I already guessed all that.

There was something else, too, something that made *me* feel guilty. Very, very guilty. It happened just a few days ago when I was passing Colhouns'. Cecil called to me. He was standing in the porch. It was as if he was waiting for me.

After slipping me another bunch of comics that he'd taken from under his jumper, he whispered something to me which at first took my breath away and then made me weep uncontrollably as I left him standing there.

'Dickie,' he'd said, 'I'm very sorry to hear about your Uncle Jimmy being killed. Nobody deserves to die like that. Will you tell your ma and Liam and the twins I'm sorry? It was a terrible thing that happened.'

'Thanks, Cecil,' I said, but I could hardly answer him. 'Thanks, Cecil,' I said again, 'I'll tell them.'

I couldn't look at him. I turned away.

Here was Cecil Colhoun saying this stuff to me about Uncle Jimmy. Cecil Colhoun, whose da, the B-man, had been killed last year by the IRA. And I knew who'd killed him. And Cecil knew that I knew. Now *he* was telling me how sorry he was. I couldn't hack it. I rushed up the Terrace, sobbing my heart out, and I didn't care if anybody saw me. I kept running, flustered, across Creggan Road, through the gap into Thompson's Field and past the new B-man's hut. And I didn't stop until I reached the far side. There, I fell on my knees with shame. Minutes later, when I stood up and took some deep breaths, I knew I had a couple of very important things to do. I ran the whole way back to Rosemount and straight to Deeneys'. Joey and Hughie were behind the shop counter with their ma. She looked a bit concerned when she saw the state I was in but she didn't say anything. I nodded to the twins to come outside. I then gave them instructions. Something very important that I wanted them to do for me. And to say nothing to anybody. But before I left, I went back into Mrs Deeney and asked if I could help her out in the shop on Saturday afternoons, starting next week, and then every Saturday as well, when I went to the College. She burst out laughing and said I had the job. And that I had a nerve on me.

'If you work from two o'clock to six o'clock,' she then told me, 'I'll pay ye thruppence an hour, because the boys here could do with the extra help.'

'Thanks, Mrs Deeney,' I said as I headed for the door. I was delighted, and on the way back home, I worked it out that I'd be earning a shilling each Saturday. Brilliant. That would easily pay for all the pens and pencils and jotters and exercise books that I'd need. The text books would be got out of the scholarship money. I ran the rest of the way home, feeling good, but I knew I'd feel even better in about fifteen minutes, especially with the help of Joey and Hughie Deeney.

***

They were waiting for me in the lane at the back of our house. That was the plan. I'd already slipped upstairs without anybody hearing me. Up to the bedroom. I lay on the floor and dragged out the stuff from under the bed. The leather schoolbag with the jotters and pens and ink and everything in it. The things that Uncle Jimmy had given me for passing the College exam. I didn't want them. But I knew who would. I moved quietly down the stairs and out through the kitchen into the yard. Joey and Hughie were there as ordered. They took the bag from me and ran up the lane towards Creggan Road. I shut the gate after them and walked casually into the house and out to the front porch. Nobody noticed.

Ten seconds later, the twin Deeneys came round the corner into Rosemount Terrace. They walked down as far as Colhoun's and knocked at the door. I said a prayer that Mrs Colhoun would answer. She did. I couldn't make out what exactly Joey and Hughie said to her when they handed over everything for Cecil, but I'd told them to say that it was a wee present for him for getting the Foyle College Scholarship Examination. But not to say where it came from. If she knew, she'd have dumped it all. I held my breath. I could see her nodding. That was a good sign. She held out her two hands and took the stuff. The twins then left, waving to her as they went. Job done. Before she went back into the house, Cecil's ma looked up and down the Terrace. She had a big beaming smile on her face. She didn't spot me. And just at that split second, it crossed my mind that Uncle Jimmy could be turning in his grave. Right now. I tried to imagine it. Him watching his present to me going to a B-man's son.

***

Kate and Laura still had to go to work every day, because if they didn't, there would be no money in the house to get food. They had already lost three days' pay because they'd had to go to Donegal with my ma, to Aunt Minnie's, for Uncle Jimmy's wake and funeral. Me and Liam hadn't been allowed to go, so we'd to stay in Mrs Fatso Lardo's. Danny Doherty thought it was great, us staying in his house and sleeping in his bedroom. But we hated it. The smell in the room was terrible and Liam cried every night for my ma.

Now it was her that was crying, every day and every night since she came back from Donegal. And she didn't do dinners for us anymore. I had to make pieces for her, and for me and Liam, all day, until Kate and Laura came back from work.

Mrs Doherty came down sometimes with a pot of dinner, but it was always rotten. And Liam would never eat it. At other times, the girls would cook a meal, but mostly it was just chips we got that the twins brought home with them from Harley's. When me and Liam complained, they just told us to shut up, that we were lucky to get anything to eat at all.

It was after about a week of getting rotten food, and when we were sick to death of chips, that Liam came up with the idea of giving the girls the money he had left over from the ten bob after we'd gone to the pictures and all. I'd forgotten that he had dosh left, and I'd forgotten as well that I still had the other ten bob that Liam had given me. With all that money, they could buy good food that would keep us going for a good while, but I told Liam that we couldn't very well just go in and hand it over to them and say something stupid like maybe we'd found it in the street or something. Liam agreed, so we came up with a plan. We'd get the money and put it all together at the back of a drawer in the sitting room. Then five minutes later, we'd take it out again and tell them that we'd found it there when we were looking for something else. We'd run in together, into the living room, shouting with excitement about what we'd discovered. And that's exactly what we did. They couldn't believe it. They said it was like getting two weeks' wages. They were so delighted they didn't even wonder how the money came to be in the drawer. That suited us.

***

Liam stayed with my ma when I went down to the chapel every day for a week to practise for the Mass. Father Donohue showed us how to do everything. One day when I was leaving, Father Mooney stopped me and said how sorry he was that Uncle Jimmy had been murdered. He said murder was a terrible crime. I thanked him but I didn't know what else to say, and I thought it was still strange that nobody else, except Cecil Colhoun and the police, had mentioned anything about the killing since it happened. Some people in the street just whispered behind our backs about it. I knew that by the way they shut up when we were passing them.

After the last day of the Mass practices, I lit three candles before I left the chapel. One for my da, one for my ma and one for me, Liam and the twins. I threw a threepenny bit into the box. I hadn't any money for a candle for Uncle Jimmy, but I'd already said a prayer earlier that he wasn't in hell.

But a great sadness came over me on the morning I was to serve my first Mass. My ma told me she couldn't go. That she wasn't feeling up to it. And I wasn't to worry, because Laura would stay home with her. But it was great anyhow to have Kate and Liam and Danny and Kevin and the twin Deeneys there. All lined up in the front pew. With Eva and her ma sitting behind them. I even saw Bap Kelly over in the side aisle. Everybody was watching. I felt proud. And I wondered if Philson was in the congregation, because the other three boys he'd trained were on the altar as well. Maybe he was in the side aisle, too. Behind a pillar. In case I would see him.

After the Mass, Eva and her ma came to our house for a cup of tea. I was chuffed. Mainly because of Eva being there. And it cheered my ma up a bit, because Mrs Johnston stayed for a good while and chatted to her about everything under the sun. Mrs Johnston visited our house a lot after that. And sometimes when they talked about Uncle Jimmy, both of them cried. It was at times like this that Liam headed upstairs, and me and Eva went into the sitting room to look at books or play cards. Anything to get away. We couldn't hack the tears anymore.

Yesterday, Eva confided in me that her ma was afraid sometimes, especially when her da shouted at her. She said he seemed to get very angry for no reason that she knew. She even said that he frightened *her*, too, sometimes, the way he looked at her with his eyes blazing. She mentioned all this to me over in the park. But it was something else that Eva told me that has stayed with me since. I could hardly sleep last night thinking about it. And it's about the worst thing you could think of, because it *could* mean that her da is a murderer. And if I'm right in thinking that, I really don't know yet what to do about it. Because if it *is* true, and I blabbed, then Mr Johnston could be hanged. And how would Eva feel about me then?

CHAPTER 26

I Always Kept My Promises

The talk leading up to this stuff about Eva's da began when we were sitting in the park yesterday evening. The sun was still shining and we were glad to be away from all the crying in the house. In the two houses. It was nice there, quiet, with very few people about. I liked being with Eva, even when we weren't saying much.

'It was great goin' to the pictures, Dickie,' she said, 'and then the chips and sausage afterwards. Everybody had a great time.'

'Aye, it was lovely, Eva,' I replied, hoping that she wouldn't mention what had happened afterwards at the reservoir. About us conking out, I mean. She didn't.

'And it was great, too, the whole gang being there, even your old friends, Billy and Cecil.'

'It was smashin' to see them again. I missed them, Eva. That's why I asked them to come. That's why I organised it all.'

'Great idea, Dickie. Would ye like to do it again?'

I stared at her.

'Well, not really,' I said quickly, 'it was just a wan-off. Do ye mean the whole lot of us, Eva?'

'Aye, Dickie.'

'Naw, Eva, I don't think so. It would be hard to organise it again. And anyway, it would be too dear. But maybe you and me could go to the pictures ourselves someday, just you and me? I've got a job in Deeneys' shop working every Saturday and I earn a

243

shilling for the half-day. That means I could afford the flicks now and again. And maybe chips afterwards.'

'Thanks, Dickie, that sounds great. You and me could have a great time, but I was thinkin' more of the whole gang goin' again, just wan last time before the holidays are up. Maybe some day in August.'

She was beginning to annoy me a wee bit, because I'd already told her that it wouldn't be easy to organise. And then there was the question of the money.

'If it's the money you're worried about, Dickie, there's no need, because *I'll* pay for it all this time.'

You'd have thought she'd been reading my mind on the money score.

'It would be too much, Eva, you couldn't afford all that.'

'I could, Dickie, I've got loads of money.' And as she spoke she reached into her frock pocket and took out a ten-bob note. She stretched her hand over to me with the money, but I pushed it away.

'Naw, Eva, it'd be too much.'

'Not at all, Dickie, it wouldn't be too much. As a matter of fact, there's plenty more where that came from. You take that now and organise the whole thing, and if ye need extra, I'll get if for ye.'

I couldn't believe what I was hearing. I knew that she was being too generous. And that if she had money and savings, she should keep it all for herself and not be spending anything on the gang.

'Ye must have been savin' a long time, Eva. Does your da give ye a lot of pocket money?'

'Naw, Dickie, he doesn't, just the odd penny when I need it.'

'So it's your ma, then, Eva, that gives ye the dough?'

'Naw, Dickie, my ma never has much for herself. My da just gives her about enough to buy food and other stuff that we need for the house. He's wile stingy, ye know.'

I didn't want to know and I was getting a bit embarrassed

when Eva was telling me all this stuff. But even though I didn't want to be nosey, I just had to ask her out of curiosity – right out, in fact – where she was getting the money from.

'My da's tool box. In the cupboard under the stairs, Dickie,' she said straightaway. 'It's stuffed with money. Bundles of it. Twenties, tens, fivers, pound notes and ten-shilling notes. He's hardly goin' to miss a ten bob or two out of that, is he?' And she laughed when she said it.

But I didn't. I went weak at the knees. And I felt myself beginning to tremble all over. I lay back on the grass to try and control it. That helped a bit. But my mind was racing with thoughts that I couldn't believe I was thinking. Mad thoughts. Stuff that couldn't possibly be true. Not in a million years. Or could it? When I got my wits about me after a bit, I asked Eva, as casually as I could, if the money had been there for a long time, and was that where her da's savings were kept? And if that wasn't being nosey, I was thinking, what was? But I needed to know.

'Naw, Dickie, it wasn't there a month ago, because I went to get a screwdriver or something out of it for my ma and there was no sign of money then. But the other day when I was lookin' for a hammer for her, there it was, stuffed with dough.'

I took a couple of deep breaths before I could speak again.

'Does your ma know the money's there, Eva?'

'Naw, Dickie, naw, I didn't tell her. I didn't think that would be wise, and don't you be sayin' anything about it, Dickie, won't ye not? Promise me.'

I mumbled something, but I promised nothing, because if what I was hearing was true, and what I was thinking was true, I knew it wouldn't be wise to give a promise like that. Because I always kept my promises. Now all I could say to Eva was that I would think about her plan for the pictures and all and let her know soon what I decided. She seemed satisfied with that. Without saying anything else about money or about pictures or about the gang, we left the park and headed home.

Later on when me and Liam were in bed, he kept nattering on about him being an altar boy when he got older, and about how he was going to form his own gang next year, and about him going to the College the same as me, and about this, that and the other thing, and stuff that I didn't hear anymore because I wasn't listening. I wasn't listening because my mind was almost spinning out of control. And I knew why. But I couldn't stop it. Because I had a very, very big problem to deal with. And you can't listen to people rambling on when you have serious stuff on your mind. And this could be very serious indeed. A matter of life and death.

But what to do about it was another matter. And that's what was now making my head whirl. Trying to work out what I should do. The word blab kept coming to the front on my mind. It was either that or say nothing. But I'm not a blabber. Then again, I was thinking, if I didn't tell somebody, my head would burst, because there's blabbing, and then there's blabbing. What I mean is that the second kind of blabbing, about life and death stuff, would be totally different from the first kind of blabbing.

Pains were now shooting from the front of my head to the back of my head thinking about all this, and I knew I wouldn't get to sleep this night if I didn't work out what I should do. And I knew I had to do something. Before long. Otherwise, I would go mad altogether.

I liked Eva Johnston a lot, and I liked her ma, too, but I knew very little about Constable Johnston, except that maybe he killed my Uncle Jimmy. Maybe. And if I went to somebody and told them what I now know, about the money in the tool box under the Johnstons' stairs, and it turned out to be the cop's life's savings, then I could be in very big trouble. And so would Eva, too, for telling me about it. And whoever I told, I'd also have to tell them about the money that used to be in the suitcase, in our attic, that my Uncle Jimmy probably took with him, without the suitcase, when he ran out of our house in a rage. And that would certainly set the cat among the pigeons. But you couldn't very well tell somebody one part and not the other. It wouldn't make sense. The whole thing was such a bloody dilemma. But I still knew that I'd have to have a plan before I went to sleep.

It was Liam's snores that interrupted my thoughts for now. But I was glad that he was asleep. It gave me more quiet time to think. But within minutes, after his snoring stopped, even that quiet time was interrupted when I heard something that I thought I'd never hear again. Or should I say someone. Someone that I'd thought I'd never see again. First, it was like a sound that I'd heard before. Often. And it came from the street, somewhere in the distance, from the Creggan Road direction. Within seconds, the sound got louder. It had moved into Rosemount Terrace. And my heart leapt. And I knew what it was. And who it was. My da. Singing his head off. At the top of his voice he was booming out the rebel song that he loved. And I pinched myself to make sure that I wasn't asleep. And dreaming.

I jumped out of my bed and rushed to the window, slid it open and looked out. There he was with a bag over his shoulder and a wee brown suitcase in his hand, staggering down the street and blaring out the familiar words of *Kevin Barry*. And I didn't care if he wakened the whole Terrace. Or if he was as drunk as a skunk. He was home.

I'd leave it till tomorrow for me and Liam to see him, because I could now hear the squeals of excitement from downstairs. And that would be enough for him tonight. As I climbed happily into the warm bed beside Liam, I realised that the pain in my head was gone. And the spinning and swirling in my brain was gone. And as I lay back on the pillow on the verge of sleep, I knew that I had probably found the solution to my big problem about Constable Johnston and that money. And Uncle Jimmy and *that* money. And about the murder of Uncle Jimmy. And, if it *was* the same money, somebody was bound to know then that the cop was involved. The solution was simple. And I wouldn't be blabbing. Tomorrow morning, after I'd served Father Mooney's Mass, I'd tell him everything. And I mean everything. That's what I would do. He'd sort it all out. Because it was too much for me to deal with. I didn't want any more headaches when I saw my da in the morning. And if spilling everything to Father Mooney was really blabbing, so what? Because this really was a matter of life and death. And I knew in my heart that Eva and Mrs Johnston would eventually understand why I had to do it.

EPILOGUE

On the following morning, Constable Johnny Johnston stood in the doorway of his house, cupping a lit cigarette in his right hand as if he didn't want anybody to know he was smoking. He wasn't a happy man. Far from it. And hadn't been since his transfer here from Belfast last year. Now, in fact, he was in a continual state of agitation and anxiety, brought about, he felt, by circumstances not all of his own making.

The rot had begun to set in some time ago when he sensed that his wife, Eileen, was losing interest in him. At first, she'd gone gradually quieter, only speaking to him when it was totally necessary, and just about mundane things. He'd blamed himself in the beginning, putting her lack of interest in him down to his long hours of work and his constant tiredness. But then the truth came out, at least to him, and things turned a lot more sour. But he didn't yet face her with what he knew. He wanted her to own up, to admit what she'd been up to. To come clean. She didn't. And he was losing patience with her.

It began with him finding some letters under the mattress, on her side of the bed; seven in all. Letters from that IRA man Jimmy O'Donnell, even though he could never prove that he was in the Movement. Oh, aye, and then there was the clandestine liaison with the same boyo, in this very house. And he'd only found that out thanks to the Colhoun woman's young son, Cecil. It made his blood boil thinking about it. And it made him squirm uncomfortably.

Obviously he'd known about O'Donnell being an ex-boyfriend

in the past, eleven or twelve years ago, but not until he'd discovered the letters had he realised that he hadn't got over her. And maybe she hadn't got over him, either. The sooner he got her and Eva out of this place the better. That's what Constable Johnston was thinking right now. Back to Belfast. Back to civilisation. And out of this godforsaken hole.

And he began to squirm again when he thought of his wife now going to visit O'Donnell's sister down the street, probably sympathising with her about her brother's death. He took a deep breath when he dwelt on it, because he couldn't bring himself to think of the death as murder. That's the way it was being described, but that's not how it had been. He'd been killed all right, but not murdered. Killed by a large rock that he'd fallen on, with the force of the attack on him from behind. At the reservoir.

He'd tailed him that night, from the town, over the Lone Moor Road and eventually up Bligh's Lane. He'd then parked the police car and followed on foot. O'Donnell was obviously heading for the border, just a mile or so away. Across a few fields and he'd be there. But O'Donnell had taken a sudden and unexpected right turn at the upper basin as if he'd decided to make his way back to Rosemount.

Jimmy O'Donnell had quickened his pace down the path towards the lower reservoir. Aye, that's where he was probably going, all right, back to the Terrace to make a final plea with Eileen to go away with him. It had made him see red at the time, his mind already disturbed by the image of the two of them together. And spurred on by what he was thinking, by the realisation of what O'Donnell was up to, he'd gone into a violent rage. Attacking him from behind. There had been no shout of surprise or a struggle. It was over in a second. O'Donnell had fallen forward and struck his head on a jagged boulder.

Killed outright.

Head bashed in.

An accident, Johnston had kept saying to himself. A freak accident. But not murder. Not in Johnston's book anyway. He'd just wanted to challenge him, maybe even give him a bit of a beating. And warn him to lay off. But it was too late.

And when he'd searched the dead man's pockets for a weapon which he could later claim made *him* the victim, he was at first disappointed that he'd found no gun. But that disappointment soon turned to utter disbelief, then to excitement when he'd found the money. And afterwards, when he'd stuffed all the stolen notes into his own pockets, he'd unfeelingly and coldly pushed O'Donnell's body into the water, hoping that it would sink. Permanently.

He remembered walking back to his car with a lighter step, and with no feelings of guilt, for two of his problems had just been solved. One, he'd got rid of O'Donnell, and two, by the looks of it, he now had enough money to buy his own house. In Belfast. He could easily get a transfer. If only Eileen would go with him.

As Constable Johnston flicked the butt of his dead cigarette into the street, he saw that young ruffian Dickie McCauley passing by. Normally in situations like this, the boy would deliberately avert his eyes and not acknowledge him, but this time, he noticed young McCauley's gaze, and although it was a fairly fleeting one, it had still lingered. Straight at him. It was a disconcerting moment for Johnston, to say the least, for as their eyes had met, he'd seen in the boy's face a certain sort of defiance and accusation. The incident had made his heart skip a beat. And for good reason, for Johnston was too long a cop to play this one down. He'd seen that selfsame shrewd look on colleagues' faces in the barracks on many an occasion when they knew they were on to something important. He immediately felt troubled. And apprehensive.

Before going back into his house, he definitely felt a growing trepidation as he continued to watch young McCauley walking the rest of the way down the street. His thoughts were racing and for some reason that he couldn't fully explain, he suddenly became more fearful, for he'd definitely detected a very determined-looking threat from this young scallywag, especially when he'd stopped at the end of the Terrace and turned round to face him for at least ten seconds before moving on into Creggan Road.

And Constable Johnny Johnston was painfully aware of the boy's dogged reputation.

ALSO BY CHARLIE HERRON

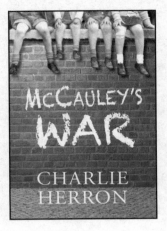

McCauley's War

McCauley's War is a fast-moving tale of life in wartime Derry as seen through the eyes of Dickie McCauley, a streetwise nine-year-old who dominates his friends and constantly outwits his elders.

Dickie's father, emboldened by news reports of German Army actions, claims Hitler will soon push the British out of Ireland, but Dickie suspects these foolish dreams are merely drunken words.

Meanwhile, Dickie's antics with his motley gang bring unwanted attention to the doorstep of his long-suffering mother. These innocent scrapes quickly tangle with much darker deeds and local politics leading to terrible consequences for the close-knit McCauley family.

A debut novel from Charlie Herron, *McCauley's War* is a poignant and compelling story, told with an absorbing mix of humour, insight and affection.

'*McCauley's War* . . . remarkably engaging and, at times, utterly hilarious.' *The Irish World*

Available from Guildhall Press at www.ghpress.com